"IT'S TIME I WAS GOING HOME."

"Not yet." Eben laid a restraining hand on her arm, checking the slight movement she made toward the door.

Maddie halted, her startled glance flying to his face, her lips parting in surprise. He found himself staring at them, remembering too vividly the taste and texture of them.

"Why not?" Her voice had a husky and disturbed quality to it.

It pleased him, especially in view of the havoc her nearness was causing in him. "We need to talk," he told her, then said to the twins, "Go on, outside with you."

Untouched by the undercurrents sizzling in the room, the twins bounded from the kitchen, made a detour to their bedroom to collect their doll Eloise, then slammed out the front door. Through it all, Eben kept his gaze locked on Maddie.

"What did you want to talk to me about?" The huskiness was gone from her voice, replaced by a note of bland interest. It told him her guard was up.

Angered by that, by the attraction she still held for him, his memories of the past—both the good and the bad ones—her insinuations that he was somehow to blame for other things, he push teeth. "Us."

D0019996

BOOK YOUR PLACE ON OUR WEBSITE AND MAKE THE READING CONNECTION!

We've created a customized website just for our very special readers, where you can get the inside scoop on everything that's going on with Zebra, Pinnacle and Kensington books.

When you come online, you'll have the exciting opportunity to:

- View covers of upcoming books
- Read sample chapters
- Learn about our future publishing schedule (listed by publication month *and author*)
- Find out when your favorite authors will be visiting a city near you
- Search for and order backlist books from our online catalog
- Check out author bios and background information
- Send e-mail to your favorite authors
- Meet the Kensington staff online
- Join us in weekly chats with authors, readers and other guests
- Get writing guidelines
- AND MUCH MORE!

**Visit our website at
http://www.kensingtonbooks.com**

SCROOGE
WORE
SPURS

Janet Dailey

ZEBRA BOOKS
KENSINGTON PUBLISHING CORP.

http://www.kensingtonbooks.com

SCROOGE WORE SPURS

Chapter I

What was that old saying—bad news comes in threes?

Eben MacCallister tried to recall the exact wording of it as his sharp eyes identified the fast-traveling Jeep Cherokee coming up the ranch lane. It was from the neighboring dude ranch, El Regalo. At this distance, trailing a cloud of Arizona dust, he couldn't make out the driver. But given his recent run of bad luck, Eben knew who it had to be.

With jaws clamped tight, he remembered that damnable letter he'd received ten days ago, the one that threatened to bring his world crashing down around him. He remembered the rage he'd felt when he finally deciphered all its fancy legalese. Rage and a cold, sick fear.

Letter in hand, Eben had slammed out of the adobe ranch house that had been the home of the MacCallisters for three generations, and piled into his old Chevy pickup. Seconds later, the tires had spit gravel as he rammed the gas pedal all the way to the floorboard and tore out of the ranch yard.

Eben remembered nothing of the drive into town, only the fury that had whipped him all the way to the bank. But every moment after that was burned into his memory as indelibly as a hot brand. . . .

Blind to the startled glances and raised eyebrows directed his way, Eben charged across the bank lobby, the *chink* of his spurs accompanying each hard strike of his heel. At the Information desk, a blue-eyed blonde, fresh out of high school, flashed him her best homecoming-queen smile.

"Good afternoon. May I—"

He forged past her desk without slowing down, leaving the girl gaping in confusion and uncertainty. A glass-walled partition gave the bank president's secretary advance warning of his approach. Like Arizona's famed saguaro cactus, Mildred Battles was tall and prickly. She planted herself in Eben's path, her expression rigid with disapproval at the sight of his dusty work clothes and clanking spurs.

Her mouth opened, but Eben didn't give her a chance to speak. "Don't try to tell me Wilder isn't in, Mildred. I saw his Mercedes parked outside."

"But you don't have an appointment," she countered with haughty disdain.

"Yes, I do. Right here." He held up the notice clenched in his fist and plowed by her, heading straight for the closed door to Billy Joe Wilder's private office.

"You can't go barging in there!" Alarmed and outraged, Mildred hurried after him.

"Watch me." Eben yanked open and charged inside.

A richly hued rug of Navaho design covered much of the spacious room's pegged wood floors, its plushness quickly muffling Eben's footsteps. Comfortable leather armchairs faced a gleaming oak desk, a silent audience for the golden-haired and silver-tongued man lounging in the green suede chair behind it, a phone to his ear and his feet propped on a corner of the desk. The conservative business suit he wore was at odds with the custom-made boots on his feet and the flashy bolo tie at his throat, fashioned in the shape of a cactus, studded with diamonds and emeralds rather than the more traditional silver and turquoise.

Not a flicker of surprise showed on his face when he saw Eben. If anything, Billy Joe Wilder looked slightly amused. "I'm gonna have t'let you go, Fred," he said into the phone. "I got somebody waitin' to see me and he looks real impatient." He smiled at the response in his ear and motioned for Eben to have a seat.

But Eben chose to stand, all six feet two inches of him towering over the desk, his blue eyes fixed on the man behind it in a hard, icy glare. He didn't bother to take off his hat or observe any of the niceties of convention. In Eben's thinking, there wasn't any room for pleasantries when it came to dealing with a predator, and as far as he was concerned, that's precisely what Billy Joe Wilder was.

Years ago the Wilder family had amassed a fortune in Arizona real estate. Now that Billy Joe had gained control of it, he was determined to quadruple it, joking that Monopoly had always been his favorite game. While the bank was among the least of his holdings, it was Billy Joe's favorite toy, albeit a powerful one.

"My plane will be there to pick you up at eight o'clock sharp. Make sure you bring those site plans, Fred," Billy Joe said in parting and hung up the phone, without changing his reclining position. His bright glance traveled over Eben, then paused on the official-looking paper, gripped by his fingers. "I see you received the notice."

"You can't do this." Fury rose up, hot and bitter, making it difficult for Eben to get the words out. "My loan doesn't come due for another five years yet."

Billy Joe Wilder folded his hands across his chest, steepling his fingers, and smiled the smile of a Cheshire cat. "I think you'd better take another look at the agreement you signed. After five years, the bank has the right to call the loan due and payable upon the issuance of a sixty-day notice. That notice is in your hand."

"You can only do that if I'm in default. And I

have never been even one day late with a payment. I can prove it."

The smugness of Wilder's smile increased a notch as he dragged his exotic-skinned cowboy boots off the desk, sat up, and reached for a folder. "Like I said, MacCallister, you'd better read it again. A default is one way the provision is triggered; a sixty-day notice is the other." He removed the document from the folder and shoved it across the desk for Eben to examine. "Page three, paragraph Five C."

Fighting dread, Eben grabbed up the document, flipped to the third page and read the cited paragraph, then read it again, a heaviness pulling at him like a weight.

"As I recall," Wilder went on, "you were advised to have an attorney look it over before you signed it, but you didn't want to spend the money for one."

Eben tossed the papers back on his desk, a muscle leaping along his jaw. "You think you've finally found a way to get your hands on Star Ranch, don't you?"

"That's a fine chunk of ground you've got there, MacCallister. Wild and rugged, full of stunning vistas and magnificent scenery. It'll be yours as long as you come up with better than a quarter million dollars in sixty days. If you don't"—he paused for effect and shrugged—"the bank's not gonna have any choice but to take it over and sell it."

"And you plan on being the buyer, don't you?"

Eben accused, his lean body rigid with anger, his voice vibrating with it.

Billy Joe rocked back in his suede chair. "I told you back when you did all this refinancing and signed the new loan—and I'll tell you again— ranching is a thing of the past. This country's in the Service Age now. You gotta cater to the needs and wants of the people—"

"The way you do," Eben cut in. "By ripping up the land to build more golf courses, condominiums, shopping centers, fancy mobile home parks with tennis courts and swimming pools, and a casino somewhere nearby to take whatever money they've got left."

A whole new anger rose up at the thought of that happening at Star, land that had been in his family for three generations, land that he had spent the last twenty-odd years of his life scrimping and saving to keep, working from dawn to dusk and beyond, sacrificing any semblance of a personal life apart from the ranch, giving up everything just to hold on to it.

"Like it or not, MacCallister, there's market for that kind of thing. The same can't be said for cattle. There's no money in ranching anymore. In fact, I can't think of a single lending institution that would make a loan to a rancher unless there was an outside income source. You don't have one, MacCallister. Which means you don't have a snowball's chance of getting a loan somewhere else."

"Why? Have you put the word out among all

your banking buddies to keep hands off of this one?"

"In some ways, you're a smart man, MacCallister," Wilder replied, and Eben noticed he didn't deny his claim.

"You think you've got me boxed, but I've got sixty days to come up with the money. And I'm giving you notice right now that you'll have it. Every dime of it."

Wilder chuckled in outright disbelief. "Sure you will. And pigs have wings, too. You could sell every cow and steer on your place and still not have enough."

Eben privately granted that was true. But the money wasn't in his cattle; it was in his horses.

After recognizing that the demand for good, using ranch horses had stayed steady while the cattle market remained poor, Eben had spent the last ten years investing his time, energy, and every cent of spare cash in establishing a herd, acquiring registered broodstock and building the necessary facilities. It had been a slow process, one of those long-term investments that had taken several years before it finally showed a profit. But he had turned that corner. The horses were making money for him. They were his hole card. But would they be a big enough one? Eben wasn't sure.

"We'll both see in sixty days, won't we?" he retorted, and turned on his heel to leave.

"I almost forgot, MacCallister," Wilder called after him. "Happy Thanksgiving."

The sarcastic taunt dogged Eben, touching off

a bitterness that consumed. It had always been like that for him—just when something he wanted had been within his grasp, it had been snatched away.

But not this time.

This time he wasn't going to lose.

All the way to the ranch, Eben had gone over the numbers in his head, calculating what he would have to sell at what price, factoring in worst case scenarios. There was no way to pare expenses; he was already operating on a bare minimum, cutting every corner he could.

After endless figuring, it was clear he had a chance—but it was a slim one.

Less than a week after getting that bad news, the phone had rung. A heaviness threatened to settle over him when Eben recalled the phone call, informing him that his sister had been killed in a car wreck. He clamped off the thought, denying that he felt anything.

But the desert grapevine had obviously been at work, spreading the news of Carla's recent death. Eben dragged his gaze away from the blue and white Jeep Cherokee. If Maddie Williams had come to offer her sympathy, he wanted no part of it.

And he wanted no part of her.

Overhead, a December sun burned strong and bright in the afternoon sky, throwing its light across the cactus-studded landscape of southern Arizona. The air was warm, with just a hint of winter's briskness carried on the wind's soft breath.

It was the kind of day that begged to be savored,

to inhale the sharp freshness of its air and admire the vivid blue of its cloudless sky.

But Eben MacCallister had no time to fritter away on such nonsense—or for company. Using his hands, his voice, and the light prod of his star-shaped spurs, Eben urged the young blaze-faced sorrel forward, taking it through the next step of its training. But the two-year-old colt liked nothing about this new lesson—not the weight of the tire tied to the rope or the sound it made dragging over the rough ground.

Snorting, the horse stopped and rolled a wary eye at the tire. Eben gave the sorrel a few seconds to look at it, then lightly dug the blunted spurs in again. The nervous gelding lunged ahead, jerking the rope. The tire jumped after him and the horse spooked.

As Eben fought to keep it from bolting, he heard the Jeep pulling into the ranch yard. The sorrel heard it as well, and swung toward the sound. Inwardly cursing the distraction, Eben threw an angry look at the vehicle when it braked to a dust-swirling stop a short distance from the corral.

There was an instant tightening of his mouth as Maddie Williams stepped out and the sun's late afternoon rays became tangled in the tawny gold of her hair. For an electric instant, his blue glance collided with the warm brown of her eyes. Then Maddie gave the door a decisive push. It swung shut with a sharp metallic *thud*.

All hell broke loose as the sorrel leaped sideways,

catching the rope under its tail and erupting in panic.

One second Eben was in the saddle, and the next, he was flat on his back beside the corral fence. Stunned by the jarring impact of the hard fall, he lay without moving, blinked a couple of times, and shook his head, trying to clear it. When he looked up, there stood Maddie, fine-boned, exquisitely patrician, and all woman.

A smile curved her lips, deepening the fanlike creases around her dark eyes. "After all these years, I finally have you at my feet, MacCallister." Amusement was in her voice, but something else was in her eyes.

Eben responded with a glowering look. "Very funny, Maddie, very funny," he muttered in ill temper, then forced his bruised and shaken body to move, fighting through the dozen protests it lodged and feeling every minute of his forty-plus years.

Hardening himself against Maddie's presence, he turned from the corral fence. In quick succession, his searching glance located his hat lying a few feet away and the sorrel horse an equal distance beyond that. His hired man Ramon Vargas had a tight hold on the gelding's reins, his slight body lifting with each anxious toss of the horse's head.

Pain stabbed from his right hip when Eben took the first step toward his hat. Grimacing, he shortened his stride and limped over to it, winced again at the soreness in his back when he reached down to scoop up his hat.

"You okay, *Señor* Mac?" Ramon's expressive black eyes studied him with concern.

Eben answered with a curt nod and reached for the reins, never once questioning how the Mexican had slipped so quickly into the corral and caught the horse—just as he had never asked anything when Ramon had shown up at the ranch ten years ago looking for work. To this day, Eben had no idea where Ramon lived, how old he was, whether he had a family—or a green card. He had arrived at a time when Eben was up to his ears in debt and too short of cash to pay the going wage. Ramon had agreed to work for less. Much less. Eben had hired him on the spot, then later taken on Ramon's cousin Luis under the same terms.

Passing the reins to Eben, Ramon stepped away. The still skittish sorrel danced sideways, shying away from him. Eben talked to the horse in a soft, crooning voice that had soothed many a fractious animal.

"Easy now, you fool-headed horse," he murmured. "Better start calming down before I decide you aren't worth all this time and trouble, especially when a kill buyer's ready to pay eight hundred dollars for you." Eben worked his way up the reins and laid a gentle hand on the quivering horse. "Didn't like the feel of that rope under your rump, did ya? Better get used to it. Someday it'll be a full-grown cow at the end of it instead of a tire."

He concentrated on the horse and steadfastly ignored the tall, slender blonde at the corral fence. Twenty years ago that would have been impossible for him to do. Twenty years ago Maddie had been his sweetheart, the girl he planned to marry. Today she was the wealthy widow of Allan Williams, and Eben was older and infinitely wiser to the ways of women.

There was no softness or sentimentality in him, and Eben was proud of that.

He continued to stroke the gelding, waiting for the trembling to ease before he swung back into the saddle. As his toe sought the opposite stirrup, his glance strayed to Maddie, noting her dryly amused look. There was a time when she would have watched him with undisguised adoration, a time when he would have shown off for her. It irritated Eben to remember that.

At the corral fence, Maddie watched as Eben resumed the horse's lesson, starting with the basics to restore the gelding's confidence. He concentrated the whole of his attention on the task, never once glancing in her direction, shutting her out as effectively as if he had slammed a door on her.

She studied him with cool eyes. Eben MacCallister was desert-lean, with a face as hard and stony as the jagged mountains beyond him. His eyes were as blue as the sky and as piercing as the sun, and his hair was a dark mesquite brown, with the first smattering of gray showing at the temples. He was a man of contradiction—at times incredibly harsh and unforgiving, and other times, amazingly gentle and loving.

It was the harsh side he was showing her now. It was hardly fair to say he was giving her the cold shoulder—he was more like a glacier, determined to freeze her out.

Once, the sharp sting of his rejection would have sent her running in tears. Now, it merely stiffened her resolve and turned her stubborn. Simple patience wasn't likely to be rewarded either. Maddie knew she could stand there until the stars came out, and still he would go about his business, all the while ignoring her.

Recognizing that she had only one choice—to force Eben to seek her out—Maddie pivoted away from the fence and struck out for the adobe ranch house.

Made out of the sandy soil that surrounded it, its walls blended into the desert landscape. Narrow posts of sun-bleached tree trunks supported the wide, ramada-like porch that encircled the structure.

Her steps slowed as she neared its front door, a flood of memories rushing back. Maddie wasn't as adept as Eben at blocking them out, but she pushed on. She wasn't about to run from Eben—or the past.

But she was caught up in the past the minute she stepped inside the house that had once nearly been her home.

After working with the green gelding another ten minutes, Eben managed a successful circuit of the corral with the tire in tow and called it enough.

He dismounted at the gate, passing the reins to a waiting Ramon.

He turned toward the fence and paused, instantly stiffening. Maddie wasn't there.

"Ramon, where did Mrs. Williams go?" he demanded.

"La señora, she go to *la casa."*

Anger surged as Eben jerked his glance toward the adobe ranch house, shaded on the west by a clump of palo verde trees. He wanted Maddie in his home about as much as he wanted the plague.

In two strides, he vaulted the corral fence and struck out for the house, his long legs eating up the ground, his spurs chinking with each step. The flagstone floor of the encircling ramada porch echoed with the hard strike of his boots. He jerked open the screen door, stepped into the tiled entry, and paused there, his glance scouring the living room with its cream-plastered walls, exposed vigas, and Mexican-tiled fireplace. From the kitchen came the distinctive clink of ice cubes. Cursing silently, Eben followed the sound to its source.

Maddie stood by the kitchen counter, the picture of at-home elegance in a sage green blouse of brushed silk and slacks of beige linen, a gold chain belt circling her waist. Her wheat blond hair was cropped shoulder length, swinging loose about her face in a style that was sheer simplicity and perfection.

"You made yourself at home, I see," Eben observed tightly.

"Once it was my home—in a manner of speaking."

He didn't want to be reminded of that. "What are you doing here, Maddie?"

"I was thirsty. I knew if I waited for you to offer me something to drink, my hair would turn gray. So I fixed myself some lemonade." With a graceful wave of her hand, she gestured to the squeezed lemon halves on the countertop.

Maddie didn't bother to remind him of all the times in the past when she had had a pitcher of lemonade waiting for him at the end of a hard day. It was a memory that lay between them, along with a thousand other bittersweet ones.

Making the lemonade had been a deliberate act on her part. She had wanted to evoke the past, and let him know that she remembered it was a favorite drink.

"You know that isn't what I meant. Now, what do you want?"

Studying him, Maddie replied, "The old Eben MacCallister, he used to smile now and then."

"I don't have time to play clever word games with you, Maddie," he said with impatience. "Save them for your Eastern guests."

"It's always business with you, isn't it?" She held up a hand to check any response. "That was a rhetorical question, MacCallister. I already know the answer to it."

After taking a brief sip of her lemonade, Maddie picked up a second glass and handed it to him before moving by, leaving him in the wake of her expensive perfume. It wafted to him, vibrant and wild like some rare desert bloom.

When she reached the opposite corner, near the phone, she swung back to face him, negligently leaning a hip against the counter. He felt the old lick of desire, and fought it.

"As it happens, I'm here on business, MacCallister. But you should already know that. Or don't you listen to the messages on your answering machine." Maddie tapped a long, coral-lacquered nail on the machine's flashing red light that indicated messages had been left. "It's obvious that you don't erase them. You have two days' worth here. Shall I play them for you? You have five from me, two from an attorney in Tucson, one from someone named H.D. in Texas, and two from Billy Joe Wilder at the bank."

"You couldn't resist snooping, could you?" His glance raked her. "Despite the classy hairstyle, the designer labels inside your clothes, and the two-hundred-dollar perfume dabbed behind your ears, you still haven't learned anything about manners."

She smiled at his insult. He couldn't possibly know that the clothes were a kind of defense against him. "That's because I had lessons in rudeness from the master—you."

"Flattery will get you nowhere, Maddie." His voice had an edge to it.

"That doesn't surprise me. It never did," she replied. "And I wasn't really snooping—just checking to make sure your machine was working."

"Right," Eben scoffed, then sipped at the ice-cold lemonade. His mouth instantly puckered at the styptic tartness of it. "Good grief, didn't you put any sugar in this?"

"Not in yours," she said with a Cheshire smile, her dark eyes sparkling with laughter. "I'm surprised you noticed, though. As sour as you are, I assumed you had been baptized in lemon juice."

"That's a child's prank, Maddie. Grow up." He walked over to the open cannister and added three rounded spoons of sugar to the glass, then stirred to dissolve it in his drink.

"Once upon a time, MacCallister, I honestly thought I was to blame for the way you've grown so cold and cynical. Now that I think about it, though, you never did joke around—or even smile all that much. Your idea of a date was a moonlight ride. You hated spending money on anything, even an engagement ring. It was always work with you. Work, work, work."

"What choice did I have?" he challenged with a show of temper. "It was the money I earned that put food on the table. It sure as hell wasn't my father."

"By all means, let's blame your spendthrift father," Maddie retorted, annoyed by his attitude. "At least he knew how to laugh and enjoy life."

"He was so busy enjoying it, he damned near lost this ranch."

"Wouldn't that have been awful," Maddie murmured in deliberate mockery.

Eben stiffened. "A MacCallister has owned Star

Ranch for one hundred and twelve years. That means something to me."

"It definitely meant more than I did."

"There was a time when I'm not sure that was true," Eben recalled to his bitter regret.

She raised a delicately arched eyebrow in skepticism. "Really?" she murmured coolly. "How long were we engaged, MacCallister?"

His expression closed. "I don't remember."

"I do," she replied, fighting the old pain of that memory. "Five years, seven months, and twenty-one days. I was a little dense back then, which is why it took me so long to realize that, deep down in your heart, you really didn't want to marry me. And I didn't even have a ring to throw in your face."

His lips came together in a cold, tight line. "You know damned well that we couldn't have gotten married sooner. Not when I didn't know from one month to the next whether we would have a roof over our heads."

"I wasn't marrying you to get a roof or a house or a ranch. I wanted you," Maddie declared in an explosion of feeling. "I wanted to help, to work at your side. I wanted us to build something together. But not you. You expected me to sit quietly in the corner and wait. I would have turned blue with mold by now."

Stung by the accusation, Eben lashed out, "Instead you became an old man's decoration."

Fighting mad, she came at him. "Don't you dare say one word against Allan. He was a good man and a good husband, the best friend I ever had in my life." She jabbed a finger against his chest, emphasizing each point. "If you were half the man he was, you might have been worth waiting for."

"How would you know? You didn't hang around to find out."

That stopped her. She pulled in her temper and eyed him coolly. "We both know, if I had waited for you, I'd still be hanging around."

"Really?" he countered dryly.

"Yes, really. Maybe you'd better listen to those two messages from Billy Joe at the bank." Maddie wagged two fingers in his face before sauntering past him to perch on a corner of the long table. "There's a rumor floating around the desert grapevine that the bank is calling its loan due. From the messages Billy Joe left for you, I suspect it's more than just a rumor. Something tells me you should have looked more closely at that loan agreement before you signed it."

"It'll be a cold day in hell when I'll let Wilder and his greedy band of developers get their hands on Star." But there was a telltale flicker of worry in his eyes.

Maddie saw it. "What will you do, Eben?" Her voice softened with concern.

"That's my business." He downed a big swallow of the lemonade. "It's long past time that we got around to yours. What is it that you want?"

Chapter II

It took Maddie a full second to make the switch in topics. "Horses," she began.

"Sorry," Eben cut in. "But I don't have any half-dead horses for your Eastern *guests* to ride." Sarcasm underlined the word.

"Good, because I'm not interested in buying any half-dead horses. But I am in the market for a couple with cow sense," she countered, then curtly reminded him, "In case you've forgotten, we still run cattle on El Regalo."

"I suppose they supply atmosphere for your high-paying guests," he concluded with a note of derision.

Her eyes narrowed on him. He was baiting her, and Maddie knew it. "If I didn't know better, I'd think you were jealous of the money I make off them," she parried his jibe.

"Hardly," Eben scoffed. "I want no part of your dudes or their bratty kids."

"Just how many cows are you carrying now?" Maddie challenged.

"Under a hundred head. There's no money in cattle these days," he admitted. "You're lucky to break even on them. But a good ranch gelding with cow sense and performance potential will bring top dollar."

"Top dollar is what I'll pay—assuming, of course, that you have anything cowy," she added dryly. "And please don't trot out that goosey sorrel gelding and try to pawn him off on me as trained. I wasn't born yesterday."

"No, you have too many wrinkles for that." His glance flickered to the fine sprinkling of them around her eyes and mouth. "It comes from turning forty, I guess."

"You always were good at saying exactly the wrong thing," Maddie declared through gritted teeth.

"I suppose your late husband was too much of a gentleman to notice the lines."

"On the contrary, Allan was just too much of a gentleman to comment on them. But then, tact never was your strong suit, MacCallister. As I recall, you always were brutally blunt." Pausing, she tipped her head to one side, once more puzzled by his contradictory nature. "Every time I see you working with a young horse, I'm surprised by your patience and gentleness. You never get mad when a colt becomes confused and frightened. You're always quick to restore its confidence. You're firm but never rough, always calm and reassuring. Why can't you be that way with people, Eben?"

His answer was quick and typically blunt. "Because they aren't worth the effort. But a well-broke horse will bring good money."

"Money. Is that all you think about?" Part of her still found it hard to believe that.

"Money is all I need. It's all any man needs," he declared smoothly.

"There are a lot of things in this life much more important than money, things that money can't buy." Maddie knew that truth well.

"Such as?" he taunted.

"Such as loyalty, affection, love."

"I don't know—Williams bought you."

Her fingers tightened their grip on the glass. She came close—so very close—to throwing the lemonade in his face. Maddie took a long, deep breath and pressed her tongue against her teeth while she carefully set the glass down and counted to ten.

"I don't know why I ever felt sorry for you, MacCallister," she stated. "Oh, it's true you had a rough time of it growing up, with your mother dying when your sister was born and your father spending money he didn't have, burying this ranch in debt. All the responsibility fell on your shoulders—the chores, your sister Carla, and the bills, ultimately. I used to think it was terrible that you never had a chance to be a child and dream silly dreams, but you always said dreams were foolish. Worse than that, you believed it.'' Which was truly sad. "I guess that's why you were so furious when Carla ran off, chasing her dream to be a recording star.''

Eben had no desire to talk about his sister, yet the old hurt came tumbling out. "No, I was furious because she took all the cash we had, over three hundred dollars, enough to carry me through the winter. Some Christmas gift that was from my dear sister.''

"Carla was only seventeen,'' Maddie argued. "She was young. She made a mistake. You had no call to cut her out of your life the way you did.''

He looked at her with cold blue eyes, downed the rest of the lemonade in his glass, then turned and dumped the ice cubes in the sink. "That's history. It doesn't matter anymore.''

"Just what is that supposed to mean?'' Maddie folded her arms.

"It means she's dead.'' He hadn't meant to tell her that. He didn't want to talk about Carla and take the chance on opening the door on things he didn't want to feel.

"What?'' Maddie stared at him in open-mouthed shock, stunned by the news.

He turned, his dry glance skimming her. "She and her husband were killed in a car crash four days ago.'' Eben gave her the cold facts, without adding that was the extent of his knowledge.

"Her husband. Carla was married?''

"Obviously."

Lost in her own memories of the adolescent Carla she had known, Maddie didn't hear his cynical response. "She was always singing," she recalled. "No matter what else she was doing—washing dishes, cleaning stalls, mothering an orphaned calf—there she'd be singing—or plucking out chords on that cheap Mexican guitar. You got that for her, remember. We were down in Nogales, and you traded that old watch with a cracked crystal for it."

"It turned out to be a waste of a good watch, didn't it?"

She looked at him, stung by the caustic note in his voice. "I'm surprised anybody bothered to notify you when Carla died." Maddie turned away, suddenly irritable and restless.

"She had me listed as next of kin. Probably thought I'd pay for her funeral." Eben used harshness to conceal the pain he didn't want to feel. But he was haunted by that voice on the phone, a stranger's voice that had first confirmed Eben was Carla's brother, then hit him with the news she had been killed in an accident. The voice had gone on talking, but Eben had stopped listening. When the man on the phone—obviously some sort of religious nut—made some comment to the effect that his sister had wanted him to have hope and joy, something had snapped inside him, unleashing a savage anger. That's when he had replied that he would take them as long as he didn't pay for Carla's funeral. Even now, anger was all Eben would allow himself to feel.

"By that, I take it that you aren't paying her funeral expenses," Maddie guessed coolly.

"Of course not," he replied, unmoved by the cutting disapproval in her voice. "You said you wanted to buy some horses. If you're finished with your trip down memory lane, I'll show you what I've got."

"Thanks, but no thanks. I've changed my mind." Maddie snatched her lemonade glass from the table and hurled its contents into the sink in a release of temper.

"I beg your pardon?"

She whirled on him. "No, you don't. You don't beg anybody's pardon. And to think I actually felt sorry for you when I heard what Billy Joe was doing. You do realize that he has subtly put out the word to every lending institution in the state that you are a bad risk. You're going to have to come up with a ton of cash if you plan on keeping this ranch."

"I am well aware of that."

"Lots of luck, MacCallister." Maddie turned on her heel and stalked out of the kitchen.

"I make my own luck, Maddie. I always have and I always will." Eben trailed after her at his own pace.

"You'll have to. It's for sure no one will lift a hand to help you." She stopped at the front door, her dark eyes snapping with anger. "Including me."

His pride rose up in instant resistance. "I don't recall asking for any help from you."

"No, you didn't. You never do. But I was prepared to give it just the same." That's what made her angry; she had actually come hoping to help. "We need at least two good cow horses at El Regalo, but it'll be a cold day in Hades before I'll buy them from you."

Too late Eben remembered how badly he needed money, and made an attempt to swallow his pride. He couldn't afford to lose any sale. "You won't find better horses than what I've got."

"I'll take that chance." Maddie gave the screen door a hard push. It flew open, banged against the building, and came flying back. Eben caught it before it slammed into him. "You can say what you want against your father, MacCallister, but people around here loved him. You, on the other hand, don't have a single friend in this whole county."

"I don't need any." He followed Maddie outside. "And the only reason people liked my father was because he was free with money."

"Nobody can say that about you, can they?" she mocked. "You squeeze every dime until blood runs out of it."

"That's wrong, I suppose."

"It isn't wrong, but it isn't right either." Arguing with him seemed suddenly pointless. He was so stuck in his ways it would take dynamite to budge him—or an act of God.

"Really? Then if it isn't wrong or right, what is it?" Eben challenged.

"It's empty." She looked at him, saddened by what she saw. "But that's what you are—empty. You take, take, take and hoard, hoard, hoard, and what have you got when you're all done? Nothing. Even if you somehow manage to hold on to this ranch, all you'll wind up with is an empty house and a bunch of sand, dirt, and prickly cactus. No wife, no children, no laughter, no love—you've sacrificed all of it for this." Her outflung arm made an encompassing sweep of the scene before them, indicating the sprawling desert valley and the jagged mountains that rimmed the horizon. "It was a bad trade, MacCallister. Can't you see that?"

Briefly he looked across the tawny land that was at once irresistible and treacherous. Then his gaze swung back to her. "You walked out on me, Maddie."

"I didn't walk; I ran." She looked away, a bitterness edging the corners of her mouth. "Lust was the deepest thing you ever felt for me."

"What did Williams feel?"

"That does it." She glared at him. "You have finally succeeded in driving me away just like you've driven everyone else."

"Am I supposed to feel bad about that?" Eben taunted.

"We've already been over that, MacCallister. You don't feel anything except heat or cold."

"I guess I'm lucky that way." The corners of his mouth lifted in a smile meant to infuriate.

"You may think you're lucky, but you are

wrong—and you don't even know it. That's what is so sad. I feel sorry for you, MacCallister.''

"I don't need your pity.''

"That's what you think,'' she fired back. "If there is any justice in this world, you'll get precisely what you deserve.''

"And that would be—'' He bit off the rest of his words, his attention claimed by a dark sedan barreling up the dusty ranch lane. "Who the hell is that?''

"I sincerely hope it's Billy Joe Wilder,'' Maddie sniped. "I'd like to be around when he sticks the knife in your back.''

"I always knew you were a bloodthirsty little witch,'' Eben snapped as he stepped from beneath the ramada's shade, his glance centering on the midnight blue Lincoln.

A child's face peered from a rear window, its expression all wide-eyed with wonder when the car rolled to a stop near the house. Eben counted two more heads in the backseat. As if he didn't have enough trouble on his plate, now some tourist family had gotten lost on their way to one of the dude ranches in the area. It had happened before.

When the driver's door swung open, the angry squawl of a baby mixed with a chorus of small voices chiming under it, "Are we here?'' "Is this it?''

A tall, dark-haired man stepped out, the clean-cut, preppy type, wearing the smug polish of a career professional that Eben detested. "Hello, I'm—''

Eben didn't let him get any further. "This isn't

a dude ranch, mister." At the same instant, the rear passenger door opened and a little blond-haired girl in a pink ruffled dress jumped out, followed immediately by her mirror image.

"Look, there's horses just like Mommy said." All excited, the first girl pointed a pudgy finger toward the animals in the paddocks.

"Get those kids back in that car," Eben ordered crisply. "I don't take guests here. This is a working ranch."

"There seems to be some confusion here," the man began.

"It's all on your part, if there is," Eben cut in, determined to get this family on their way and out of his hair.

"I'm Spencer Davenport with the firm Hughes, Hughes and Davenport." The man's smile faltered at Eben's lack of response. "Didn't you get my message? You are Eben MacCallister, aren't you?"

"I'm MacCallister." He frowned, puzzled that this stranger would know him. "What message was that?" he asked as Maddie came up beside him.

"I think he means the one on your answering machine," she said, then directed a smile at Spencer Davenport. "It was a bit garbled."

"I was afraid of that. I was calling from the airport."

A seven-year-old boy slid out of the car and joined the two small girls. The baby inside shrieked in rage.

"Tad's mad," the girl on the right declared.

"Real mad," the left one added. Saying nothing,

the boy simply glowered at Eben, his eyes dark with suspicion and wariness.

With nerves strung tight as a barb wire fence, Eben turned a hard look on the attorney. "What exactly was the message you left?"

"That I was picking up your sister's children and bringing them here." The answer was delivered in a matter-of-fact tone that indicated he thought it was obvious.

"My what?" Anger and shock warred for supremacy in Eben's voice. Never once had it crossed his mind that Carla might have had children.

"Your sister's children." Turning, Spencer Davenport reached inside the car and came out with a manila envelope. "Here are all the legal documents confirming your appointment as their guardian, per your late sister's wishes. You also have their birth certificates and various other papers that you may need."

"This is all a mistake. It has to be." Eben grabbed the envelope.

"I hope not." Maddie's dark eyes laughed at him.

"Are you Mrs. MacCallister?" the attorney inquired while Eben tore the envelope and rummaged through the sheaf of papers inside.

"Thankfully, no. I'm just a neighbor." All smiles, she turned to the children. Bending slightly, she asked, "What are your names?"

The boy glared at her in silence, his sandy eyebrows lowering another notch to increase the hooded effect. "Dillon is the oldest. He's seven."

The attorney inched toward the trunk. "The twins are four. One is—why don't you tell the nice lady your names, girls?"

"I'm Joy," the one on the right promptly asserted, not the least bit shy.

"I'm Hope," her sister proclaimed.

"Momma called us that—"

"—'cause we were born on Christmas Eve—"

"—just like Baby Jesus," Joy beamed with a proud smile.

"Momma said that's what—"

"—Christmas was all about."

"Hope and joy."

"And that's us."

Hope and Joy. Eben had a sudden sinking feeling, remembering that voice on the phone telling him that Carla had wanted Eben to have hope and joy. It hadn't been a spiritual wish. The words had been capitalized.

Without a pause, Hope added, "We look alike."

Before Maddie could agree, Joy declared, "But we're really not."

"Joy has freckles on her nose." Hope pointed to them.

"Hope doesn't have any." The girl shook her head, blond curls swinging about her shoulders.

"But I got a strawberry on my leg. You want to see?" Hitching up the dress's ruffled skirt, Hope thrust out her right leg to show Maddie the birthmark on her thigh.

Maddie admired it, conscious all the while of Eben poring through the papers, the baby's angry

cries in the background and the attorney dragging
suitcases and boxes out of the trunk and stacking
them on the ground. The scene was absolute may-
hem. And she couldn't imagine anyone who
deserved it more.

"Is that your little brother in the car?" she asked.

The freckled Joy nodded. "His name's Tad."

"We flew in a plane," Hope inserted.

"Tad didn't like it," Joy explained, blond curls
swinging again with the sideways movement of her
head.

Hope heaved an adultlike sigh. "Tad doesn't like
anything."

"Momma said he's a trial."

Sadness instantly rounded Hope's blue eyes.
"Our mommy and daddy died."

Joy nodded. "They're in heaven."

Hope hurried to add, "They're angels."

"Momma sings."

"Daddy can't sing—" Hope inserted, clearly
troubled by the thought.

"—but he plays the fiddle—" her twin reminded
her.

"—and the guitar and the banjo," Hope recalled, brightening.

"I bet he could learn to play the harp real quick,"
Joy declared with certainty.

"I'll bet he can, too," Maddie agreed, touched
by their simple faith.

Joy darted a curious look at Eben, then cupped
a hand to the side of her mouth and whispered
loudly, "Is that our uncle Ben?"

Seven-year-old Dillon poked her in the back. "Don't you know anything? His name's Eben, you silly goose."

Hands on her hips, Joy turned on him, indignant. "I am not a goose."

"Me neither." Hope matched her twin's pose.

"And you aren't supposed to call us names either." Joy stuck out her tongue at him, then paused and looked back at Maddie. "He is our uncle, isn't he?"

"He certainly is." Maddie's smile ran from ear to ear.

Dillon eyed him with wary distrust. "He doesn't want us," he stated. "I can tell."

Eben shot him a look and hardened himself against any feelings of pity for these orphaned youngsters. With all the trouble he had and the deadline he was under, he had neither the time nor the money to take on these four, and he saw no reason to pretend otherwise. The boy had obviously sensed that.

"Smart kid," Eben murmured.

His observation sailed right over the twins' heads as Joy rushed to deny her brother's claim, "Uncle Eben does so want us."

"He's our uncle." Which seemed to settle the issue in Hope's mind.

At the rear of the Lincoln, the attorney lifted a folded stroller out of the trunk and gave the lid a downward push. As it lowered automatically and closed with a soft click, he propped the stroller against a pile of suitcases and reached into the backseat. The baby's cries stopped in midwail, a sudden and blessed silence falling over the scene.

"Tad doesn't like to be alone," Joy explained when the attorney backed out of the car, holding a red-cheeked and dry-eyed baby well away from him.

Tad was a hefty boy, somewhere around six months old, with soft, pale brown hair and a Gerber face. He gurgled happily, chubby arms and legs churning in gleeful abandon.

"It makes him mad," Hope added.

"He's a trial," the twins chorused together.

Still holding the baby away from him, the attorney walked straight to Maddie. She started to reach for the baby, then caught a whiff of his dirty diaper and did a palms-up sweep toward Eben, indicating the lawyer needed to give young Tad to him.

Eben barely had time to shift the mass of documents into one hand before the lawyer pushed the baby into his arms. Automatically he wound his left arm around young Tad, drawing him tight to his chest.

For an instant, the two stared at each other in surprise. Then Eben recoiled from the diaper's rank smell, making a face, and Tad let out an ear-splitting wail that showed a new front tooth.

The sight of Eben with their little brother seemed to cement things for the twins. Both came over to him; only Dillon stayed back, viewing him with suspicion.

"Tad poohed his diaper," Joy explained unnecessarily.

"He won't stop crying—" Hope warned.

"—'til you change him," Joy finished.

The laughter that had been just below the surface bubbled from Maddie's throat when she saw the stricken look on Eben's face. She threw back her head, releasing an explosive burst of laughter. It rang through the air, rich with humor.

"I wish I had a camera so I could have a picture of your face right now," she declared in a voice still riddled with it.

Glaring at her, Eben checked an angry retort as the baby stiffened and arched away from him, dangerously overbalanced. Hurriedly Eben put a supporting hand behind its rigid back, crumpling both the envelope and its documents in the process.

"Better not hold him too tight," Joy cautioned, her eyes widening with certain knowledge.

"Or it'll squish out the sides—" Hope explained.

"—and make a real mess," Joy added, making a slight face at the thought.

"Tad's a—" they both began.

"—a trial, I know." An irritated Eben finished the already familiar phrase. "I got the message."

Maddie smothered another laugh and looked away, catching sight of the young attorney as he struggled to conceal his own amusement.

"Otto Grimes in Branson is handling the disposition of your sister and brother-in-law's estate," he told Eben, managing to attain a measure of sobriety. "If you have any questions, you need to contact him. His address and phone number are among those papers. Good luck." With a saluting wave, he headed for the Lincoln.

"Wait a minute." Eben all but bellowed the words, the baby crying in his ear. "You can't go off and leave me with these squawling brats."

"Sorry." The attorney shrugged, raising his voice to make himself heard above the baby's cries. "Like I said, if you have any questions, talk to Otto Grimes. Our firm's just the local liaison." With that, he climbed into the car and closed the door.

Craning her neck to look up at him, a blond-haired Joy patted his thigh. "Uncle Eben, I gotta go potty." She stood with her knees squeezed tightly together and an anxious look in her eyes.

"Oh, for God's sake," Eben muttered under his breath, then looked at Maddie. "Can you—"

Holding up her hands, she took great delight in cutting off the request. "Oh, no, you don't. I'm out of here, MacCallister. You are strictly on your own."

She walked away, leaving him with an angry, bawling baby, a little girl hopping anxiously in front of him, a second one on the verge of doing the same, a distrustful boy looking on, and a pile of luggage in the yard. Maddie had no doubts at all that Eben would be able to cope with the situation, but oh, how she wished that she could stay around to watch.

Just the thought of it had her laughing again.

Chapter III

The baby's cries quickly drowned out the taunting ring of Maddie's laughter. With jaws clenched, Eben wavered on the edge of going after her and wringing that swan-slender neck of hers. Before he succumbed to the impulse, a hand tugged insistently at the leg of his jeans.

"Uncle Eben, I gotta *go,*" came the forceful declaration.

"Me, too," a second voice claimed.

Eben started to look down at the pair, but that brought his nose too close to the baby's dirty pants. Worse than that, he felt a telltale dampness on his shirt sleeve. It confirmed what his sense of smell detected—the diaper was leaking all over the place.

"The bathroom's in the house." He jerked his head in the direction of the front door.

The two girls were off in a flash. Their departure brought a fresh note of rage to the baby's wail.

Eben fixed the baby with a glare. "Will you quit that bawling before you break my eardrum?"

The loudness of his voice startled the baby into a split second of silence. Eyes blazing with temper, he stared back at Eben and let loose an even louder scream.

"The girls are right. Tad won't stop crying 'til you change him," the seven-year-old boy stated with a definite smirk.

That was becoming increasingly clear to Eben, but he was loath to admit it. Instead he stated, "There has to be a diaper bag mixed in with all that luggage. Get it and bring it in the house."

The boy didn't move. "You're supposed to say please."

With the baby screaming in his ear, Eben was out of patience. "Just get the bag, kid."

"My name's not kid. It's Dillon," the boy fired back, but he spun on his heel and stalked over to the pile of luggage.

Satisfied that his order was being obeyed, Eben started to turn toward the house, then spotted Ramon near the barn and yelled to him, "You and Luis get up here and bring all these bags in the house!"

From the doorway came a panicked voice, "Uncle Eben, we can't find the bathroom."

Turning, Eben swore softly and succinctly, furious at Maddie for leaving him to deal with this chaos alone. He charged inside and herded the twins to the only bathroom in the house, conscious all the while of the diaper's stench and the spreading dampness on his arm. When he passed through the living room a second time, Dillon came in the front door, half-carrying and half-dragging a bulging blue diaper bag.

"Bring that into the kitchen," Eben snapped the order over his shoulder and kept walking.

In the kitchen, he tossed the crumpled documents and their envelope on the countertop, snagged a couple of clean dishcloths out of a drawer, and took them to the sink, wetting them under the faucet. Elsewhere in the house, a toilet flushed. The water coming out of the faucet went from a full-force gush to a narrow stream while the baby continued to cry in his ear, his little body stiff with rage.

Dillon came into the kitchen, lugging the diaper bag. One of the twins was right behind him. Sparing the boy a short look, Eben crossed to the long kitchen table that was a relic from the ranch's glory days. A cracked and frayed oilcloth that was nearly as old as the table covered its scarred surface.

"Get me a clean diaper out of the bag," he told the boy.

When Eben started to lay the squawling baby on the table, the little girl looked at him with widened eyes. "You aren't going to change Tad's dirty diaper on the table, are you?"

"Uugh, gross." Dillon made a face of revulsion

as the second twin bounced into the room. "Who would ever want to eat off it again?"

Grudgingly Eben conceded the validity of the boy's point and changed directions, lowering the baby to the floor—only to find himself staring into another pair of shocked blue eyes.

"You aren't going to change his diaper on the floor, are you?" the second twin exclaimed in dismay.

"It's dirty," the first one protested, aghast at the idea.

"So is your brother," Eben growled.

As a concession to the children's offended sensibilities, Eben snatched a towel off the rack and spread it on the floor, then laid the baby on it. Both girls nodded in approval.

Still screaming, the baby flailed the air with his arms and legs, broadcasting the malodorous smell straight into Eben's face. All three children gathered around as Eben unsnapped the legs to the baby's blue corduroy pants, already stained a yellowish brown in places—just like the sleeve of Eben's shirt. The smell triggered memories of all the times he had changed his baby sister's diapers when he was just a boy.

"Tad's got pooh all over him," one of the twins observed. "See."

"He's even got it on his little shirt," the second one pointed out.

"You're gonna have to change his clothes, too." The first one sighed in commiseration.

"I noticed," Eben muttered. An audience was

the last thing he wanted right now. Dodging the baby's soiled and kicking legs, he searched for the diaper's safety pins, muttering, "If you would just hold still for two minutes, I could find the pins and get this off you."

Beside him, Dillon snorted. "There aren't any pins. Haven't you ever changed a diaper before?"

Too late Eben realized this was one of those disposable diapers with adhesive tabs at the sides. Locating one of the tabs, he informed Dillon, "I'll have you know that I was changing your mother's diapers when I was seven years old. I'm not exactly new to this business."

But his technique was definitely a little rusty, Eben acknowledged—although only to himself.

When he ripped back the second tape, the baby's cries stopped, the last one dissolving into a kind of gurgle of relief. The silence was like a blessing.

But it didn't last as the girl crouched on his left proclaimed, "We told you Tad wouldn't stop crying—"

"—'til you changed him," the second one finished the sentence.

Ignoring their chatter, Eben lifted back the diaper, using the clean corners to wipe as he went. The mess was everywhere.

"This is worse than a calf with the scours," he muttered to himself.

"What's the scours?" One of the twins tipped her head to the side, peering at him curiously.

"You're looking at it," Eben replied.

Grabbing the baby by the ankles, he lifted his

bottom off the dirty diaper and held it up while he wiped the worst of it off the baby, then rolled the diaper into a wad and handed it to the boy.

"Throw this away." With a nod of his head, Eben indicated the tall plastic wastebasket at the end of the kitchen counter.

Dillon scowled at him without taking it. "You're supposed to say please."

Irritated, Eben gave him a narrow look. "I'm the one who taught your mother manners, so don't be giving me any lessons in them, kid."

"My name's Dillon, so don't be calling me kid," the boy snapped right back, eyes blazing beneath his beetling brows. "And don't worry—I don't want to be here any more than you want us here."

Without another word, Dillon snatched the dirty diaper out of Eben's hand and stalked to the wastebasket. Eben stared at him, taken aback by the venom in his voice. But the kid had read him right: Eben didn't want them here. He was sorry their parents had died; that was something he wouldn't wish on any kid. But Carla's children or not, they were strangers to him. After the way she had treated him, it wasn't right that his sister had dumped them on him. Just as soon as he got the baby cleaned up, Eben intended to do something about getting them off his hands.

"Dillon didn't mean that, Uncle Eben." A small hand patted his shoulder in comfort.

"I did so!" Dillon hurled the diaper into the wastebasket in sharp punctuation.

The other twin picked up the first one's initial

thought, continuing it as if her brother hadn't spoken. "He's just talking mean 'cause—"

"—he's upset about Mommy and Daddy."

"He misses them a lot."

"So do we."

It was like being trapped between two stereo speakers, with sound bombarding first one ear then the other. Seeking to halt it, Eben ordered, "One of you get a clean diaper out of that bag."

"Please," Dillon inserted in a sarcastically nasal voice.

Eben shot him a look. Fortunately neither of the twins paid any attention to their brother, as the one on Eben's left scurried to do his bidding. In the meantime, he picked up a wet dishcloth and began the task of cleaning the baby. From the living room came the tramp of booted feet into the house, signaling the arrival of Ramon and Luis with the luggage.

"You need to use these wipeys, Uncle Eben," one of the twins instructed, pulling a plastic container out of the diaper bag and holding it out to him.

"They already got soap in 'em," her sister explained, taking it and opening the container's flip-top cap, then tearing off a premoistened wipe for him.

The clean scent of it was a welcome change from the diaper's stink. Eben gladly took it and used it to finish washing the baby's behind while the first twin went back to rummaging through the diaper bag.

"Here." She dragged out a green receiving blanket and tossed it to Eben. "You better put that over Tad."

"Yeah," the second girl agreed. "Or else he might pee on you."

"That's 'cause he's a boy," the first explained, assuming an adultlike air.

Recognizing the wisdom of the suggestion, Eben took the blanket and draped it over the baby. A small hand instantly grabbed a corner of it and jammed it in his mouth.

"Here's some lotion." She held out a plastic bottle.

"That's to put on Tad's bottom—" The other stereo speaker kicked in.

"—so it doesn't get all red and sore."

"He cries when it does."

"We don't want that to happen." Not when the baby had finally stopped his bawling. Eben took the lotion and smeared it over Tad's bare bottom.

"Give this to Tad." The girl passed a teething ring to her sister.

"He likes to chew on it." Deftly she extracted the blanket corner from the baby's mouth and replaced it with the teething ring.

"That's 'cause he's getting another tooth."

"The diaper," Eben prompted, recapping the lotion bottle.

Instead the girl pulled a small white T-shirt out of the bag. "You'll need to put this on him. And this." She reached back in and hauled out a pair of brown coveralls with a teddy bear appliqued on its front.

"Is there a diaper in there or not?" Exasperated, Eben sat back on his heels and landed squarely on the blunted points of his spurs.

He arched off them, swearing. "Ouch! Dammit."

Dillon immediately howled with laughter. "Did you see that? He sat on his spurs. They poked him right in the butt."

Both girls rushed to him with motherly concern. "Did you hurt yourself, Uncle Eben?"

"Let me see." The second tried to examine him and ascertain the extent of his injury.

He brushed them both off with a gruff, "Just get away from me. I'm fine, okay?" Reaching back, he unbuckled the spurs and shoved them across the floor, out of the way.

"Are they real sharp?" One of the twins went to inspect them. A gasp of surprise came from her when she picked one up. "Hope, look," she called excitedly to her sister. "They're Christmas spurs!"

"They are!" Hope touched the star-shaped rowel with a kind of awe.

"Put that down. They aren't to play with," Eben ordered sharply. "And they aren't Christmas spurs either."

"They are, too. See." The first twin hurried to show him. "It's got a star—"

"—just like the star that shined over Befflehem," her sister finished.

"—when Baby Jesus was born."

Eben snatched the spur from the girl's hand and

pushed it back with its mate. "It has a star because this is Star Ranch. It has nothing to do with Christmas."

"But it could."

"Well, it doesn't. Now find me that damned diaper, Faith or Hope or whatever the heck your name is."

"It's Joy." She thrust her nose close to his face. "See the freckles."

"I'm Hope," the other girl declared.

"Fine." At rope's end, Eben dragged a hand down his face and gave up. "Just give me the bag. I'll find the damned diaper myself." He grabbed the strap and pulled the bag closer to him.

"You said a bad word again," the freckled Joy informed him with a primly censurous look.

"Momma said you shouldn't do that," Hope scolded.

"Yeah." A still-gloating Dillon joined in the criticism. "When you swear, you're supposed to get your mouth washed out with soap."

"All three of you are gonna hear a lot more swearing if you don't back away and give me some room." Eben cast a warning glance at them.

"Oh-oh," Dillon laughed in mock fear. "I think the big guy's mad."

Joy was instantly contrite. "We didn't mean to make you mad, Uncle Eben."

"We just wanted to help," Hope explained, the corners of her mouth taking a downcast turn.

"Honest."

"I have had all your help I can stand." Eben

went through the unzipped diaper bag, digging through the toys, bottles, clothing and assorted baby paraphernalia, looking for a clean diaper.

"Señor Mac?" Ramon spoke from the doorway, interrupting the search.

"What?" The demand exploded from him.

Ramon hurriedly pulled off his straw cowboy hat and held it in front of him. Luis hovered directly behind him, his expression as startled and wide-eyed as his cousin's.

"We bring in the bags," Ramon explained quickly. "Was there something else you wished us to do?"

"No. Go on back to work." Eben waved them away and went back to his search, half-convinced he was never going to get this kid's diaper changed.

"The chores, they are all done. We go home now," Ramon told him.

"Fine." Distracted, Eben didn't see the baby roll onto his stomach and awkwardly push onto his hands and knees. His first warning was a glimpse of a bare bottom high in the air. "Come back here, you little squirt."

He grabbed the baby before he could crawl away, his big hands picking up Tad and laying him back on the towel. The baby squealed in delight as if it were a game and immediately started to roll over again.

"Oh, no, you don't." Eben caught him again. This time he kept a hand on the baby's stomach to hold him down. Gurgling with laughter, Tad

wiggled and kicked. "Will you hold still?" Eben
growled.

"Tad thinks you're playing," Joy advised him.

"He's real ticklish," Hope added with a grin of
her own.

"That's his problem, not mine." Still keeping
his hand on the squirming and giggling baby, Eben
resumed his search for the elusive diaper.

"Do you want us to watch Tad?"

"Tad's fine," Eben replied. "Just leave us both
alone."

"But we don't got nothin' to do."

"Find something." At last he located a clean
diaper all the way at the bottom of the bag.

"Can we watch cartoons?"

"I told you—I don't care." Unfolding the diaper
required both hands, giving the baby a chance to
make another escape.

"Where's your television?"

"I don't have one." Eben grabbed a leg and
rolled a gleefully squealing Tad back onto the
towel.

"You don't have a TV?!" the twins chorused in
shocked dismay.

At the news, Dillon flopped onto a kitchen chair,
the picture of bitter dejection. "I knew I didn't
want to come here."

"But—everybody's got a television," Joy protested.

"How come you don't?" Hope wanted to know.

"Because it's a waste of good money," Eben
stated flatly.

"TV's don't cost that much," Dillon scoffed.

"They do when you start adding on the price of a satellite dish, installation and hook-up fees, plus the monthly subscriptions." Eben listed the reasons while he struggled to get the diaper on the squirming baby. "You start figuring all that up and you'll find it's very expensive."

"If we can't watch TV, what are we supposed to do?" Joy asked in a forlorn voice.

"You can do what I did when I was a kid—go outside and play," Eben answered with sorely tested patience.

"We can't," Joy told him.

"We got on our good dresses," Hope explained. "We'd get 'em all dirty."

In Eben's mind, the solution to that was obvious. "Then go change your clothes."

"But we don't know where our old clothes are," Joy protested.

"Why don't you try looking in the suitcases?" Eben suggested with dry disgust. "They're all in the living room."

"Which ones, Uncle Eben?"

"Oh, good grief," he muttered under his breath, then motioned to Dillon. "Take your sisters into the living room and help them find their clothes."

"Why do I have to take them?" Dillon complained with a put-upon look.

"Because I said so," Eben stated, in no mood for an argument over it. "Now, go. All of you."

Sulking in protest, Dillon dragged himself off

the kitchen chair and plodded toward the living room. The twins skipped alongside him.

"Dillon, would you find my purple jeans?" Joy asked.

"And I want my 'Little Mermaid' shirt," Hope delcared, drawing an instant protest from her sister.

"No, let's wear our 'Pocahontas' ones."

Hope shook her head. "They don't go with purple jeans."

"It does so."

"No, it doesn't. Dillon, tell her you aren't supposed to wear Pocahontas with purple jeans."

Tuning out the receding voices, Eben concentrated on getting the diaper on Tad, then set about removing the baby's dirty shirt and searching out a clean set of clothes. None too expertly, Eben got the squirming infant dressed, laid him back on the towel, and stuck the teething ring in his little hand.

"Stay there," he ordered, rising to his feet.

Tad cooed happily and waved the ring in the air while Eben crossed to the kitchen counter. Retrieving the crumpled documents, he smoothed them out and shuffled through them until he located the telephone number for the lawyer in Branson.

With the number in hand, he walked over to the phone, picked up the receiver, and punched out the numbers. As he listened to the first ring, metal clanked on the kitchen's tiled floor. Eben glanced back to see the baby, off the towel, grabbing the leather strap to the spurs he'd left lying on the floor.

"Oh, no, you don't, buster." Eben moved to rescue them from the baby's clutches, but the telephone cord didn't reach that far.

Hurriedly he laid the receiver down, scooped up the baby, took the spur away, and snatched up the receiver in time to hear a woman's voice saying, "—offices of Grimes, Norris and Brown, attorneys at law. Our office hours are from eight-thirty A.M. until five P.M. The office will be closed from twelve noon until one P.M. If you would leave your name, telephone number, and a brief message, we'll get back to you as soon as possible." A long tone droned in Eben's ear, followed by a *beep*.

Eben fired a glance at the wall clock and mentally calculated the difference in time zones. The office was closed for the day.

"That's great. That's just great," he muttered and slammed the receiver down in frustration.

The twins ran back into the kitchen, one of them dressed in a garish lime green top and purple jeans and the other in neon pink shorts and a beige T-shirt emblazoned with a svelte Indian maiden and a raccoon. Obviously they had agreed to disagree about what to wear.

"Uncle Eben, we're hungry," the one in purple announced.

"You got any cookies?" the neon pink twin asked.

"We like Oreos best."

"I like to lick the centers."

"I like to dunk mine in milk." The girl in the purple jeans had freckles on her nose. Which meant she had to be Joy.

"You're out of luck," Eben informed them. "I don't have any cookies—Oreos or otherwise."

"But we're hungry."

"All we had on the plane was a dry old sandwich."

"We got to eat something—" Joy insisted.

"—or we'll die." Hope flung up her hands in dramatic emphasis.

"That's too bad. You'll just have to wait until suppertime," Eben said.

"When's that?"

"What are we gonna have?" Hope cut to the important issue.

"How about pizza," the freckled and purple-clad Joy suggested with bright-eyed excitement.

Their chatter was nonstop. There was no escape from it. Listening to them, Eben had the uneasy feeling they probably talked with their mouths full. There was no doubt about it—they couldn't leave soon enough to suit him.

"We're having chili." He had a large bowl of it in the refrigerator.

Hope screwed up her face in distaste, the strawberry birthmark on her leg clearly visible below her shorts. "I don't like chili," she told him.

"Me either." Joy shook her head.

Eben started to tell them they would eat it and like it, then thought better of it. With the way his luck was running, they would probably get sick and throw up all over the place.

He sighed in defeat. "What do you like to eat?"

"We like lots of things," Joy assured him.

"No, they don't," Dillon said from the doorway. "They only like pizza, hot dogs, and hamburgers or else macaroni and cheese."

"Hamburgers it is, then," Eben replied.

Chapter IV

The amusement that had carried Maddie away from Star Ranch faded by the time she reached the elaborate entrance gates to El Regalo Guest Ranch. The drive had given her too much time to reflect on her meeting with Eben and all the things that had been said *before* the children arrived.

In some ways, Eben had reacted exactly as she had expected he would. After all, she had known from the start that he wouldn't be glad to see her. But she had thought that once he learned the purpose of her visit, he would be a little grateful.

But not Eben.

What on earth had she hoped to gain by going there? Maddie wondered for about the tenth time.

Unfortunately the more she examined her motive, the less pure it seemed.

Yes, Maddie knew the bank, i.e. Billy Joe Wilder, had given Eben notice that it was calling the loan due; hence, Eben would need a lot of cash fast if he hoped to keep the ranch. Yes. El Regalo was in the market for a couple of good cow ponies. Buying them from Eben seemed a logical way to fill that need and help Eben at the same time. It was a simple case of neighbor helping neighbor; the past was the past, wasn't it?

Except none of that explained why Maddie had gone to see Eben herself. And she knew it.

Buying horses for the ranch was the job of Sam Adams, El Regalo's head wrangler; her only responsibility was to approve the amount of the purchase, not select it. It wouldn't have been out of line for Maddie to recommend that Sam Adams buy the needed horses from Eben. But she hadn't been content to do that. No, she had insisted on going there herself.

Why? The reason was painfully clear—so she could have the satisfaction of watching Eben's face, knowing that he needed this sale—that indirectly he needed her. It had been a kind of sweet vengeance for the past.

Like it or not, the old hurts were still there. The old feelings of rejection. Time hadn't healed them as completely as Maddie had believed.

Her mind flashed back to that moment when the young gelding had spooked and Eben had landed on the ground not far from her. In her

head, Maddie could hear the words she had said—
"After all these years, MacCallister, I finally have
you at my feet."

At the time it had been merely a clever thing to
say. She hadn't recognized the truth in them; she
hadn't recognized that she secretly wanted Eben
at her feet, begging—for what? Mercy? Help? For-
giveness?

And if he had pleaded for any of those things,
would she really have been glad? Something told
Maddie the satisfaction would have been very
fleeting.

It was a sobering thought, one that left her feeling a bit ashamed of herself. The feeling intensified
when Maddie remembered those four children
and recalled that last glimpse of them—the baby
screaming in Eben's ear, one of the twins tugging
at his pant leg, and the boy looking on, aloof and
distrustful.

She had been so busy laughing at Eben's predica-
ment that Maddie had given little thought to the
children's. To lose both their parents, then be
taken from their home and thrust into the care of
a stranger, all in a matter of days—it had to be
traumatic.

And she had just walked away. How could she
have done that?

An hour and a half later, Eben was on his hands
and knees under the table, mopping up spilled
milk and chucking pieces of broken glass into a

dustpan. The baby sat on Dillon's lap, squealing and banging a spoon on the table.

Joy poked her head under the table. "Hope didn't mean to make a mess, Uncle Eben. Honest," she told him for the tenth time.

"The glass just jumped out of my hand," came Hope's tearful explanation.

"That's 'cause your hands aren't big enough to hold it," Dillon stated with an older brother's superior knowledge. "I told him he needed to give you two smaller glasses or you'd drop them. I was right."

"I don't have any smaller drinking glasses," Eben muttered through clenched teeth.

"You'd better get some, or all the ones you've got will wind up getting broken," Dillon stated matter-of-factly.

Eben tossed the last large chunk of glass into the pan and grumbled to himself, "What I need to do is get rid of the four of you."

"Do you want some more paper towels, Uncle Eben?" Sliding off her chair, Joy put one foot on the floor. "I'll get them for you."

"You get back in that chair!" Rising up, Eben cracked his head on the underside of the table. Pain shot through him in an explosion of colors. "Ouch, damn!"

"Are you okay, Uncle Eben?" Joy peered under the table again, all anxious concern.

"Yes—no thanks to you." Wincing, he rubbed the throbbing crown of his head. "For once, just do as you're told and stay in that chair. How many times do I have to tell you, there's broken glass down here? You'll cut yourself on it and bleed all over the place."

"No, I won't."

"She's wearing shoes," Hope reminded him.

"I don't care what she's wearing," Eben snapped. "Now, just sit up to the table and eat your hamburgers."

A moment of actual silence followed, broken only by the clatter of plates and Tad's testing shrieks. After the bedlam of the last hour and half, the quiet seemed beautiful to Eben. He had almost forgotten how wonderful silence was. Unfortunately it didn't last as a squabble broke out above his head.

"You give me that ketchup, Dillon," Hope demanded.

"You want it. You get it," he taunted.

Joy looked under the table again. "Uncle Eben, Dillon won't give us the ketchup."

"I can't eat my hamburger without ketchup," Hope declared.

"Dillon, give your sister that ketchup bottle." Eben tossed the milk-sodden paper towels onto the broken glass in the dustpan.

"How can I when I'm holding Tad?" Dillon responded in a fine show of innocence.

"Never mind," Joy said in disgust. "I'll get it myself."

As Eben backed out from under the table, dustpan in hand, Joy stood up on her chair seat. He lifted his head above the table at the same moment her fingers closed around the neck of the ketchup bottle. Their eyes locked.

"Sit down in that chair before you knock something else over," he ordered.

"I never knocked nothing over. I'm Joy."

"Sit down right now!" Eben thundered, completely out of patience.

In her haste to do as he said, Joy let go of the ketchup bottle. It teetered unsteadily for an instant, then crashed onto Eben's plate, splatting pork and beans as ketchup spurted across the table into Tad's face and Eben's hamburger catapulted into the air. He grabbed for it and missed. The patty separated from the mustard-smeared bun and cartwheeled onto the floor, scattering pickles and onions in three different directions.

Tad squealed with glee and clapped his ketchup-splattered hands while Dillon hooted with laughter at the sight, and Hope giggled wildly. A stern-faced Joy stood on her knees and struck a combative pose, hands at her waist.

"It's all your fault," she told Eben, yelling above her siblings' laughter. "You shouted at me!"

"You're damned right I shouted at you," Eben yelled right back. "That was my hamburger that went on the floor!"

"You can have mine, Uncle Eben," a giggly Hope offered.

He took one look at the bun-shredded hamburger on her plate and roared, "Who in his right mind would want yours?!"

"Isn't this just the ideal scene of family bliss."

Maddie paused inside the kitchen doorway, observing the scene with open amusement.

Startled by the sound of her voice, Eben swung around and inadvertently tilted the dustpan, spilling broken glass and sodden towels onto his chair seat. He swore furiously at the new mess.

"Tch, tch, tch." Maddie clucked her tongue in mock reproval, laughter sparkling in her eyes. "Such language in front of the children. You should be ashamed of yourself, MacCallister." She calmly crossed to the sink and wrung out a wet dishrag.

"What are you doing here?" Eben glared.

Maddie stopped halfway to the table, an eyebrow arching in droll challenge. "Do you want me to leave? If you do . . ." She paused, letting the thought dangle.

In that split second of hesitation, images of the mess on the floor, the table and chair flashed through his mind. Eben's anger crumbled like a house of cards before a desert wind.

"Dear God, no," he said with feeling.

"Poor Eben." Behind the glint of amusement in her brown eyes, there was a look of genuine sympathy.

"Careful," he warned when she started to walk past him. "Don't step on the hamburger."

Bending, she picked it up. "Whose is this?"

"Mine," Eben admitted, then saw the quick mocking arch of her eyebrow and pointed an accusing finger at Joy. "I didn't do it. She knocked the ketchup bottle on my plate."

"He shouted at me," Joy spoke up in her own defense.

"Dillon started it." Hope glared at her older brother.

"He wouldn't give Hope the ketchup," Joy explained to Maddie.

"Yeah, well, you dropped your glass of milk first," Dillon jeered the reminder.

"That's 'cause it was too big for me."

"Yeah," Joy quickly agreed with her twin. "Uncle Eben should have given us smaller ones."

"I don't have any smaller ones," he repeated in exasperation. "How many times do I have to tell you that?"

Maddie raised her hands, calling for quiet. "Children, children." Her pointed glance included Eben in the group. "Accidents happen all the time. It doesn't matter whose fault it is. We still have to clean up and go on."

"With these kids, accidents turn into chain reactions," Eben muttered before scooping the onion and pickle slices off the floor and dumping them in the dust pan.

"Most chain reactions require some sort of catalyst," Maddie reminded him in a mocking undertone.

Joy's sharp ears caught her softly voiced comment. "What's a cat'lyst?" she asked with a puzzled frown.

"It's an instigator," Maddie replied easily.

Joy's frown deepened. "What's a 'stigator?"

"A troublemaker."

"I'm not a troublemaker," Hope declared with a vigorous shake of her head.

"I never said you were," Maddie assured her, then suggested, "Why don't you get a washcloth from the bathroom so I can wipe the ketchup off Tad's face and hands."

Before Hope could hop to the floor, Eben spoke up sharply. "Sit down and don't move. There might be glass on the floor yet."

"Eben, she has shoes on." Maddie smiled at his extreme caution.

"That's what Hope told him," Joy was quick to point out.

Maddie wagged a reproving finger at her. "No tattling."

Dillon instantly began to chant, "Joy is a tattletale. Joy is a tattletale."

"I am not!" Her hands went to her waist again.

"You are so." He stuck his tongue out at her.

Joy appealed to Eben. "Make him stop that, Uncle Eben."

"Oh, good grief," Eben muttered, rolling his eyes heavenward.

"Dillon's a 'stigator, isn't he, Uncle Eben," Hope stated, pleased with herself for remembering the word.

"That's enough out of all of you." Out of the corner of his eye, Eben saw the smile Maddie was struggling to hide. It only irritated him more. "Hope, go get the washcloth like Maddie told you," he directed. "Just be careful and don't fall."

"Okay." Hope slid off the chair and walked with

deliberate slowness away from the table, then broke into a run when she reached the doorway.

"Walk," Maddie called after her.

But the admonishment came too late. Gingerly Maddie lifted the ketchup bottle out of Eben's plate and wiped off the worst of the smashed pork and beans. More were splattered on the patterned oilcloth.

"Joy, bring me that roll of paper towels off the counter, would you?" she asked.

"Sure." Eager to help, Joy jumped down and dashed to the counter.

Within minutes, the mess was cleaned and order was restored. "Do you see how easy it is when everyone helps," Maddie chided Eben.

"If you think this is all so easy, little Miss Pollyanna, you can fix me something to eat." Eben pulled out his chair and sat down. "In case you haven't noticed, I'm the one that worked all day— and they are the ones with food on their plates. Mine's in the garbage."

"I'll make a deal with you, MacCallister." As always when he annoyed her, she called him by his surname.

"What's that?" He eyed her with suspicion.

Maddie lifted the baby off Dillon's lap and set him on Eben's. "If you feed Tad, I'll fix you some supper. Deal?"

"There isn't any more hamburger thawed." Eben obligingly dipped the spoon in the jar of baby food.

"In that case, you'll have to be satisfied with

bacon and eggs," Maddie replied, opening the refrigerator door.

By the time Tad had eaten all he wanted, Maddie set Eben's plate before him, overflowing with three perfectly basted eggs, a double rasher of bacon, and a side of buttered toast. Nothing had ever looked so delicious to him. Eben started to tell her so, then caught her smug you-thought-I'd-forgotten-the-way-you-liked-your-bacon-and-eggs-didn't-you? look. It checked the compliment on his tongue.

"It's about time," he grumbled instead and handed the baby to her.

"Your gratitude is overwhelming, MacCallister. Next time I'll sprinkle tabasco sauce on your food." She snatched the washcloth off the table and wiped at Tad's hands and face, sticky with strained chicken and pureed pears.

"We both know there won't be a next time, Maddie." Eben cut into an egg with his fork, piercing the yolk.

She stiffened for an instant, then relaxed, murmuring a cool, "How very true."

"I'm done eating, Uncle Eben." Joy pushed her plate back.

"Me, too," As always, Hope followed suit.

"What are you telling me for?" Eben frowned.

" 'Cause you need to 'xcuse us," Joy explained.

"You're excused," he said with a wave of his fork.

Both of them remained in their chairs. "What should we do now?" Joy asked.

He gave her a blank look. "Leave, I suppose. How should I know what you're supposed to do?"

Hope turned sad eyes on Maddie. "Uncle Eben doesn't have a TV."

"And we can't play outside—"

"—'cause it's dark."

"If we can't watch TV—"

"—and we can't play outside—"

"—what are we supposed to do?"

"That is a problem, isn't it?" Maddie agreed solemnly.

Joy released a long, weighty sigh. "It's a big one."

"Can you think of something we can do?" Hope turned bright eyes on Maddie.

"How about helping me with dishes?" Maddie suggested.

"We could load the dishwasher," Joy offered eagerly.

"Yeah, we know how," Hope chimed in.

"That's wonderful. Unfortunately, your uncle Eben doesn't have a dishwasher," Maddie explained.

"Jeez," Dillon declared in disgust. "What kind of place is this? He doesn't have TV, he doesn't have a microwave, and now he doesn't have a dishwasher."

"Yeah, but he's got a real fireplace—" Joy reminded him.

"—with a chimney and everything," Hope rushed to add.

"On Christmas Eve—"

"—we can hang up our stockings—"

"—and Santa can fill them with lots and lots of

presents," Joy finished with a dramatic flourish of hands.

"You can forget that idea right now," Eben informed her. "Santa won't be coming here."

"Why not?" Joy looked horror-stricken.

"We been good," Hope promised with an insistent bob of her head.

"Santa, Santa, Santa." Dillon mocked, then turned angry. "I've told you and told you—there's no such thing as Santa Claus. It was always Mom and Dad who put presents under the tree. Now they're dead and you aren't ever gonna get any more presents."

Chapter V

At the end of Dillon's bitter outburst there was a moment of utter silence in the kitchen. Maddie shot a glance at Eben and saw the look of approval he directed at Dillon. Irritated, she turned to the twins, determined to restore their belief in Santa. But neither girl appeared the least bit ruffled by their brother's denial of him.

Looking at him, Joy released a sigh of annoyance. "You always think you know everything, Dillon."

"But you don't," Hope asserted.

"Momma explained about all that," Joy declared.

"Sometimes moms and dads have to help—"

"—when Santa's in a jam."

"He used to do it all himself—"

"—but there's too many kids now."

"It's a pop'lation thing," Hope concluded.

Dillon snorted in derision. "Mom only told you that to keep you believing a little longer. It isn't true."

"It is so!" Joy argued.

"Is not," he jeered.

"Is so!"

Before it turned into an is-so, is-not shouting match, Maddie intervened. "That's enough of that. No more fighting."

"But he's wrong," Joy protested.

"Then, he'll find that out, won't he?" Maddie reasoned.

But Dillon refused to let that be the last word. "You're the ones who are gonna find out that you're wrong."

"That's enough, Dillon." Maddie pressed a silencing hand on his shoulder.

But Eben took Dillon's side. "Let the boy talk."

"Keep out of this, MacCallister," Maddie warned, her sharp glance cutting to him.

"Why should I?" he demanded, his head rearing back. "You certainly aren't doing these girls any favor by perpetuating the myth."

Joy frowned at the word. "What's a myth?"

"Don't you pay any attention to—" Maddie began.

Eben broke in, "A myth is a story people make up in their heads. Christmas and Santa are just a scheme some retailer came up with to sell merchandise."

Joy gasped in dismay. "You don't believe in Christmas?!"

"But you got to, Uncle Eben," Hope insisted.

As he opened his mouth to reply, Maddie cut in, "One more word out of you, MacCallister, and I'm out of here. And when I go, I'll take the crib back to the ranch with me."

"What crib?" Eben frowned.

"The one I brought for Tad. Or hadn't you thought about where this baby is going to sleep tonight?" Maddie challenged as young Tad yawned and rubbed his face.

Eben dodged the question rather than admit he hadn't thought that far ahead. "What are you doing with a baby crib?"

"We always keep a couple at the ranch in case we need one for our guests. We don't encourage families with infants to bring them when they vacation at El Regalo, but it happens." The baby snuggled against her, his action touching off a whole tide of warm, maternal feelings that had been too long denied. Maddie slid her hand a little higher on his back and rocked him from side to side. "As soon as you're done eating, you can unload the crib and set it up in your room—"

"My room? Why does he have to sleep there?" Eben demanded, the frown deepening on his bluntly chiseled features.

"So you can hear him if he wakes up in the night, of course."

Lowering his head, Eben grumbled something under his breath. In some ways, he hadn't changed at all, Maddie decided, and yet, he had changed a lot. That was a contradiction, she knew, but that didn't make it any less true.

For too many years, Eben had been driven by the need to make a success of the ranch. Many had thought he couldn't do it, including Maddie. But he had rescued it from near bankruptcy through sheer hard work and a careful pinching of every penny, denying himself things that most people regarded as necessities. Out of pride, he had pretended he didn't need them—as he had pretended he didn't need many other things.

That was the problem. For too long he had pretended to be tough, cold, and uncaring; now, he actually believed he was.

She wondered if Eben remembered telling her about the times when his baby sister Carla had cried in the night and he had taken her out of the crib and put her in bed with him. He had been the one who took Carla to school that first day, helped with her homework, taken her shopping at the thrift stores for new clothes, and vetted her boyfriends. Carla had always been quick to admit that Eben had raised her.

From everything both Eben and Carla had told her about their father, Maddie had gotten the impression that Johnny MacCallister—Johnny Mac to his friends—would have made a great doting uncle, always joking and teasing, showering them with useless gifts. But as a parent, he couldn't be bothered with the day-to-day responsibilities of fatherhood.

He'd had much the same attitude toward the ranch—he had liked owning it, but not running it. As a consequence, Eben had stepped in to fill the void, first assuming responsibility for his sister, then, ultimately, the ranch.

Maddie wasn't at all surprised that Carla had left her children in Eben's care. In its own way, it was a testament to the parenting job he had done with Carla.

"Where are we gonna sleep tonight, Uncle Eben?" Joy wanted to know.

"Yeah," Hope said to echo the question, then added a second one of her own, "Are we gonna sleep in your room like Tad?"

Eben choked on a bite of bacon. "Absolutely not!"

"Then where?" A worried, little crease appeared on Joy's forehead.

Sensing that the children had long ago exceeded the limits of Eben's patience with their endless questions, Maddie took pity on him and suggested, "We'll sort out which bedroom you'll have later. Right now, let's all pitch in and get these dishes started while your uncle finishes eating. Dillon, you can wash. Joy can rinse and Hope can dry."

Dillon objected indignantly to his inclusion. "I'm not helping. Guys don't wash dishes," he declared with certainty.

"Around here, guys do everything," Eben was

quick to inform him. "They cook and clean, wash dishes, and make beds."

"I'll bet you don't do all that stuff. You're just saying that," Dillon taunted.

"You'd be wrong, because I do it all."

"Yeah, right," Dillon mocked.

"You haven't seen any housekeeper around here, have you?" Eben challenged.

"No, but—"

"That's because I don't have one. What's more, I don't need one," he stated.

Personally, Maddie thought that point was debatable. In her opinion, the house was overdue for a thorough cleaning. True, the floors were swept, the furniture dusted, and the countertops were spotless, but the curtains were badly in need of washing, the woodwork needed to be wiped down, and the cupboards needed to be cleaned and new shelf paper installed. Wisely, she refrained from telling Eben that.

"In case you forgot, I fixed that hamburger you ate," Eben continued, determined to make his point with Dillon. "It's only right that you help with the cleaning up. So, get over there and start washing dishes." He waved him toward the sink. "And take your plate and silverware with you."

Dillon gave him a sullen look, then grudgingly gathered his dirty dishes and carried them to the sink. The twins arrived there ahead of him, eager to get to work. There was a problem, though.

"We can't reach the sink," Joy announced in frustration.

"We're too short," Hope complained.

"What are we gonna do now, Miss Maddie?" Joy turned to her.

"Why don't you bring your chairs over here and stand on them? And just call me Maddie. You don't have to say 'Miss.' It makes me feel old."

"But Momma said that we should." Joy's blond curls bounced with the emphatic nod of her head.

"She said it showed the proper 'spect," Hope added, stumbling a little over the last word.

"Your mother was absolutely right," Maddie assured them. "But as long as you have my permission not to use 'Miss' before my name, then you are still showing the proper respect, okay?"

"Okay," they chimed and ran to get their chairs.

To Dillon's disgust, he discovered he needed a chair as well. Soon all three had their chairs drawn up to the sink counter and were about their individual tasks while Maddie looked on, holding the drowsy baby in her arms.

When Eben added his dishes to the slowly dwindling stack, Dillon muttered, "I don't see why we didn't use paper plates. Then we could've thrown them away when we were done eating, and we wouldn't have to be washing all these ucky dishes."

"Because paper plates cost money, that's why," Eben replied, then turned to Maddie. "Is your Jeep unlocked?"

She nodded that it was, then glanced at the heavy-eyed baby in her arms, a softness automatically entering her expression at the sight of him. "As sleepy as Tad is, I think he'll be ready to use the crib as soon as you get it set up."

"With luck, they all will," Eben murmured dryly, his glance encompassing the other three children and lingering a moment on the talkative twins.

"You gotta give Tad a bottle when you put him to bed," Joy was quick to inform Maddie.

"Else he'll cry," Hope added the warning.

"Great," Eben muttered, and headed out of the kitchen. Three steps into the living room, he came to an abrupt stop. Recovering, he thundered, "What happened in here? It looks like a cyclone hit."

He stared at the jumble of opened suitcases and strewn clothes that transformed the once-tidy room into a scene of chaos. Maddie came to the doorway, with all three children hot on her heels. Dillon and Joy dripped water from their wet hands.

"I wondered if you had seen this," Maddie murmured, hiding a smile.

"Seen what?" Joy looked around the room in perfect innocence.

"This—" Eben appeared to search for the right word. "This mess! There are clothes everywhere."

"We had to change out of our good dresses," Joy began with utter unconcern.

"But we didn't know where our old clothes were," Hope inserted.

"So we had to look."

"Don't you 'member?"

"I remember, all right," Eben snapped. "But did you have to go through every single suitcase?"

Joy's shoulders lifted in a small shrug. "Hope couldn't find her pink shorts."

"Heaven forbid that she wear something else," Eben muttered to himself, then gestured impatiently at the mess. "As soon as you get those dishes done, you get in here and clean this up."

"We'll straighten up while we look for their pajamas," Maddie promised as the baby fussed in her arms, then diverted the subject. "There's a mattress pad and a sheet lying on the front seat. Be sure you bring those in when you unload the crib."

"Gladly." Pajamas, sheets, mattresses, all equated with sleep in his mind. And sleep meant some peace and quiet at last. Eben crossed to the front door, more convinced than ever that he wanted his house and his life back. It couldn't happen soon enough to suit him.

Forty-five minutes later, he had the crib set up in his room, ready for the baby. Eben briefly toyed with the idea of simply closing the door and leaving Maddie to cope alone. But he knew she would come looking for him, dragging the kids with her.

Guided by the sound of jabbering voices, Eben made his way to the living room. He paused a minute, unnoticed, and surveyed the stacks of crudely folded clothes that brought a hint of order to the chaotic jumble of suitcases, boxes, and bags littering the room.

With a shift of attention, his glance skipped over the chattering, stereo twins and briefly touched on a sullen-faced Dillon, flopped in one of the chairs, disinterestedly spinning the wheels on a miniature race car. Moving on, it came to rest on Maddie, bouncing a cranky baby in her arms.

Eben was pleased to see that she no longer projected an aura of unflappable competence. Her hair was mussed; there were wet spots on her silk blouse from the baby's drool; and a tail of her blouse hung outside the waistband of her slacks. Despite the easy smile she showed the twins, Maddie looked a little bit frazzled.

He liked that—and the glint of relief that flashed in her eyes when she saw him. "How come you guys are still up?" he challenged, walking the rest of the way into the room. "I expected you to be in bed, sound asleep by now."

"We might as well be in bed," Dillon grumbled as he rolled off the chair. Rising, he tossed the race car back onto the seat cushion. "There's nothing else to do in this dumb place."

Before Eben could respond, the twins crowded around him. "But we couldn't go to bed, Uncle Eben," Joy declared earnestly.

"We didn't know which room was ours," Hope explained.

"But we found our jammies." Joy held up a purple-flowered pair.

"And Eloise." Hope clutched a worn and bedraggled doll in her arms. Obviously Eloise.

"Eloise always sleeps with us," Joy explained.

"Lucky Eloise," Eben murmured dryly.

But the sight of the doll evoked unwanted memories of Carla and the pigtailed doll she had carted with her everywhere. Betsy was her name. The two had been virtually inseparable. Carla had slept with her, bathed with her, eaten with her, played with her—they even attended the first day of school together. For years afterward, Betsy had occupied a place of prominence on Carla's bed—in fact right up until the day his sister left, taking Betsy with her—and leaving Eben behind.

"Where are we going to sleep, Uncle Eben?" Hope asked with a serious and concerned frown, looking at him with eyes as blue as Carla's had been.

"Maddie will show you." He was more determined than ever to have no part of them.

Instead of throwing him a dirty look for volunteering her services, Maddie thrust the tired and crabby baby into his arms. "In that case, you can put Tad to bed. His little sleeper is on the arm of the sofa, along with a clean diaper. I have a bottle of milk warming on the stove. You'd better check and see if it's ready."

The baby took one look at Eben, screwed up his face, and broke into hiccoughing little sobs. "The feeling's mutual, kid," Eben muttered as he automatically patted the baby's back in a fruitless attempt to soothe him.

"Does it matter which rooms they have?" Maddie asked.

"Put them anywhere you want," he said, but inwardly he knew where she would put them. He didn't stay around to watch, instead heading for the kitchen, determined to get the bottle planted in the baby's mouth as soon as possible.

Maddie watched him go, then turned to the children. "Come on, the bedrooms are this way." She herded them into the wide hallway.

"Which one's ours?" Joy wanted to know, gazing at the row of doors.

"Yeah, which one?" Hope skipped sideways.

"This one right here." Maddie opened the second door on the left. "This is where your mother slept when she lived here."

"Momma slept here?" Joy gave her a wide-eyed look.

"Really?" Hope echoed her sister's surprise.

"Yes, really." Maddie smiled, warmed by the sudden excitement in their eyes. Reaching inside, she flipped on the wall switch.

Light spilled over the room's canopied bed. Its dainty nightstands, dresser, and vanity table were all painted white and trimmed with touches of gold gilt. The suite was one of the more extravagant gifts Johnny Mac had given his young daughter years ago, buying it with money earmarked for a new breeding bull. At the time, Eben had been beside himself over the loss of a new bull but Carla had been thrilled with her new bedroom set. What little girl wouldn't be?

The twins took one look at the room and went into ecstasy, dashing from the canopied bed to the vanity table. Its ruffled skirt was layered in little girl shades of purple and pink.

Only Maddie noticed the absence of Carla's things, the snapshots, show ribbons, and school mementos that had once cluttered the vanity mirror. The school banner and George Strait pictures were missing from the walls, as well as the bulletin board littered with more photos, class programs, competition ribbons, and "Far Out" cartoons.

Eben had stripped the room of all traces of Carla after she left, as if to erase her existence from his mind. But Carla's children made that an impossibility now.

"This is the most beautiful room in the whole world." Joy climbed onto the curved-back vanity chair to gaze into the mirror.

Hope bounced on the bed. "Dillon, aren't you going to come look?"

"Yeah, this is where Momma fixed her hair." Joy primped in front of the mirror, patting her blond curls.

But Dillon didn't budge from the doorway. "What's to see?" he grumbled. "It's just a dumb ole bedroom."

"But it used to be Momma's," Hope reminded him, hurt by his disinterest.

Ignoring her, he lifted a sullen glance to Maddie. "Are you gonna show me my room now?"

Convinced that Dillon's show of ill temper was symptomatic of the grief he felt over the loss of his parents, Maddie longed to reach out and gather him into her arms. But when she attempted to slide a consoling hand on his shoulder, he pulled back from her, rejecting it with a glare. The look reminded her that she was virtually a stranger to him. He wasn't about to share his feelings with her.

"I thought you might like to sleep in the room next to your sisters'." Maddie didn't add that it had been Eben's old room.

"Fine." He peeled away from the door.

"I'll show you—" Maddie began, moving after him.

"I can find it myself," he snapped, rejecting her company.

"All right, but I'll come in later to tuck you in," Maddie insisted and watched as he pushed open the door to the next room.

"I'm too old to be tucked in." His hot glance was riddled with contempt. "That stuff's for babies."

With that, he stepped into the room, hit the light switch, and shut the door, making it clear she was neither wanted nor welcome. Yet, Maddie suspected that, deep down, it was all a bluff. Whatever the case, she was going to tuck him in—whether Dillon liked it or not.

Getting the twins ready for bed proved to be a challenge, due partly to their excitement over the room and partly to the long list of rituals that had to be performed. After they had their pajamas on and their teeth cleaned, each one wanted to sit in front of the vanity mirror while Maddie brushed their hair, insisting that their mother had always done that before they got into bed.

Maddie quickly discovered the rhythmic stroke of the hairbrush had a calming effect, and recognized the wisdom behind the practice. By the time she had finished, both girls were thirsty.

Two glasses of water later, they finally knelt

beside the canopied bed and said their prayers in that alternating fashion that came so natural to them.

As always Joy went first, "Now I lay me down to sleep—"

"I pray that God's angels watch over me—" Hope continued.

"—and keep me safe all through the night—"

"—and wake me up with morning's light."

"God bless Mommy—"

"—and Daddy in heaven."

"And God bless Dillon—"

"—and Tad—"

"—and Hope—"

"—and Joy."

"And Uncle Eben, too," they added in unison. "Amen."

Both scrambled to their feet. Halfway onto the bed, Joy remembered with a gasp, "We forgot Maddie." She grabbed her sister's arms and pulled her back down. Hurriedly they knelt again. "And God bless Maddie, too."

"Amen," Hope added.

"We're sorry," Joy said when Maddie drew the covers over them.

"We didn't mean to forget you," Hope explained.

"I know you didn't," Maddie assured them, both moved and amused by their earnestness.

A troubled frown settled over Joy's face. "How come Uncle Eben doesn't believe in Christmas?"

Startled by the unexpected question, Maddie

searched for an answer. "It isn't so much that he doesn't believe—"

"He said he didn't," Hope reminded her.

"I know—"

"We've got to do something about that," Joy decided.

"But what can we do?" Hope wondered, clearly worried.

Well aware that was a question without an answer, Maddie suggested, "Why don't you think about it tomorrow? Right now, you need to close your eyes and get some sleep."

"You've got to read Eloise a story first," Joy informed her, touching the doll nestled between them.

"Yeah, Mommy always reads her a story before she goes to sleep," Hope added.

"Is that right?" Maddie suppressed a smile and pretended to puzzle over a new thought. "What did your mommy do on nights when Eloise was too tired to listen to a whole story?"

Joy thought about that and said, "Sometimes she just sang to Eloise."

"She did? Well, I can't sing as well as your mother, but I'll try. Okay?"

"Okay," they agreed quickly.

"But you'll have to close your eyes," Maddie informed them. "I can't sing if anybody watches me."

Obediently they closed their eyes. After the second time through Brahms' "Lullaby," both girls were asleep. Turning out the light, Maddie tiptoed from the room and went next door to check on Dillon.

He was already in bed, eyes tightly closed, feigning sleep. Following her instincts, Maddie went through the motions of adjusting the covers around him, then lightly smoothed a lock of hair off his forehead.

"Good night, Dillon," she whispered, then slipped quietly from the room. As she stepped into the hall, Eben came out of the large master bedroom. "Is Tad asleep?" Maddie asked softly.

"Finally," he muttered without stopping. "Somewhere in the kitchen there's a glass of Chivas with my name on it."

Chapter VI

Smiling at the harried and slightly desperate edge to his voice, Maddie followed Eben to the kitchen. He went straight to the cupboard, took a fifth of scotch from the top shelf, blew the dust off its cap, and reached back for a glass. He paused in mid-motion, glancing over his shoulder at Maddie.

"Do you want one?"

"Please." She went to the refrigerator to fetch some ice cubes.

"Do you hear that?" Eben poured three fingers of scotch into a highball glass.

"What?" Maddie turned, listening for the baby.

"The silence," Eben replied, his lips curving. "I've never heard anything so beautiful in a long time."

"Honestly, Eben, it wasn't that bad." Maddie shut the refrigerator door and carried the plastic bucket of loose cubes over to the counter.

"That's what you think." He tipped the scotch bottle into the second glass. "When they weren't talking, I swear they were either yelling, fighting, or crying. It was insanity around here."

"It was hectic," Maddie conceded, reaching in front of him to drop a handful of ice cubes into each glass. "But I actually enjoyed it."

Eben started to scoff at her claim; then he saw her face and the happy sparkle in her eyes. She had never looked more beautiful, more alive. The sight seemed to snatch the air right out of his lungs. He didn't like it that she still had that effect on him.

"You mean that, don't you?" he realized, looking away.

"You sound surprised." She turned at right angles to the counter and rested a hip against it. "You shouldn't be. We always talked about having a big family."

"Six children, at least," Eben recalled—along with too many other memories, the kind that heated his blood and made him want what she had once given only to him. He tried to shove all those thoughts and feelings back into the past, where they belonged.

"We ended up compromising on six," she reminded him, "because the house only has seven bedrooms and you didn't think our children should have to share a room."

He even remembered his reasoning for that. "Everybody's entitled to some privacy."

He handed her a glass of scotch, their fingers briefly brushing. His skin tingled from the contact, disturbing him. Seeking to banish the sensation, Eben picked up his own glass.

Before he could raise it to his mouth, she clinked her glass against it. "To old memories," she said in toast, a warm smile on her lips.

"Yeah." He downed a big gulp of scotch and felt the lava burn of it flowing down his throat.

Maddie took a ladylike sip of hers, then used a forefinger to idly stir the cubes in her glass. "If there's one thing I regret," she said, her thoughts turning inward, "it's not having children."

She stood close to him. Too close. Eben needed to step away, put some distance between them. But it was as if his feet were rooted in the floor. He couldn't move. Not even a centimeter.

"I was always surprised that you and Allan didn't have a whole brood of kids." He deliberately mentioned her late husband, needing to hear his name to quash this resurgence of old memories and old feelings.

She glanced at her drink, the warm glow fading from her expression. "Unfortunately Allan couldn't have children."

Eben took perverse satisfaction in the news that her late husband had been sterile. "You could have adopted."

"We talked about it," Maddie admitted with a small, dismissing shrug that signaled an end to this discussion. She enforced it by switching subjects. "I think Dillon is having a hard time dealing with the loss of his parents. He's angry, confused—and frightened, too. You'll need to be patient with him, Eben."

"Someone else maybe, not me," he stated, swirling the liquor in his glass, rattling the ice cubes, his nerves grating at the mere thought of Carla's children.

"Eben, he needs *you*," Maddie stressed. "You are his uncle."

"That's his bad luck." Eben tossed down another swallow of scotch.

Maddie gave him an incredulous look, a frown forming. "Eben, I don't think you understand—these children are your responsibility now."

"Not for long, I hope."

She opened her mouth, closed it, then murmured tightly, "I know I shouldn't ask because something tells me I'm not going to like the answer but—exactly what do you mean by that, MacCallister?"

"I mean—that if all goes well, I'll have them packed and gone by tomorrow," he replied in a voice hard with purpose. "It will probably mean losing a day's work, but that can't be helped, unfortunately."

"A whole day's work, now wouldn't that be awful?" she mocked.

"You're damned right it will," Eben declared, a deep furrow of irritation creasing his brow.

"Eben MacCallister, those are Carla's children

in there.'' Maddie thrust a finger in the direction of the bedrooms.

"That's right,'' he shot back. "They're hers, not mine.''

"But she left them in your custody.'' Turning, Maddie snatched the crumpled documents off the counter and held them up. "Or had you forgotten about these papers that gave you custody?''

"Not at all. Those papers grant me full authority over those kids. Which means I can do whatever I want with them.''

"And what would that be?'' she demanded, clearly angry.

"Dump them on some other relative, of course.''

"What other relative?''

"I don't know yet,'' he admitted, unconcerned by that. "I'll find that out tomorrow when I talk to the lawyer who drew this stuff up for Carla.'' Eben flicked a hand at the documents Maddie held. "I figure the man Carla married is bound to have a family somewhere—parents, sister, an aunt, maybe a cousin.''

"And what if he doesn't?''

"He will.'' That was a possibility Eben refused to consider.

"Don't you think that if Carla and her husband wanted some other relative to raise their children, they would have appointed that person as their guardian instead of you?'' Maddie reasoned.

"I don't care what they wanted or didn't want. Those kids are not staying here!'' On that point, he was emphatic.

"Why not?"

"Because I said so," he flashed, his temper rising to match hers.

"That is not a reason, MacCallister."

"You want a reason?" he challenged. "I can give you about a hundred of them. In the first place, I've got a ranch to run. And if I have any hope in hell of keeping it, I've got thirty two-year-olds and nineteen three-year-olds to get trained and ready for sale by the middle of January. And when I say trained, I don't mean broke to ride, I mean I've got ten damned good cutting prospects out there and about the same number of reining prospects. I'm talking horses that are competition quality."

"So?"

"So?!" Eben couldn't believe she said that. "So, you figure it out. Working each horse only twenty minutes every other day means I'm in the saddle at least eight hours. On top of that, I still have cattle to check, chores to do, and who knows what else? You should know how it is on a ranch, Maddie."

"What does any of that have to do with the children?" She carefully laid the papers on the counter in a studied effort to control her anger.

"What does it have to do with it?!" Eben flung up his hands. "Good grief, Maddie, you saw what it was like tonight with those monsters. It will be impossible to get any work done with the four of them underfoot."

"What you are really saying is that the children are inconvenient. You simply don't want to be bothered with them." The coolness of her voice turned her words into an accusation.

He set his glass down on the counter, then turned and looked her straight in the eye. "As matter of fact—no, I don't want to be bothered with them."

"Eben MacCallister, you are not only heartless, you are also incredibly selfish." Maddie glared at him, her fingers tightening around her drink until her knuckles turned white with the pressure.

For an uneasy moment, he thought she was going to throw the contents in his face. Instead, she turned and shoved the glass onto the counter with an abruptness that sent the mixture of scotch and water sloshing over the rim. Pushed by anger, she swept over to the table, then swung back to face him, her arms folded high and tight. The only thing missing was a tapping toe.

"I don't see it as heartless, Maddie," he replied. "As far as I'm concerned, it's the only logical answer."

"Don't talk to me about logic," she flared. "If logic ruled the world, men would ride sidesaddle, never astride."

That stopped him cold for an instant. "Where on earth did that come from?" He frowned.

"It came from a lifetime of dealing with men," she retorted. "Every time a man wants to convince somebody about something, he starts talking about logic—as if men were the masters of it."

"All right, forget about being logical. Try realistic," he countered. "I don't have either the time or the money to raise four kids."

"Yes, you do," she shot back quickly. "You just don't want to spend it on them."

"Why should I?" he argued. "They're nothing to me."

"They are your nieces and nephews."

"They are strangers, Maddie. We never saw each other until five hours ago," he reminded her. "They don't know me, and I don't know them. What's more, I don't like them."

"You have made a conscious decision not to like them," Maddie corrected. "That's more than just sad, MacCallister. That's pathetic."

Stung by her censure, Eben turned, grabbed the bottle, and poured more scotch into his glass. "I don't know why I'm talking to you about any of this," he muttered in ill-temper. "None of it is your business."

"Feeling a little prick of conscience, are you, MacCallister?" she taunted.

"No, I'm not!" he denied vehemently. "Do you have any idea how much it costs to raise four kids these days? I can't afford to keep them."

"It's back to money again, isn't it?"

"Yes, it's back to money. Like it or not, you need it to live. Maybe you don't know what that's like, but I do," he stated. "I've lived like that and I'm not doing it again."

By the end of his impassioned declaration, much of her anger had faded. Until that moment, she had forgotten how much Eben had hated being poor, and understood how much he feared it happening again. Financial security was vital to him. It was the reason he guarded his pennies so carefully today. There was nothing she could say that would change that. To argue money was futile.

"I don't blame you for feeling the way you do," Maddie said at last. "But I don't think caring for Carla's children will put you in the poor house."

"Maddie, there are four of them. Count them." Eben ticked them off on his fingers. "One, two, three, four."

"In other words, you might consider keeping them if there were only three?" She knew that wasn't what he meant, but she had to batter at him with something.

"No, of course not."

"Two, then?"

"No."

"One?"

"Haven't you been listening to me?" Eben demanded with impatience. "If I don't clear at least three hundred thousand on the sale of my horses, I can kiss this ranch goodbye. And if I don't get them fully trained, they aren't going to bring that kind of money, registered stock or not. Would you tell me how I'm supposed to get those horses ready with those kids constantly underfoot? They aren't even old enough to wipe their own noses."

"Couldn't you hire a qualified trainer to help you with the horses?" Even as she suggested that, Maddie guessed the answer.

"With the kind of fees those guys charge, I can't spare the cash, let alone the time it would take to find one."

"What about Luis or Ramon? Couldn't they—" she began.

Eben shook his head. "They have more work than they can handle now, taking care of the mares, halter-breaking the weanlings, checking on the cattle and the yearlings. On top of that, they don't know the first thing about teaching a horse the fundamentals of spins, rollbacks, and sliding stops. They would be more apt to ruin a horse."

"I see." She searched for another option, another argument.

"Face it, Maddie," he said. "Billy Joe Wilder has a gun to my head. I either come up with the money to pay off the mortgage or I end up with no roof over my head, no income, no job, and nothing to show for all the years I worked and fought to keep this ranch. I'm not going to let that happen, not when I can do something about it," Eben stated grimly. "Which means those kids can't stay here. Tomorrow morning, they are leaving, and that's final. I—" He checked the rest of the sentence, his glance shooting past her as a flicker of shock registered in his expression.

Turning, Maddie saw Dillon standing in the doorway. The corners of his mouth were pulled sharply down. An angry scowl hooded eyes that were filled with bitterness and hurt. There was no need to wonder how much Dillon had overheard. His expression made it clear he had heard enough to know that Eben intended to send all of them away tomorrow.

"Oh no," Maddie murmured in distress, glancing at Eben in silent appeal.

The line of his mouth hardened in tightness, a contrast to the glimmer of regret in his eyes. "What are you doing out of bed?" He directed the question at Dillon, his voice stern with impatience.

Dillon pulled out the ready excuse. "I got thirsty."

Maddie took a step toward the sink. "Let me get you a glass of water," she said, anxious to somehow repair the damage they had done.

"I'll get it myself." With stiff, brisk strides, Dillon marched to the sink.

Stretching onto his tiptoes, he reached the water glass and held it under the faucet, then stretched again to turn the handle on the cold water tap. The silence in the room was as thick and awkward as the tension. Maddie darted another glance at Eben, but the grim set of his features hadn't changed.

After taking a small sip of water, Dillon emptied the glass in the sink and clunked it on the counter, then turned and marched back across the kitchen floor, looking neither to the right nor to the left.

At the doorway, he paused and directed a hooded glare at Eben. "You'd better stop talking so loud, else you'll wake my sisters," he warned and walked off.

Maddie knew at once it wasn't thirst that had brought him to the kitchen; it was the sound of their raised voices.

"He heard us, Eben," she murmured with guilt. "He knows."

"It's just as well." He picked up his glass, a muscle working along his jaw.

"He's only a little boy, Eben," she protested. "He's just lost both his parents. He's hurting, and we've hurt him more."

"It couldn't be helped." He downed a swallow of scotch.

But this time it didn't have the desired, numbing effect. The regret Eben felt still tasted as strong as before. He walked over to the table and sank onto a chair, fighting a weariness that was as much mental as it was physical.

"But you must know how he's feeling, Eben," Maddie reasoned, determined to stir his compassion. "You were his age when you lost your mother."

Unwillingly he looked back into his own past. There were blurred recollections of the funeral, the steady stream of friends and neighbors stopping by the ranch, and a tiny, squawling baby with tons of downy, black hair.

He had only one sharp memory of those days immediately following his mother's death—the night he couldn't sleep, when the ache had gone so deep, he couldn't stand it anymore. At seven years old, he had understood the finality of death, but the grief he felt had been a new thing. Painful and frightening.

He had gone looking for his father, needing the love, the comfort, and reassurance of his presence.

Eben had found him in the kitchen, sitting in this very chair, weeping uncontrollably. He had stood there for a long time before his father noticed him. When he did, his father had wept all the harder.

"What am I gonna do?" he had cried. "Dear God, I miss her so much, Eben. How am I ever gonna take care of that baby without her? How am I gonna do anything? I can't. I just can't."

"I can help, Daddy." Eben had rushed to his side, frightened by the depth of his father's anguish and the hopelessness he voiced.

"You don't understand," his father had sniffled, dragging fingers through his hair, then leaving them there, cupping the back of his bowed head. "It's too much. Don't you see? It's all too much without her. I can't do it. I can't."

Instead of being consoled and comforted, Eben had been the one to do the consoling and comforting. There had been no sharing of grief, no sharing of loss. Eben had come away as empty and lost as he had been when he first entered the kitchen.

And it hadn't been the last time.

"Life is hard," he said to Maddie. "The kid might as well learn that early."

"It shouldn't have to be this early," she disagreed with a quick shake of her head.

"In a way, it makes him luckier than most." Eben stared into his drink, the memory fresh, hardening him to Dillon's plight. "Sooner or later, everybody has to learn you have only two choices in life—to toughen up or knuckle under."

"You toughened up, didn't you?" Maddie stood

near his chair, studying the small shifts and changes in his expression.

"I wasn't about to knuckle under." Dryness twisted his smile. "Not when my father provided such an excellent example of someone who had."

"Your father had his good points, Eben." Her voice softened with the gentle words.

A heavy sigh came from him, weighted with annoyance and weariness. "I don't want to talk about him, Maddie," he said. "Not now."

"You've had a hard day, haven't you?" She murmured.

"That's a mild way of saying it." The breath he exhaled was loaded with irony.

Maddie stepped behind him. An instant later, Eben felt her hands slide onto his shoulders, her fingers searching out the muscles that had constricted into iron bands of tension. For an instant he stiffened under the massaging pressure, resisting the relief they offered. But it felt too good, and that ease was something he needed.

Once, this had been a nightly ritual between them, the first step in a familiar pattern that always ended in each other's arms. Memories flooded back, stirring awake the old needs and desires. They tunneled through him, briefly causing him to forget that this was not yesterday.

As he had in the past, Eben captured one of her hands and pulled it forward, studying its long, slender fingers and clear lacquered nails.

"Such an expert hand," he murmured in an echo of words he'd spoken a hundred times before.

He felt her tremble in awareness. It was an old signal of her willingness to be held and loved, one as familiar to him as the desire that stirred through his loins. He knew what came next—what always came next.

But instead of drawing Maddie onto his lap as he once would have done, Eben stood up and let her hand slide from his grip.

"Why did you come back, Maddie?" His hard gaze searched her upturned face, seeing too many things he hadn't wanted to find there.

"To bring the baby crib, of course." Her voice had a breathy quality to it, a reaction to his nearness.

"That isn't what I meant," he said and reworded the question. "Why did you move back? Why didn't you stay in Scottsdale after Allan died?"

"You make it sound as if I returned only yesterday." Her smile chided him. "I've been living at El Regalo for almost a year and a half now."

Irritated by her evasive answers, Eben demanded, "Why didn't you stay in Scottsdale? From all I heard, you were the darling of Phoenix society."

Maddie laughed at that. "If I was, then it was probably because I didn't care whether they accepted me or not."

He felt his temper rising and fought to control it—along with all the rest of his emotions. "You used to be more direct with your answers, Maddie."

She shrugged that off. "Maybe I thought the answer was obvious. We lived in Phoenix because Allan's business was there. But I am not—and never have been—a city girl. You, of all people, should remember how much I love the desert, the harshness of its beauty and the vibrancy of its skies."

"People change." His glance critically skimmed the expensive silk blouse and impractical linen slacks. "You clearly have."

"You're looking at the clothes," Maddie told him. "They are different than what I used to wear, that's true. But the person inside them hasn't changed all that much, except to grow a little older."

"Maybe." Eben wasn't convinced of that.

"Why did you ask?" She cocked her head, a glimmer of amusement in her eyes. "Did you think I came back because you were still here?"

He wasn't about to admit he had wondered that very thing. "Did you?" he challenged instead.

"I honestly don't think I did. In fact, I was certain I was over you. Now . . ." She let the pause lengthen as she ran her gaze over his face, a wondering and a doubt in her eyes.

Without warning, Maddie cupped a hand to his cheek and jaw. Surprise held him motionless. A fraction of a second later, she rose up, her lips moving onto his in an exploring fashion, as if seeking an answer to the questions that had been in her eyes.

Automatically Eben responded, changing the angle to do some exploring of his own. But it didn't take him long to discover that nothing had changed, not the hunger she had always aroused in him or the rush of feelings.

The urge was there to take the next inevitable step and forget that Maddie had left him and married another man. He grabbed at that memory and the anger that accompanied it with all the desperation of a drowning man.

But before he could push her way, Maddie broke the contact and stepped back, looking dazed and breathless, her eyes locked on his.

"The old magic is still there, isn't it?" she marveled softly. "I think I knew it would be." Her eyes darkened with regret and something else. Pain? "But it isn't enough, Eben. It wasn't before, and it isn't now."

"Why?" he said, then silently cursed himself for asking, for opening the door to the past even a crack.

"If you still don't know the answer to that, there's no point in explaining, Eben. You wouldn't understand anyway."

Maddie briefly held his glance, then looked away and ran a smoothing hand over her hair. It was a self-conscious gesture, one he recognized from long ago. "It's time I went home," she said, then shot him a glance full of her old sauciness. "Are you going to walk me out to my Jeep, or did you abandon simple courtesies at the same time you threw away any sense of humor?"

"I should have," he grumbled and trailed after her when she moved to the door.

"You don't have to come with me, you know," she mocked over her shoulder.

"I just want to make sure you actually leave," he lied.

The softness of her laughter drifted back to him as she pushed through the door and stepped into the crispness of the desert evening. She paused beneath the jewelry of the night sky.

"Too bad I didn't leave after I dropped off the crib. Then you could have put the children to bed by yourself," she teased.

Wisely Eben made no reply to that and lengthened his stride to draw level with her, slipping the ends of his fingers inside the pockets of his jeans. Darkness had thrown its layers of mystery over the land. Overhead, the sky was incandescent with the diamond sparkle of a million stars, breathtaking like the woman beside him. To his regret, her closeness tugged him.

"I've been thinking," Maddie murmured, her voice automatically dropping to a hushed level amid all this stillness. "You were right, Eben."

That was a first, coming from her. Eben nearly said so, but the night had cast its mood over him, silencing the jibe that would have inevitably led to more. Oddly he didn't want to argue.

"About what?" he asked instead.

"The children," she said after a long and pregnant hesitation. "They will be better off living somewhere else."

"Really?" He cocked an eyebrow, skeptical of this turnabout.

"Yes, really—although I didn't think so at first," she replied in a voice that was briefly dry with amusement, then turned serious. "But you really don't have the time to take care of them. And heaven knows, you don't owe anything to Carla, not after the way she treated you—running off without a word, taking your savings, leaving you to cope with everything by yourself. When you think about it, it took a lot of gall to put the responsibility for her children on you."

"You're telling me," he agreed on a breath of disgust.

"At least now, you'll finally be able to get even with her."

"What do you mean?" Eben frowned, the remark striking him wrong.

"Isn't it obvious?" she countered. "Carla turned her back on you, and now you're turning your back on her children. In a way, it's poetic justice." Maddie opened the door to the Jeep Cherokee and slid behind the wheel, then glanced at Eben before closing the door. "I'll come by sometime tomorrow to pick up the crib."

"Sure." He nodded absently, clearly distracted by her comment.

As she drove out of the ranch yard, Maddie recalled that last glimpse of Eben's face and the vaguely troubled look it had worn. She smiled in satisfaction, glad she had remembered how bull-headed he could be. At such times, the easiest way to persuade him to change his mind was to totally agree with him.

The trick was to be convincing.

She crossed her fingers. Tomorrow she would find out exactly how convincing she had been.

Chapter VII

A frightened scream shattered the silence, jolting Eben out of a sound sleep. He sat bolt upright in bed, confused for a moment by the muted wails and murmurs coming from another part of the house.

Then he remembered—the children.

Smothering a groan, he wiped a hand over his face and peered at the clock on his nightstand. It was two in the morning. Muttering a string of curses under his breath, Eben threw back the covers and rolled out of bed, determined to silence all the noise before Tad woke up and he ended up walking the floor trying to get him back to sleep.

Eben's jeans lay across the chair in the corner. Grabbing them up, he jammed a foot through one leg, hopped a couple steps to get his balance before sliding his left foot down the other leg. He hastily zipped them as he went into the hall.

It was no surprise at all when he discovered the sobs and soothing voices emanated from his sister's old room where the twins were. Irritated, he stepped into the room, hitting the wall switch.

"Who's doing all this crying?" His gaze narrowed suspiciously on Dillon, seeing the hands that tightly gripped the arms of a sobbing twin. "What are you doing here? Did you start this?" With a tweak of conscience, Eben remembered the conversation Dillon had overheard.

The other twin rushed to explain, "Hope had a bad dream."

Before Eben could respond, Dillon gave him a fierce look. "Go away. We don't need you." The boy hurled the words, then gathered the sniffling girl into his arms. "Sssh, it's okay, Hope. It's over. I'm here now. You're safe."

The scene and the words Dillon spoke evoked memories of his own childhood, reminding Eben of the many times when he had ventured into this very room to comfort his sister after a nightmare wakened her. Drawn by those memories, he crossed to the canopied bed.

"She had a dream, did she?" he repeated for something to say, conscious of the empty feeling of his arms.

"Uh-huh," Joy confirmed. "A real bad one."

"A bear was gonna get me," Hope sobbed against Dillon's pajama top.

"He was gonna eat her," Joy added, wide-eyed at the thought of that.

"How would you know?" Eben turned a dubious glance on her.

Joy gave an exaggerated shrug, burying her neck in her shoulders and lifting both hands palm-up. "I just know that's what she dreamed. Mom says it's 'cause we're twins."

"The bear's all gone, Hope," Dillon assured his sister. "I chased him away for you."

"He might come back," she sniffled.

"If he does, I'll just chase him away again," he replied in his most determined voice.

"But he's bigger than you are, Dillon," Joy told him.

Dillon rolled his eyes in exasperation. "Will you shut up, Joy?"

"But he was." Hope pulled out of his arms, exposing her tear-streaked face.

Eben intervened, gently pushing the girl back onto her pillow and drawing the covers around her. "It was nothing but a bad dream. It wasn't real. You can forget about it and go back to sleep now."

"But I don't want to go back to sleep," Hope said in a whimpering voice.

Joy nodded wisely. "She's afraid she'll dream about the bear again."

"If you do, then just dream something larger and meaner into your dream and have him chase the bear away," Eben said, echoing the same advice he had once given the girl's mother all those years ago.

"Yeah," Dillon agreed quickly, a glint of impish wickedness in his eyes. "Dream Uncle Eben into it, Hope. He's big enough and mean enough to scare away your silly old bear."

"Do you really think so?" Hope asked, turning anxious eyes to him.

"Uncle Eben's as mean and tough as they come," Dillon promised almostly gleefully.

A testing shriek came from the master bedroom.

"Oh, oh, Tad woke up," Joy murmured, casting a concerned glance at Eben, reminding him, "He doesn't like to be alone. You'd better go get him right away," she warned.

"I'm going, but you two better get to sleep." He pointed to the twins, then hooked a thumb at Dillon, indicating the door. "And you, go back to your own bed. The girls will be fine."

Before Eben made it to the master bedroom and the crib, Tad let loose with a full-blown scream that was pure outrage. It stopped the minute Eben loomed over the crib. The baby looked at him and gurgled a laugh, glad to discover he wasn't alone.

"You may think this is playtime, buster, but you're wrong," Eben told him.

He lifted the happy, cooing baby out of the crib, shifted him into the hook of one arm, then reached back into the crib and fished around, looking for the pacifier. A waving fist smacked him in the mouth.

"Ouch." Wincing, Eben straightened and

pushed the baby's hand down. "Don't pick a fight with me. I happen to be bigger than you are."

Tad gave him a bright-eyed look, then squealed gleefully and jabbered something unintelligible, but the hand stayed down. Resuming his search for the pacifier, Eben bent over the crib again. Just as his fingers closed around the pacifier's hard plastic back, a smaller set of fingers grabbed a handful of chest hairs and pulled.

With a strangled yowl, Eben dropped the pacifier and seized the offending hand, prying it loose from his hair. "You little devil," he muttered, ready to swear it was mischief he saw sparkling in the baby's eyes.

He retrieved the pacifier from the floor, washed it off in the bathroom sink, and popped it in the baby's mouth. Tad sucked happily on it, then spit it out the instant Eben laid him down in the crib. Patiently Eben slipped it back in his mouth while Tad was still working up a protesting wail.

"No more games, kid. You go back to sleep," Eben ordered, in a much softer voice than he'd intended.

Before he could draw his hand away, small fingers wrapped themselves around his thumb, as tenacious in their grip of it as they had been when they seized the clump of hair on his chest. It wouldn't have required much effort to pull free of it. Eben wasn't sure why he didn't—or why he stood beside the crib, watching those little eyelids droop, spring open, then droop again. When he finally removed his hand, Tad's eyes were closed.

He padded over to the door, listened, but all was quiet in the rest of the house. Leaving the hall light on and the door open a crack, Eben slipped off his jeans and climbed back into bed. After punching his pillow into shape, he laid his head on it and closed his eyes, feeling the tiredness wash over him.

Within seconds, he heard the murmur of little voices and the faint slap of bare feet hitting the floor. He tracked the progress of those feet along the hallway and tried to convince himself it was one of the twins making a trip to the bathroom.

But the footsteps stopped outside his door. An instant later, light from the hall flooded into his bedroom.

"Uncle Eben?" came the tentative query.

Groaning, he levered up on one elbow. "What now?" he growled, keeping his voice low.

Both twins stood in the doorway, backlit by the hall light, their faces in shadow.

"Can we sleep with you?" one of them asked with a confidence that told him it was the freckled one, Joy. His suspicion proved correct with her next words. "Hope's still scared the bear'll get her."

Something told him he wasn't going to get any sleep unless he agreed. Deciding that turnabout was fair play, Eben did some blackmailing of his own.

"All right," he agreed. "But on one condition— there is to be no talking. If I hear a peep out of either one of you, you're heading straight to your own bed. Is that a deal?''

There was one vigorous and one hesitant nod, but neither twin said a word in reply, as if fearing that it would be cause for banishment.

"All right, then." He threw back a corner of the covers. "Come on over here and climb in."

Giving her sister's hand a tug, Joy led Hope to the bed. The light from the hall glistened on the girl's still damp cheeks. Eben had a glimpse of their sheen an instant before she scrambled into bed and dived under the covers, turning to snuggle up close to him.

Startled by that, Eben was slow to notice when Joy scampered back to the door, partially closed it to block the light, then ran back to the opposite side of the bed and lifted the covers.

The instant he felt the draft of air on his naked back, he twisted around to peer over his shoulder. "What are you doing?"

She paused and went through the motions of locking her mouth shut with an invisible key, then pointed to the bed, indicating her intention to sleep on that side.

"What's wrong with sleeping over here with your sister?" Eben frowned in irritation.

Joy adamantly shook her head and pointed again to the empty space on his right. Eben started to argue, then gave up, muttering, "Get in, then."

Flashing him a quick smile, she jumped into bed. Instead of sliding under the covers, Joy crawled over to him and smacked a kiss on his cheek, then mouthed a "good night."

Sandwiched between the twins, Eben stared at the ceiling and wondered whether he would get any rest at all. He consoled himself with the knowledge that tomorrow he would be packing them off to some unsuspecting relative.

The alarm clock was set to go off at five in the morning.

Tad went off at ten minutes 'til.

Groggy with sleep, Eben stretched an arm over a curly blond head and slapped twice at the alarm's off button before he identified the source of the noise. Grumbling to himself, he shifted away from one clutching twin and crawled over the second, then stumbled to the crib. Tad stood at the rail, bawling his head off, tears streaming down his red cheeks.

"Do you always have to make so much racket?" Eben lifted the baby out of the crib and breathed in the unmistakable odor of a dirty diaper.

"He probably needs his diaper changed," came another familiar voice.

Glancing back at the bed, Eben saw Joy sitting up, looking as rumpled and bleary-eyed as he felt. Beyond her, Hope stirred restively.

In no mood to cope with both the twins and the baby, too, Eben replied, "I already guessed that. Now, go back to sleep before you wake up your sister."

Without a word, she scooted under the covers again. Halfway to the door, Eben remembered the alarm, went back, and shut it off, then snatched his jeans off the chair and padded into the living room. After digging through the baby's things, Eben came up with a clean diaper.

More adeptly than the first time, he got the diaper changed, then went about the task of warming some milk while Tad fussed and gnawed hungrily on his own fist. Making coffee for himself with only one hand free proved to be a trick, but somehow he managed. While the baby sucked noisily on the bottle, Eben took that first reviving sip of his morning coffee.

"I guess you take after your father," he told the baby. "With any luck, the others will be like Carla. I had to practically drag her out of bed in the mornings," he recalled with a remembering smile, then worked to banish further thought of his sister.

Less than a minute later, Eben heard the telltale slap of bare feet in the hall and knew his run of bad luck wasn't over. Sure enough, Joy trotted into the kitchen, followed by Hope, who was still rubbing the sleep from her eyes.

"I thought I'd better tell you—" Joy began, then stopped. "Oh. You already fixed Tad a bottle. That's good, 'cause he always wants one right away in the mornings."

Eben sighed. "I thought I told you to go back to sleep."

"I did. Then Hope woked up and we decided to come help you."

"She doesn't look awake to me." Eben studied the other twin as Hope climbed onto a chair and yawned widely, showing him all of her teeth.

"She is," Joy asserted blithely.

"How come she isn't talking, then?" he challenged, arching one eyebrow.

"Her mouth doesn't work good in the mornings," Joy replied easily.

"It's a pity yours doesn't," he mumbled to himself.

Her sharp ears caught that. "Oh, mine always works good."

"I noticed."

Crossing to his chair, Joy hovered over the baby, stroking his head and talking baby talk to him. Delighted with the attention, Tad waved and kicked, grinning between sucks of milk.

After checking to see how much milk was left in the bottle, she informed Eben, "You'd better burp him, Uncle Eben."

"I will in a minute," he told her, half-irritated that a four-year-old was giving him instructions on the care of a baby.

Shrugging that he had been warned, Joy turned and walked to the refrigerator. "You got any juice, Uncle Eben?" Pulling hard, she opened the door to look for herself. "Hope wants some."

"That's too bad, because I don't have any juice," he replied a little curtly.

"Want some milk instead, Hope?" she asked.

Before Hope bobbed her head, Eben knew what

was coming next and got to his feet, saying, "I'll get it."

"I'll get the glasses." Joy dashed back to the table, grabbed a chair, and dragged it to the cupboards, then climbed onto the chair seat.

"Forget the glasses and use the coffee mugs." Propping the refrigerator door open with a shoulder, Eben lifted the pitcher of milk from its resting place on the top shelf and set it on the counter.

"Do you got any Fwuit Loops, Uncle Eben?" After taking down two cups, Joy stood on her knees atop the counter and started opening cupboard doors.

"Any what?" With one hand holding the baby firmly against his shoulder, Eben poured milk into the mugs with the other.

"Fwuit Loops," she repeated.

"It's a kind of cereal." Dillon's faintly superior voice came from behind him.

One look at the boy advised Eben that a night's sleep had done nothing to improve Dillon's attitude. "No, I don't have any Foot Loops," Eben told Joy.

Dillon snorted a laugh. "It's *Fruit* Loops. It's kinda like Cheerios except it tastes like fruit."

"I still don't have any." As Eben put the milk back in the refrigerator, the baby let out a loud belch, then looked at Eben and grinned.

"What kind of cereal do you got?" Joy asked, giving up her search of the cupboards.

"Just oatmeal."

"Oatmeal," Dillon scoffed. "Man, are you ever in trouble."

The certainty in his voice worried Eben. "Why?"

He jerked a thumb at his sisters. " 'Cause those two won't eat anything but cereal for breakfast."

"Then, they'll have to eat oatmeal." Satisfied that he had the problem in hand, Eben sat down in his chair, shifted the baby into the crook of his arm, and picked up the bottle to finish feeding him.

Joy screwed up her face. "We don't like oatmeal."

"That's all I have," he replied.

"Why?" Hope finally broke her self-imposed silence.

"Because that other stuff is too expensive." Which was reason enough for Eben. "Anyway, it's junk. It isn't good for you."

"But we like it!" Joy protested.

"We hate oatmeal," Hope pouted, while Dillon all but snickered.

"We aren't gonna eat it either," Joy declared.

"If you try to make us—" Hope began.

"—we'll throw up."

Faced with open rebellion, Eben gave up. "All right, all right, no oatmeal. Okay?"

"Okay," Joy agreed, all smiles again. "What are we gonna have instead?"

Eben glanced at the kitchen window, seeing the darkness beyond it. "The sun isn't even up yet," he groaned.

"But we're hungry," Joy said brightly, still perched on the kitchen counter.

"What do you want to eat—besides the cereal that I don't have?" he added, testy and not bothering to hide it.

"What have you got?" Joy countered.

It was too early for this, Eben thought. Mornings were a quiet time—a time to reflect on the things that needed to be done, a time to line out the day's work while drinking that first cup of coffee. And there sat his coffee, rapidly going from lukewarm to cold. As for planning out the day, he hadn't had time to string two thoughts together before these kids barged in, unraveling his whole routine.

Just a few more hours, Eben told himself. He just had to get through this; then he'd have them out of his hair and have his life back.

Bolstered by the thought, Eben dragged in a breath and began listing the breakfast choices. "Toast, eggs, bacon—"

Joy never let him finish. "Pancakes. Can you make us pancakes, Uncle Eben?"

"Yeah, we like pancakes," Hope declared.

"Momma used to make them for us on Sunday—"

"—and sometimes when we were extra good."

Eben inserted, under his breath, "That must have been rare."

For once, Joy's sharp ears didn't hear that. "She made the bestest pancakes in the whole world."

"I don't like the ones you get in rest'rants," Hope said with a decisive shake of her head.

"Can you make pancakes as good as Momma's?"

Hope rushed to assure him, "It's okay if they're only almost as good."

"I happen to be the one who taught your mother how to make pancakes," Eben informed them.

"You did?" Joy's eyes widened in a mixture of amazement and delight.

"Would you make some for us?"

"Please," Joy added, stretching out the word.

"Yes—" he began.

Hands clapped in celebration amid squeals of "Goody, goody, pancakes, pancakes" that came so rapid-fire that Eben had no idea which one said what. Before he could draw a breath, the scene erupted before his eyes, turning the kitchen into a hive of activity.

Bounding off her chair, Hope raced to the refrigerator to get the syrup while Joy scrambled onto her knees and began going through the cupboards to set the table for breakfast. The clatter and clang of silverware and dishes competed with the slamming of doors and the scrape of chair legs.

All of it was overridden by the arguments over who was to do what and why. In between, they pushed and prodded at Eben to get the pancakes started.

Too late he realized there were varying degrees of peace and quiet. Standing at the counter, mixing up the batter, a chair on either side of him and one twin jumping down while the other climbed up, Eben found himself longing for the relative quiet of those first moments when Hope hadn't been awake enough to talk and only Joy had chattered away.

"Do you need eggs next? I'll get 'em." Off went Joy, leaping from the chair and accidentally shoving it against a leg already sore from yesterday's fall off the horse.

Eben sucked in a pained breath as his leg buckled from the blow. Meanwhile Hope climbed onto the opposite chair and grabbed the Bisquick box to examine the picture on the front of it.

"This isn't what Momma used, Uncle Eben," she said with a look of grave concern. "Hers had pancakes on it."

"This is what I use," he told her, then called to Joy. "I'll get the eggs myself. Don't—" He didn't bother to complete the sentence when he saw Joy trotting back to the counter carrying the egg carton. He took it from her before she decided to try to climb onto the chair with it.

Hope tugged at his sleeve. "Can I get the next thing?"

"No."

"I can stir," Joy told him.

"Good. Go stir up some air at the table."

"Some air?" She frowned in bewilderment.

"Oh, no," Dillon groaned in sudden despair. "Somebody get me a towel or something. Tad just spit up all over me."

"I'll get it." Grabbing her chair, Joy dragged it to the sink.

"No, me." Hope raced to pull her chair there, jockeying with her sister to be first.

For once, Eben ignored the shouting and arguing, the thuds and thumps, the splashes and splatters. He was satisfied with his little corner of peace that allowed him to whip up the batter and pour the first pancake on the griddle without any helping hands getting in his way.

"How come I always have to watch Tad?" Dillon protested from his seat at the table. "Why can't they do it? There's two of them."

" 'Cause we're not big enough—"

"—or strong enough."

"Jeez, Hope, you're just smearing it all over," Dillon complained.

"I'll do it," Joy offered.

"You'll just end up making it worse, Joy. Give me that rag. I'll do it myself." Dillon plunked the baby on the floor near his chair. "Play with Tad and make sure he doesn't crawl off somewhere."

"Tad needs his playpen."

"It isn't here yet," Dillon replied, then moaned again, "Jeez, why does he always have to spit up on me?"

"How come his playpen isn't here yet?"

"How should I know? Ask Mrs. Evans," Dillon snapped.

Eben perked up at that. "Who's Mrs. Evans?" He flipped the first pancake.

"She's our Sunday school teacher," Joy explained. "She's kind'a old."

Hope paused in the midst of a game of pattycake with Tad. "Sometimes she smells funny."

Eben let that pass. "Why would she know about the playpen?"

"Because she was gonna pack up our toys and stuff and ship them to us." Dillon craned his head around, trying to see the large wet stain on the shoulder of his pajama tops.

"If she shipped it, how's it ever gonna get here?" Joy frowned in bewilderment. "There isn't any water."

"It isn't coming by boat, you goose," Dillon declared in disgust.

"You said it was."

"I did not," he denied.

"Yes, you did," Hope asserted on Joy's behalf. "I heard you."

"All I said was—they're shipping it. It's probably coming by truck."

"Well, which is it?" Joy demanded, arms akimbo. "A ship or a truck?"

"I told you—by truck. Jeez, you're so dumb, Joy."

"I am not."

"You are, too."

"Am not!"

"All right," Eben interrupted the exchange, grabbing a plate off the table and sliding a golden brown pancake onto it. "Who wants the first pancake?"

Both twins scrambled to their feet, singing out in unison, "I do. I do."

Eben set the plate on the table and left them to argue it out while he poured another circle of batter onto the griddle. Behind him came the jostling of chairs, followed by a rare silence. Turning, he saw the twins staring at the pancake on the plate.

A freckled Joy gave him a reproachful look. "This doesn't look like the ones Momma makes."

"A pancake is a pancake." Eben frowned and waved the metal turner at the plate. "That's what you've got."

Hope regretfully shook her head, disputing that. "Momma makes little baby ones for us."

"That's 'cause you're babies," Dillon taunted.

Joy rose instantly to the bait. "We are not!"

"We just got little mouths," Hope insisted.

"Look," Eben intervened again, attempting a little fast-talking to solve the problem. "That pancake started out as a bunch of little ones, but they all ran together and turned into one big one."

"Well, we like little ones best," Joy informed him.

"Too bad. Eat that one and make the best of it." He turned back to the griddle.

"No thanks. You can have it, Dillon." She shoved the plate toward him. "Uncle Eben can make another one."

"Uh-uh." Dillon pushed the plate back and went to work again cleaning the spot on his clothes. "My pajamas still stink. I can't eat anything with them smelling like this."

"If it's that bad, take them off," Eben told him, then paused, his glance running over the three of them, all seated at the table. "Who's watching Tad? Where is he?"

Gasping in alarm, Joy scooted off her chair, then stopped and looked under the table. "It's okay." She straightened, wearing a big smile. "He's under the table, playing."

"One of you keep an eye on him," Eben ordered.

A muffled "Sure" came from Dillon as he pulled the pajama top over his head. A second later it sailed through the air, landing in a corner.

"Are mine ready yet?" Joy crawled back onto her chair and stood on the seat to see the top of the stove. When she spied the pancake on the griddle, she sighed in dismay. "Uncle Eben, you made another big one."

"This one's mine." Something told him it would be futile to argue that pancakes tasted the same regardless of their size. "I'll make yours next. How many little ones do you want?"

"Three."

"I want three, too," Hope inserted.

Taking the plate with the first pancake, Dillon picked up the syrup bottle and made like a rocket. "Three, two, one—blast off!"

He lifted the bottle high in the air, then turned it upside down over his plate and made a crashing sound when he squeezed out the syrup.

Most of it landed on the pancake.

Eben closed his eyes to the sight. Only a few more hours, he thought.

The phrase became like a mantra.

Chapter VIII

Sitting astraddle Eben's leg, the baby eyed the coiled telephone cord with interest, watching it dip and sway. The instant it swung within his reach, Tad grabbed it, squealing with delight. Eben was too stunned by the news he had just heard to notice the small hand tugging at the cord.

"Wait a minute," he said into the phone. "Are you telling me the man didn't have any family? That's impossible. Somewhere there has to be a mother or a father, an aunt, a cousin. Someone."

"It's logical to assume that," the attorney agreed. "However, as I explained a moment ago, your sister's husband was abandoned as a toddler. The authorities were never able to determine the identity of his parents. He grew up an orphan. You are the children's only *known* living relative, Mr. MacCallister.''

"That can't be," Eben murmured, gripped by a sense of doom.

"I'm afraid it is.'' The attorney sounded half-amused.

"But you don't understand, Grimes,'' Eben protested. "These kids can't stay here. I don't have time to look after them. I have a ranch to run."

"No doubt, you will have some difficult adjustments to make—"

The baby pulled hard on the cord and yanked the receiver away from Eben's ear.

"Hold on a minute, Grimes,'' he yelled toward the mouthpiece, then struggled for possession of the phone cord.

When he finally jerked it loose from the baby's fingers, Tad screamed in temper, his hands flying up and his body arching against the encircling arm.

"Do you hear that, Grimes?'' Eben demanded, unleashing some of his own anger. "This is what I'm up against. Here I am holding a squawling baby in my lap, the morning is already half-shot, and I have two hired men finishing up chores that I should have had done before they got here. Put yourself in my position and tell me how you would get any work done if somebody suddenly dumped four kids on you.''

"You must have a cook or a housekeeper—someone on your ranch who—"

"This is a bachelor outfit, Mr. Grimes. There's just me and two hired men to do it all." Unspoken

was that January deadline hanging over his head—
the one with dollar signs attached to it.

"In that case, I suggest that you advertise for a
live-in housekeeper or a nanny—"

"Do you have any idea how much that would
cost?" Eben declared. "Just feeding and clothing
four kids is expensive enough. Now you're expecting me to pay somebody to look after them?
I don't happen to have that kind of money to throw
away."

"Throw away," the attorney repeated, his voice
taking on a definite chill. "Is that the way you look
at it, Mr. MacCallister?"

"What other way is there?" Eben countered in
challenge.

"It is obvious to me, Mr. MacCallister, that you
have absolutely no sense of family duty or loyalty,
so I won't waste my breath reminding you that
these children are your nieces and nephews. But
by law, they are now your responsibility. I strongly
advise you to take that responsibility very seriously
because, I assure you, the courts will. Good day."

There was a sharp, disconnecting click, and the
line went dead. Furious, Eben slammed the
receiver down and rose from the chair with a sud-
denness that had the baby first gasping in surprise,
then gurgling with pleasure.

In one stride, he was at the counter, riffling
through the assorted papers and legal documents,
searching for something that would give him a
name, another option. A white, business-sized envelope fell to the floor, landing near his feet.

Bending, Eben scooped it up, the sudden dip and rise drawing another surprised gurgle of laughter from Tad. Eben paid no attention to him and concentrated on the envelope, its thickness telling him there were papers inside.

He ripped the sealed flap and extracted the sheets inside. The baby instantly made a grab for them, but Eben was quick to move them beyond his reach. The instant Eben saw the handwritten date in the upper-right-hand corner, everything inside him froze.

He stared at the precisely scrolled letters, an example of nearly flawless penmanship, fully legible with each letter flowing artistically into the next, all graceful curves and strong lines. It was Carla's handwriting. Eben had reviewed too much of her schoolwork in the past, read too many notes she had left for him not to recognize it even though it had been years since he had seen it.

A thickness clogged his throat, making it impossible to swallow as he dragged his gaze from the date in the corner, indicating the letter had been written nearly a year ago, to the opening salutation.

"Dear Eben," it read, and the tightness in his chest increased, the pressure squeezing at him. "I hope you never read this—"

Pain erupted in a swamping fury. Refusing to read another word of it, Eben crumpled the letter and jammed it back in its envelope, then stuffed it into a cabinet drawer, needing to get it out of his sight.

Trembling with a kind of rage he didn't fully

understand, he slammed the drawer shut, then turned his hot eyes upward. "This is all your fault, Carla," he accused hoarsely. "If you hadn't run off, I wouldn't be in this mess—I wouldn't be stuck with these kids. If you had just stayed"—he searched for the right words to add, but only one thought came to him—*you would still be alive.*

Pushed by a rawness that demanded physical action, Eben stormed from the kitchen without noticing Dillon, flattened against the wall near the doorway. He charged across the living room and out the front door, letting it slam shut behind him.

When he reached the flagstone ramada, grains of desert sand bit sharply into the bottoms of his bare feet. Swearing furiously, Eben came to an abrupt halt, then took mincing steps, searching for a smooth place to put his tender feet.

Finding one, he paused and threw a narrow glance at the fiery yellow sun riding well above the eastern horizon. Its light flooded the land with color and crispness.

"Would you look at that sun?" he said to the baby, his voice thick with irritation. "It's nearly nine o'clock and I'm not even dressed yet—all because of you and your wretched brother and sisters."

The baby laughed and clapped his hands as if finding it all a good joke. Automatically Eben slid a hand under the baby's heavily padded bottom and shifted him to a higher position against his bare chest.

Behind him the screen door opened, and a twin

poked her blond head outside its frame. "Can we come outside, too, Uncle Eben?"

At the moment, Eben was too busy nursing his anger to notice whether the girl had freckles on her nose or not. "You can go take a flying leap in a pile of cactus for all I care," he snapped.

"Oh, goody! Come on, Hope," she called. "He said we could go outside."

Whatever peace Eben might have absorbed from the stillness of the desert morning vanished with the invasion of the twins. The baby jabbered with excitement when the two girls darted outside, still dressed in their pajamas, their blond curls all tangled and mussed.

"Can we go see the horses, Uncle Eben?" Joy walked to the edge of the flagstone porch and gazed longingly at the corral.

"Yeah, have you got a nice one we can ride?"

"Don't you dare go near those horses," he warned.

"How come?" Joy turned, disappointment clouding her eyes.

"Will they bite?"

"No, but I will if I catch you anywhere near the corrals," he stated.

"Why?" Joy persisted.

"We won't hurt them, honest."

"As noisy as you two are, you'll spook them faster than a flapping sheet," he declared.

"We know how to be quiet," a freckled Joy stated with an adultlike sigh of exasperation.

"Yeah, Momma showed us."

"You gotta hold your hand out like this," Joy extended hers, palm up and fingers tight together, "and not jerk it away."

"Horses got real soft noses."

"Like velvet."

"Sometimes it tickles." Hope giggled at the memory.

"Momma's taken us riding lots of times."

"I'll just bet she did," Eben muttered skeptically.

"You got a visitor, Uncle Eben." Joy pointed to a vehicle coming up the lane.

"Who do you think it is?" Hope wondered.

But Eben didn't have to guess. He recognized the Jeep Cherokee.

"It's Maddie," he said grimly.

The twins took up the chant. "It's Maddie. It's Maddie."

Mindless of the gravelly sand beneath their bare feet, they ran to meet the approaching vehicle. Eben stayed on the porch and watched when it rolled to a stop and Maddie stepped out, dressed in a Western-style blouse and simple broomstick skirt that swirled about the tops of her boots. She looked stunning. He was furious with himself for noticing.

Distracted by the twins' exuberant greeting, Maddie was slow to notice Eben waiting under the ramada's shade. Her breath caught at the sight of him standing there, clad in only a pair of blue jeans.

With an effort, she dragged her gaze away from the lean roping of muscles across his chest and shoulders, and lifted it to his face, taking note of the finger-tracks in his hair that gave evidence of repeated rakings.

Fighting off an attack of breathlessness, Maddie responded absently to the twins' chatter and advanced toward the adobe house. As she drew closer, she saw the anger that glittered like a blue fire in his eyes, and guessed at the cause for it. Wisely she kept the observation to herself.

"Hi. I thought I'd come early and give you a hand with the packing," she said with deliberate brightness.

"You should have called and saved yourself the trip," he told her.

"Why?" She feigned confusion, then allowed comprehension to dawn. "You talked to the lawyer."

"Yes." His clipped reply spoke volumes.

"And?" Maddie pushed for more specific information.

"And Carla's husband had no family—at least, none that the lawyer knew about."

"None at all?" she echoed, inwardly rejoicing at the news.

"None," Eben confirmed, his expression tightening in renewed grimness. "He was abandoned as a baby and raised in foster homes. Leave it to Carla to choose some motherless stray to marry."

"That means, you are the only family these children have." Maddie pretended the thought had just occurred to her.

"Family." He released a heated breath of disgust.

"Would you believe that lawyer had the gall to lecture me about family duty and loyalty?"

"He did?" Maddie decided she liked this lawyer.

"Carla certainly showed a strong sense of family duty and loyalty when she ran off with all the money and left me to get by the best way I could. Didn't she?"

"She was only seventeen, Eben," Maddie reminded him.

"That's supposed to make it all right, I suppose," he challenged.

"No. It just means you should make some allowances. We have all done things that we later regret."

"You would know that better than me." A trace of bitterness crept into his voice.

Maddie chose to ignore it. She didn't want this conversation getting sidetracked by personal issues. "What are you going to do now, Eben?"

"According to Carla's attorney, I'm supposed to hire a live-in babysitter," he recalled with renewed irritation. "Of course, he didn't have suggestions on where I could come up with the money to pay for one."

Belatedly she became aware of two pairs of ears listening closely to their conversation. Turning to the girls, Maddie suggested, "Why don't you two run inside and pick out what you want to wear today?"

"Do we have to?" Joy protested.

"Yeah, it's fun wearing our jammies," Hope wheedled.

Maddie smiled at their tactics. "I'm sure it is, but it's time you got dressed."

"Will you help us?" Joy wanted to know.

"Yeah, we need our hair brushed."

"I want mine braided."

"Can I have mine in a ponytail?"

"As soon as you're dressed, I'll come and fix your hair," Maddie promised. "Now, go find some clothes."

As one, they ran into the house. Turning back to Eben, Maddie saw him studying her with a speculating look. She was instantly on guard.

"You are really good with those kids, Maddie," he observed, but not without reason. "Why don't you take them?"

"Oh, no, you don't, MacCallister," she said quickly. "You're not pawning those children off on me."

"But you have always wanted kids." A coaxing smile edged the corners of his mouth.

It was so rare that he smiled, Maddie had forgotten the impact of it. She realized then that he was pulling out all the stops.

"Here's a ready-made family for you," Eben went on. "Goodness knows, you're better equipped to handle them than I am. You already have a bunch of kid wranglers on the ranch payroll—games, playhouses, the whole nine yards."

"I am well aware of the facilities at El Regalo, but the answer is still no," she stated firmly. "These children are your responsibility, MacCallister. Not mine."

"But they can't stay here, Maddie," he argued, his exasperation surfacing again. "I don't have time to take care of them. You know that. For god's sake, just look at me—I haven't even had time to get dressed yet."

"I can see that." Standing this close to him, Maddie found it impossible not to be aware of all that hard-muscled flesh. "It's clear that you have only one choice."

"What's that?" He eyed her warily.

Maddie hesitated, wanting to lay it on thick, but not too thick. "Since you are too poor to take care of them, you'll have to call Social Services and have someone come get them. Then they'll be the government's worry."

"I never said I was too poor." Eben seized on that phrase just as Maddie had hoped he would.

"You said yourself that you couldn't afford them. It's the same difference." She feigned an idle shrug.

His eyes narrowed on her in sharp suspicion. "You're trying to talk me into keeping them, aren't you?"

Maddie laughed. "Are you kidding? I know you. I would have more success trying to talk a mountain into moving."

"You're up to something. You're too understanding. Too agreeable," Eben accused.

"It may sound that way, but I'm simply looking at the situation and carrying it to its logical conclusion. If you refuse to keep the children and I won't take them, your only alternative is to let the government find a home for them." She struggled to sound matter-of-fact. "Of course, it's highly unlikely that they'll find a family who will take in all four of them. It's a shame, though, to think of the twins being split up."

"Nice try, Maddie. But it isn't going to work." He studied her with narrowed eyes.

"What isn't? I'm just stating the facts," she said with a look of total innocence.

"But it's the way you're saying them," he replied, his faint smile indicating he wasn't buying any of it.

Bored with all the talk and inaction, the baby began to fuss and fidget in Eben's arms. Maddie caught at a waving fist, grateful for the distraction that allowed her to avoid Eben's keen eyes.

"What does it matter how I say them?" she argued. "You know it's true. Initially the children will be placed in various foster homes until suitable couples can be found to adopt them. I'm sure they won't have any problem finding new parents for little Tad here. People prefer to adopt babies. It's the older children who will be more difficult to place," Maddie added with regret, then made an attempt to take a more positive approach. "Although, the twins are awfully sweet. Parents might be found for them. Dillon is another story, though. More than likely he'll grow up in the foster care system."

"Will you stop it, Maddie?" Eben all but growled the words.

"Stop what?" She pretended not to understand.

"Don't get cute. You know damned well what I mean," he insisted. "You're doing your best to make me feel like a heel."

She had to bite back the urge to suggest that if the shoe pinched, there was a reason. Instead, she looked contrite.

"I'm sorry," she said. "That wasn't my intention. I know what you mean, though. It's sad that it has to be this way, but you can't afford to keep them—"

"Will you quit saying I can't afford it?" Eben demanded with fresh impatience.

"Eben, for heaven's sake, I'm not going to go spreading it around that you're practically broke—"

"I am not broke!" he exploded.

"Stop being so touchy," Maddie chided. "You aren't the only rancher who is financially strapped right now. Besides, we both know that—broke or not—you are under absolutely no obligation to look after these children. Carla had a lot of nerve leaving them with you after the way she treated you."

"I doubt very seriously that Carla planned on dying so soon," Eben inserted dryly.

"Maybe not, but that hardly changes anything," Maddie replied, then paused, making a covert study of him. But his face was as stony and impassive as the desert mountains. She took a breath and played her trump card. "In a way, it's too bad that you can't keep the children. One of them might grow to love the ranch as much as you do, and

someday take over running it. As things stand
now—when you die, it will all be sold, probably
to some developer like Billy Joe Wilder and his
cohorts.''

"Now you're playing dirty, Maddie." He pushed
the words through clenched teeth.

"Why? It's the truth." But she knew better than
to push her luck. "Come here, little guy." She
lifted the baby out of Eben's arms. "I'll watch Tad
while you phone the local Social Services office
about taking the children. You shouldn't have any
trouble explaining why you want to get rid of
them.''

"I never said I was going to call them," he
reminded her.

Maddie opened her eyes wide in a questioning
look of surprise. "Have you changed your mind
about keeping the children?"

"I never said that either." His expression darkened in irritation.

"Then what alternative do you have?" Maddie
reasoned. "You can't dump them along some roadside like an unwanted litter of kittens—not without
getting arrested for child endangerment."

"I know that," he snapped.

"That's a relief," she mocked lightly and angled
toward the door. "As soon as the twins are dressed,
I'll start packing their things. In the meantime,
you can make that call."

"I'll decide when—and *if*—I will."

Secretly pleased by his reply, Maddie allowed a
small smile to show. "Look at it this way, Eben—

the sooner you make the call, the sooner they'll be gone and the sooner you can get back to work."

He looked away, making no move toward the door. Mentally crossing her fingers, Maddie opened the screen door and went inside, surprising Dillon at his listening post near the door. He started to run off, then stopped and threw his head back in defiance, his chin quivering, his eyes hot with accusation.

"Dillon, it isn't what you think," Maddie said quickly, her heart twisting with regret at the things he'd overheard.

"Yeah, right," he jeered in disbelief. "And turtles fly, too."

Joy paused in the middle of buttoning a frilly white blouse and gave her brother a superior look. "That's silly, Dillon."

Hope agreed with her. "Turtles can't fly."

"Only birds—"

"—and angels—"

"—and butterflies—"

"—and airplanes can fly."

He turned on them, venting some of his anger and hurt feelings. "I know that. You're the ones who are silly."

"I am not." As always, Joy was ready to do battle.

"You are so," he taunted.

"You're the one who is 'cause—"

"—you're still wearing your jammies," Hope finished the sentence Joy had started.

"So?" Dillon challenged.

"So"—Joy appealed to Maddie for support—"it's time Dillon got dressed, isn't it?"

"Yes, it is—" Maddie began.

Dillon never let her finish, accusing, "You just want me to get dressed so you can take us and dump us along some road."

"That isn't true—"

"Yes, it is," he broke in again. "I heard you talking out there, planning how to get rid of us. I'm not dumb like they are. I know you're going to send us away."

Joy pursed her lips in reproval, then declared, "Now you're being silly again, Dillon."

"Uncle Eben wants us here," Hope added.

"No, he doesn't. He's gonna call somebody and have them take us away. They'll put us all in different homes, and we'll never see each other again!" All the while he was yelling, Dillon was sneaking in sniffles, fighting back the tears that made his nose run.

"Uncle Eben wouldn't do that," Joy said none too certainly, automatically gravitating closer to her sister.

Quicker to believe, Hope wailed, "I don't want to go."

"You don't have to, honey," Maddie tried to reassure her.

But there was Dillon, shouting again. "You're lying! You're going to send us away. I heard you."

"Why?" Joy asked tearfully. "We didn't do nothing."

"I told you before, he doesn't want us here,"

Dillon angrily hurled the words. "He hates you 'cause you're dumb and stupid and silly!"

"I want my mommy," Hope sobbed.

The screen door came shut with an explosive *bang* that startled everyone, including Maddie. She turned with a jerk and saw Eben standing inside the entryway surveying the scene with a dark scowl.

"What's going on here?" he demanded. "What's all this yelling and crying about?"

"Dillon overheard us talking," Maddie explained tentatively while holding her breath, hoping against hope that Eben had relented. But his expression was completely unreadable.

"Dillon says you're gonna make us go away." Joy hiccoughed back a sob.

"And we'll never see each other again," Hope added with a whimper.

"As usual, Dillon is wrong," Eben stated, and Maddie released the breath she'd been holding with a rush of relief.

"You're lying." Dillon was quick to attack. "I heard you. You never wanted us here."

"You're absolutely right," Eben replied with a curt nod of agreement. "I didn't want you here, and you didn't want to come. But you're here now, which means we are stuck with each other— whether we like it or not."

Joy eyed him uncertainly. "Does that mean we're gonna stay?"

"That's what I just said," he answered, all stern and hard.

"Hope, we're gonna stay." She grabbed her sister's hands.

"Yippee! Yippee!" Together they jumped up and down in delight.

Only Dillon remained skeptical and scornful. "You're just saying that stuff to make them stop crying."

Eben locked eyes with him. "In time, you will find that I always mean what I say, kid."

"My name's Dillon. I hate it when you call me 'kid,' " he declared with force.

"If you ever stop acting like a bratty kid, I'll call you by your name," Eben told him, then paused and swept his glance over the group, commanding their attention. "Since you'll be living with me now, it's time we got a few things straight. I have some hard-and-fast rules that—"

Hope interrupted, frowning, "What's a ... rule?"

"It must be like the golden kind," Joy decided. "You mean—like we learned in Sunday school where Jesus said—"

"—we should love each other," Joy finished while Eben stared at the floor, wearily shaking his head in despair.

Hope turned earnest eyes on him. "We love you, Uncle Eben."

"Lucky me," he muttered under his breath, then picked up roughly where he left off. "For now, we'll deal with rule number one—your clothing is never to be left in the living room. Which means I want you to gather up all your stuff and take it to your rooms while I go get dressed. When I come out, I don't want to see anything here but empty suitcases and bags."

Joy's mouth dropped open. "All of this?" she squeaked in disbelief.

"But what'll we do with it?" Hope wanted to know.

Eben thought the answer to that was obvious. "Put them away, of course."

"Where?"

Joy looked totally blank.

"In your dresser drawers."

"Which ones?" Hope asked.

"Whichever ones you want your clothes in. You figure it out," Eben tossed the problem back in their laps.

"But we don't know how to put our clothes away," Joy declared.

"Momma always did it for us," Hope explained.

"Your mother isn't here anymore." He felt that tightness in his chest again and refused to acknowledge it. "You have to start doing these things because I'm not going to wait on you hand and foot like she did. You're old enough to start taking care of yourselves." He ignored Maddie's reproving look. "Now, hop to it and get your stuff out of here."

"But Maddie's gonna—"

"—brush our hair now."

"She can do that after you put your clothes away. Get busy before I decide to cut it all off."

Galvanized by his threat, the twins flew into

action, scooping up clothes and racing for their room. Dillon watched them contemptuously, then glared at Eben and plunked himself down on a chair, folding his arms in a gesture of mutiny.

"That rule goes for you, too, kid," Eben told him. "Get a move-on and start picking up your clothes."

"I'm not going to do it. And you can't make me either," Dillon taunted.

"Want'a bet?" Eben challenged in a voice ominously low.

Dillon shifted uneasily, then declared, "You aren't the boss of me."

"Unfortunately for both of us, your mother made me the boss of you," Eben replied. "I'm not any happier about it than you are. But that's the way it is. If you don't like it, you'll have to blame your mother." He caught Dillon's arm and pulled him off the chair. "Get your clothes and take them to your room."

"I hate you." Dillon glowered, jerking his arm free.

Eben shrugged his indifference. "Hate me all you want, but you're still going to abide by the rules here."

With a last, grudging look, Dillon grabbed up a bunch of jeans and headed toward his bedroom at a foot-dragging walk. Maddie watched him with worried eyes.

When he was out of earshot, she said to Eben, "Don't you think you were a little hard on him?"

He flashed her a dry, crooked smile. "What are

you complaining about? They're staying, aren't they? That should make you happy."

"Me?" She blinked, striving for a look of bewilderment.

"Don't be coy, Maddie. It doesn't suit you."

"I don't know what you're talking about," she stalled.

"In a pig's eye, you don't," he scoffed. "Your act out there might have been convincing if you hadn't laid it on so thick."

"Did I say something to change your mind?" she asked, curious as to what it might have been and hoping he would tell her.

"No. You just confirmed things I'd been thinking. So—I'll keep them and raise them—for all the thanks I'm likely to get," he added in a low mutter.

Behind them, the screen door swung open and Ramon stepped inside, hastily dragging off his battered hat. *"Señor* Mac, we have finished the morning chores," he said in his thickly accented English, then hesitated, his wide-eyed glance taking in Eben's bare feet and his state of near-undress. "Do you wish us to saddle the little bay first?"

"No." Eben paused as the twins ran back into the living room, laughing and giggling, somehow managing to turn the whole thing into a game. "I won't be working any of the horses today."

"Sí, Señor." Ramon nodded, then hesitated again, gripping his rolled hat with both hands, crumpling its rolled brim even more. "What work would you have us do?"

"You'd better ride out and check the cattle, see how they are."

"*Sí, Señor.*" With a quick bob of his head, Ramon started to back out the door.

"Ramon, wait a minute," Eben called him back, then jerked a thumb toward the chattering twins. "I need somebody to come in every day and look after these kids. Do you know anyone who might do that? A sister or an aunt, maybe?"

"*Sí, mi prima Sofía—*" He stopped and repeated the answer in English, "My cousin Sofia, she sometimes watches the little ones in our village. I will ask her."

"*Bueno.* If she agrees, bring her with you tomorrow."

"*Sí, señor.*" Pleasure lit Ramon's face as he backed up and went out the door.

Eben turned, his glance cutting to Maddie. "Happy?" he taunted. "I'm not only keeping them, now I'm hiring someone to watch them."

"Don't put that off on me. It wasn't my idea," Maddie chided, amused by the ploy.

"Well, I didn't have much choice, did I?" he countered on a cynical breath, "Not if I expect to get any work done."

Maddie couldn't argue with that. "You really should have Ramon and the others apply for their green card. One of these days the INS will show up out here. Then what will you do?"

"Who says Ramon doesn't have a green card?" Eben challenged.

"Have you seen it?"

"No, and I haven't asked to see it either. He works and I pay him for it. As long as we're both happy, it's none of the government's business."

"I don't think the government looks at it that way," Maddie suggested dryly.

"That's their problem," he said.

"They can very easily make it your problem," Maddie pointed out. "What you're doing happens to be illegal, Eben."

"Are you on some new crusade now?" he scowled in annoyance. "First it was the kids and now it's green cards. I don't have time for this, Maddie. Have you forgotten Wilder has a gun to my head?"

"I haven't forgotten—"

"Then get off my case, will you? You know what it's like getting help on a ranch. You're lucky if they're with you a year before they get itchy feet and move on to greener pastures. Ramon has stuck with me. The man's not only a hard worker, he's dependable as the sunrise."

"That's all the more reason to get him a green card," she replied evenly. "It isn't that hard, Eben. We've done it before at El Regalo—"

"Fine," Eben broke in. "Then you do it since you think it's so all-fired important."

"It is important," she insisted as a cooing Tad tried to stick his fingers in her mouth. "Both for Ramon's and Luis's sakes, as well as the children's."

His eyebrow shot up. "The children's?"

"Yes, the children's," Maddie repeated. "You need to set a good example, Eben. That's part of raising children, too."

He looked at her for a long second, then said, "In that case, if I'm supposed to be setting good examples, I'd better be getting dressed."

"You'd set a better example by helping Ramon and Luis to get their green cards," she countered with a stubborn glint in her eyes.

But Eben refused to budge. "If you think it's that important, Maddie, you do it," he told her. "I don't have time to mess with all that red tape—not with everything else I've got to do, thanks to Wilder and these four kids I'm stuck with now."

Aware there was truth in what he said, Maddie conceded the point. "If that's what you want, I'll handle it." Unlike Eben, she had few demands on her time, and considerably fewer pressures.

"Good." He scratched at the beard stubble along his jaw, then muttered, mostly to himself, "I haven't even had time to shave yet." His glance ran to Maddie. "I don't suppose I could talk you into keeping an eye on Tad while I get cleaned up?"

"Of course," she said, then remembered, "I should warn you, though, you only have one clean diaper left." She picked up the plastic Pampers sack and shook it, rattling the single diaper inside.

Eben sighed heavily. "I'll be going into town to get Dillon enrolled in school. I guess I can stop at the store while I'm there." He eyed her hopefully. "I don't suppose I could talk you into staying here and looking after Tad and the twins until I get back."

"Please?" she prompted with a teasing smile.

"Please." There was a definite edge to his voice.

Maddie laughed. "Since you asked so nicely—yes, I can stay."

"Thanks." His expression softened with a look of genuine gratitude, but it was the disturbingly warm light in his eyes that took her breath away.

At that moment, Maddie knew that, despite all his flaws, she still loved him. But she also knew that loving him wasn't enough. It never would be until Eben learned that love had to come first, and everything else second. Maybe it was a lesson the children could teach him.

Chapter IX

The first blush of dawn tinted the eastern horizon a pale pink. The dimness of its light deepened the night's lingering darkness as Eben set out from the house, the blanket-bundled baby in one arm and a pail of sudsy water in the other hand. A grumbling Dillon walked beside him swinging an empty pail while the sleepy-eyed twins stumbled along behind him.

"How come we had to get up so early, Uncle Eben?" Joy asked in a drowsy voice.

"Yeah, my eyes aren't woked up yet," Hope complained, rubbing at them.

"Because you're not old enough to watch the baby by yourselves." A horse stirred restlessly in the paddock, then whickered hopefully.

"Dillon could," Joy reminded him.

"But Dillon had to come with me. He has chores to learn," Eben replied.

"What's a chore?" Hope hurried to catch up with him, then trotted to keep pace with his long strides.

"You," he answered truthfully, but the humor of it went right over her head. Glancing down, he saw the quizzical look on her face. "A chore is a job that has to be done every single day without fail."

"Whatcha gonna do with that water, Uncle Eben?" Joy eyed the pail he carried.

"I'm going to wash the cow's udder before I milk her."

She gave him a perplexed look. "Her other what?"

"Not other—udder," Eben corrected, but it cleared up none of her confusion. He tried again. "I'm going to wash the cow's bag."

"The cow has a bag?" Her eyes popped open in disbelief.

"Is she going on a trip somewhere?" Hope wondered, a perplexed frown creasing her forehead.

Eben stifled a groan. It was much too early for one of these conversations. "Just forget it. You'll see what I'm talking about in a minute."

For once, they took his suggestion and fell silent.

When they reached the barn, Eben set the pail down and unlatched the door, then reached inside and flipped on the light. Dillon took one look inside and wrinkled up his nose at the host of strong smells.

"It stinks in there."

"You'll get used to it." Eben gave him a little shove inside and picked up the pail.

"Jesus was born in a barn," Joy remembered, looking around with interest.

"That's 'cause there was no room in the motel," Hope added.

Dillon looked back with scorn. "You two think you know everything about Christmas, but you don't know nothing. Jesus was born in a manger."

"A manger's a barn, isn't it, Uncle Eben?" Joy craned her neck to look up at him.

"Momma said it was." Which settled the matter in Hope's mind.

"Technically, a manger is the place where a farmer or rancher puts the feed for his animals," Eben explained with mixed patience. "In most barns, the manger would be at the head of the stall."

Joy turned to her brother in triumph. "See, I told you, Dillon. Jesus was too borned in a barn."

"Who cares?" Dillon grumbled.

Eben privately echoed the sentiment and sent Dillon to the feed room with instructions to fetch a can of grain, then watched to make sure Dillon took it from the right barrel.

"Have you got a manger in your barn?" Joy ran ahead to look.

"Can we put Tad in it?" Hope asked eagerly.

"Yeah, then we can play Christmas," Joy called back.

To his everlasting dismay, Eben realized that both twins were now wide awake. "No, you cannot put Tad in the manger," he refused flatly. "You are going to sit here and watch him while I show your brother how to milk a cow."

Joy ran back, protesting, "But we want to see how to milk a cow, too."

"Yeah, and you promised to show us her bag," Hope reminded him as Eben fixed a place for the baby, using hay bales for crib walls and spreading the extra blanket to cover the mattress of loose straw.

"You'll be able to see everything from here." He laid Tad on his makeshift bed and passed his bottle to Joy. "You two park yourselves right here and feed him the rest of this bottle. With any luck, he'll go back to sleep." When Dillon came out of the feed room, carrying an old coffee can, Eben waved him forward. "Come on, kid. I'll show you where to dump that; then we'll bring the cow in."

"Where is the cow?" one of the twins called.

As much as he wanted to ignore the question, Eben knew it wouldn't do any good. She would just keep asking until he supplied the answer. So he did. "Outside."

"Can we come?"

"You stay right where you are and don't make a sound," Eben ordered, then added for good measure, "You might scare the cow."

Which was far from likely. The Brown Swiss was

the best-natured milk cow Eben had ever owned. Nothing ever seemed to faze the placid and patient animal, which was why Eben had no qualms about turning a seven-year-old loose on her.

He opened the side door to the barnyard and cupped both hands to his mouth, yelling, "Ca' boss! Ca' boss!" Glancing down at the sulking boy, shoulders hunched under his jacket, Eben instructed, "Now you call her."

"Why should I?" Dillon grumbled. "You already did."

If he thought for one minute an explanation would have changed the boy's attitude, Eben would have told him that the cow needed to learn to recognize Dillon's voice. But he didn't, and said instead, "You're going to do it because I told you to. Now, hurry it up." Already Eben could hear the slow, steady plod of cloven hooves as the Brown Swiss made her way to the opened barn door.

Still grumbling, Dillon dragged his hands out of his jacket pockets, lifted them to his mouth, and yelled, in sarcastic mimicry, "Ca' boss! Ca' boss!"

A low *mooo* came from the slowly lifting darkness. "She just told you that you need some practice." Eben nudged Dillon out of the doorway, turning him back toward the barn's interior.

Dillon snorted his disbelief. "Cows can't talk."

"They talk. They just don't speak English."

"And I suppose you can understand everything they say," Dillon scoffed.

"Not everything," Eben replied as the cow's hooves struck the concrete aisle behind them.

A chorus of admiring "oohs" came from the twins when they caught sight of the fawn brown cow, her head crowned with a pair of short, curving horns. Liquid dark eyes acknowledged the praise an instant before the cow turned into her customary spot and ducked her head through the stanchion to nose at the waiting grain.

"She's beautiful, Uncle Eben," Joy whispered in awe.

"Can we pet her?"

"No, you stay right there with Tad." Eben grabbed a five-gallon bucket and turned it upside down next to the cow, using it as a milking stool.

"What's her name?" one of them asked.

"Bessie." Eben sent Dillon after the pail filled with warm, soapy water.

"She doesn't look like a Bessie," Joy informed him in a voice that remained soft with admiration.

"No, she looks like an Annabelle," Hope asserted thoughtfully.

"Can we call her Annabelle?"

"You can call her whatever you want," Eben replied with complete indifference.

Joy slid off the hay bale, tiptoed past the cow's head, took a long look from that angle, then came back, frowning hard at Eben. "Where's her bag?"

"I didn't see her carrying one when she came in." Hope shook her head.

"It's right there." Eben waved a hand toward the cow's udder, swollen with milk.

"That's her bag?" Joy frowned skeptically.

"Yup. That's where she keeps her milk. We have

to wash the outside of it before we start milking."
Eben sat down on the upturned bucket, then
looked around for Dillon and spotted him standing
well back from the cow. "Come over here, kid, so
you can see what I'm doing."

He expected an objection from Dillon for being
called kid, but Dillon's only reaction was a further
lowering of his eyebrows in a scowl. "I can see from
here."

"You're going to be doing more than watching,
kid," Eben informed him. "This is going to be a
hands-on lesson."

"How come I have to learn how to do this?"
Dillon protested again.

"Because this is going to be your job," Eben
replied. "One of these mornings you'll have to do
it all by yourself. So I suggest you get over here
and learn how it's done."

"How come we can't learn?" Joy asked.

"Yeah, how come we can't have a job—"

"—like Dillon," Joy finished.

"You've got a job—watching Tad." Bending low,
Eben squeezed the excess water out of the soapy
rag and proceeded to wash the cow's teats and
udder.

"Watching Tad isn't a real job," Joy sighed in
disappointment.

"Yeah, we want a real one," Hope agreed.

Eben had the sinking feeling they would continue to pester him until he came up with one a
four-year-old could handle. "I've got a real job for

you as soon as we finish up here," he said, thinking of one.

"Oh, goody, what is it?" Joy clapped her hand together.

"Feeding the chickens. Now, you better be quiet," he warned. "You know what I told you about making too much noise and scaring Bessie."

"Her name's Annabelle," Joy corrected, then gasped with the excitement of a sudden thought. "I know what we can do, Hope, let's—"

"—sing to her." Her equally round-eyed sister completed the sentence.

"Would she like that, Uncle Eben?" Joy asked, all eagerness.

"She would love it." At the moment, he was ready to agree to anything that would stem this incessant flow of questions.

While he taught a reluctant Dillon the rudiments of milking a cow by hand, the twins sang a fractured rendition of "Away in a Manger." The second time through, the song dissolved into a disagreement when they reached the verse about lowing cattle. Joy was positive that it meant the cattle were laying down, and Hope was equally certain they were low because they were bowing.

Eben, wisely, stayed out of the argument.

After numerous futile tuggings, Dillon finally managed to get a half-dozen puny squirts of milk into the pail. In the interest of time, Eben took over and finished milking the newly dubbed Annabelle.

By the time the chickens had been fed and hay thrown to the horses, the sun had poked its head above the horizon, brushing the eastern sky with watercolor strokes of crimson and gold. Eben wasn't the least bit surprised to note that morning chores had taken him twice as long as normal— thanks to his little helpers.

He headed for the house carrying the milk pail in one hand, with the fussing baby hooked against his opposite hip. The twins skipped alongside, one on his right and the other on his left, while Dillon lagged behind, in no better mood than when the morning had started.

"That was fun, Uncle Eben," Joy declared with a happy smile.

"Can we do it again tomorrow?" Hope asked with undisguised enthusiasm.

"We'll be doing it every single morning." At the moment, that sounded like a death sentence to Eben.

"I liked feeding the chickens," Joy told him, nodding her head in emphasis.

"How come they wouldn't let us pet them?" Hope frowned curiously.

"Don't you two ever stop jabbering?" he countered in exasperation.

Joy giggled, cupping a hand to her mouth. "Momma says I even talk in my sleep."

"I don't." Hope shook her head, sending a mass of blond curls into motion.

Dillon spoke up, "I'm hungry."

"Me, too," Joy declared.

"Can we have pancakes again?"

"Little ones."

Eben all but groaned at the thought of fixing breakfast and facing a repeat of yesterday's sticky mess. Then his eyes beheld a wondrous sight— Ramon and Luis Vargas trudging up the ranch lane, accompanied by a woman in a long, tan coat.

He stopped to wait for them, an actual smile curving his mouth.

Ramon made the introductions. "*Señor* Mac, this is my cousin, Sofia Perez."

She was younger than Eben had expected, not much more than eighteen or nineteen, with soft and dark doe eyes. A brightly colored scarf circled her face, covering all but a few inches of jet black hair. Conscious of his critical appraisal, she briefly dropped her gaze, then lifted it, giving him a shy smile.

"Good morn-ing, *Señor* Mac." She spoke in a slow, careful English that sent up a red flag.

"You do speak English?" Eben challenged, his gaze narrowing on her.

"*Sí*—yes," she hastily corrected herself. "I learn in school." Hesitating, she glanced sideways at Ramon. "I forget the right words sometimes."

"I hope you don't forget too many," Eben told her in a voice dry with reproval. "The children know only English."

Sofia nodded. "Ramon tells me this."

Dillon looked her over and turned accusing eyes on Eben. "What's she doing here?"

"She's *here* to look after you so I can finally get some work done, instead of spending all my time babysitting you four."

"We don't need a babysitter," Dillon stated.

"What do you care?" Eben challenged, then reminded him, "As of Monday, you'll be be in school most of the time anyway."

"It's a dorky school," Dillon muttered loud enough for Eben to hear and dug a toe into the rough soil, kicking at a rock. "I'm gonna hate it."

Eben ignored that and directed his attention beck to the Mexican girl. "You understand that, in addition to watching the children, I'll expect you to fix their meals and keep the house looking halfway clean?"

"*Sí*—yes, *Señor* Mac, I can do these things," she assured him quickly, anxious to make a favorable impression.

"Can you fix us pancakes?" Joy piped up, exhibiting none of her brother's reluctance over the addition of a babysitter.

"Yeah, we like pancakes," Hope echoed.

"I can eat three of them—"

"—if they're little pancakes," Hope qualified the claim.

After listening intently, Sofia turned dark, questioning eyes on Ramon. "*Que?*" He tipped his head and murmured something in her ear. Comprehension dawned in a wreathing smile. "*Sí*, I make pancakes."

When the twins cheered the news, the baby appeared to take exception to the noise. After coughing out a few sobs, as if testing his lung capacity, Tad unleashed a screeching wail. Eben tried to jiggle him into silence, but Tad only got madder.

"I will take him, *Señor* Mac." Sofia stepped forward, hands lifting.

"He's either tired, hungry, or his diapers are dirty," Eben warned.

As she reached for the baby, the front of her coat swung open. Eben stared in shock at the distinctive roundness of her stomach. By the time he recovered his speech, she was on her way toward the house, taking the children with her.

Eben turned on his hired man, accusing, "Ramon, she is going to have a baby."

"*Si.*" Ramon beamed. "It is the first for Sofia and her husband, Juan. They are *mucho* happy."

"I'll bet she's even happier to get this job," Eben challenged, grim-lipped.

The wiley Ramon made a show of pretending that he didn't understand. "Oh, *si, Señor* Mac, it is *mucho* better to have extra money before the baby is born."

"And even better if the baby is born on this side of the border, right?"

Unease flickered briefly in Ramon's expression before he shrugged slim shoulders and smiled. "Such things are in God's hands. The baby, it will not be here for many months yet."

"How many, Ramon?" Eben inquired smoothly. "Exactly when is this baby due?"

"Not until March, *señor.*"

He arched an eyebrow in sharp skepticism. "March?"

Ramon hesitated, then lifted his hand, wagging it from side to side. "March, February. *Quien sabe?*"

"You'd better know," Eben stated. "Because if that baby is born any sooner, you'll be out of a job."

"*Señor* Mac, I swear by the Virgin Mary—" Ramon began in earnest defense.

Eben waved off the oath. "We've wasted too much time talking already. Luis, take this milk up to the house and show your cousin how to strain it." He handed him the bucket, then said to Ramon, "Catch that little bay and saddle him up for me."

As the two men separated, heading in different directions, Sofia called from the adobe house. "*Señor* Mac?"

"What?" Eben barked, suddenly short-tempered.

She drew back a little, recoiling from the sharpness of his voice. "Do you wish for me to fix you some pan-cakes?"

"No!" he hollered back and felt his stomach rumble emptily. "Just scramble a couple eggs, roll them in a tortilla with some cheese, and have the kid bring it to me down at the corral."

Eben made a point to steer clear of the house the rest of the day, eating both his breakfast and lunch at the corral. It was nearly dark before he finally called it a day. Sofia met him at the door.

"*Los niños*, they have eaten. I have placed your supper in the oven for to keep it warm," she explained, then shyly nodded a good night and hurried to join her cousins.

He watched her leave, thinking that just maybe he had found the solution to this mess. Not only had Sofia fed the children and kept them out of his hair all day, she'd also fixed a hot meal for him. He was even more convinced when he found the twins half-asleep, too exhausted to chatter up their usual storm.

Fresh from the shower, Maddie slipped on a robe of champagne silk, tied the sash at her waist, then absently slicked the wet hair away from her face. Steam clouded the bathroom's mirrored walls, obscuring her reflection. Turning from it, she crossed the marble floor, retracing her steps to the bedroom.

A breakfast tray sat on the glass-topped table next to an ice blue chaise lounge. The tray and the morning sunlight flooding through the French doors to the private courtyard gave evidence that the housekeeper had already come and gone.

Maddie ignored the glass of freshly squeezed orange juice and poured herself a cup of coffee. Fragrant vapor rose from the coffee's surface as she lifted the cup to her lips and took that first sip. But the coffee did little to ease the restlessness that pushed at her.

Giving in to it, Maddie wandered to the French doors. Although the house sat well apart from El Regalo's main guest lodge with its adjacent swimming pool, tennis court, and quaint adobe guest cabins, she could see much of it from her bedroom.

On Sunday morning there was none of the usual bustle of activity that marked the rest of the week. The large corral next to the stables was empty of all but a handful of horses. There were no wranglers lounging about the stables and no riders heading out to bring the remuda in.

Here and there, suitcases sat outside cabin doors. Sunday was always a quiet time of transition when many of the guests left and new ones arrived.

Westward, beyond the buildings, was the pure flare of the desert. A blue blur of mountains rose suddenly from the dry plains, stark and stunning and rawly beautiful. But it was to the east that Maddie looked, where the morning sunlight raced yellow and hard over the land. Twenty miles away lay Star Ranch, Eben's place.

Eyes narrowed, Maddie gazed in that direction, then abruptly turned and crossed to the telephone, curiosity finally getting the better of her.

A hundred times in the last few days, she had wondered how Eben and the children were getting along. It didn't matter that it was none of her business. Every ounce of common sense warned that she was a fool to get mixed up with Eben again. She would only open herself to getting hurt a second time.

Even as she picked up the phone and dialed his number, Maddie tried to convince herself she was calling purely out of concern for the children, that this wasn't about Eben. Still it irked her that it had never once crossed his mind to let her know how the children were doing.

The man was thoughtless, insensitive, and incredibly stingy. How on earth could she possibly love him? Maddie wondered in a huff.

But the answer was easy—Eben MacCallister could also be amazingly gentle and fiercely loyal. Which was one of the main reasons he found it so hard to forgive her lack of loyalty to him.

With the receiver to her ear, Maddie took another sip of coffee and listened to the trill of the phone. Shortly after the fourth ring, a voice growled in her ear, "MacCallister here."

But it was all the crying in the background that caught Maddie's attention. "Eben, what is going on there?" She frowned in concern.

"What did you say?" he demanded, half-shouting to make himself heard above the noise.

"I said—"

"Just a minute. I can't hear you," he snapped. A split second later Maddie caught the partially muffled sound of his voice bellowing at the children. "You stop that bawling right now! Can't you see I'm on the telephone? I can't hear a word with all the racket you're making. Now, shut up!"

On the heels of that came a faint, aggressive voice that unmistakably belonged to Dillon. "Don't you yell at my sisters!"

"I'll do more than yell at them if they don't shut up!" Eben threatened. The noise had subsided to mere background sobbing when he finally came back on the line. "Sorry. Are you still there?"

"I'm still here," she said, still wondering what all the crying had been about.

"Maddie. It's you, is it?"

She instantly reacted to his disgruntled tone. "I'm thrilled to hear your voice, too."

To start your membership, simply complete and return the Free Book Certificate. You'll receive your Introductory Shipment of FREE Zebra Contemporary Romances. Then, each month as long as your account is in good standing, you will receive the 3 newest Zebra Contemporary Romances. Each shipment will be yours to examine for 10 days. If you decide to keep the books, you'll pay the preferred book club member price of $15.95 – a savings of up to 20% off the cover price! (plus $1.99 to offset the cost of shipping and handling.) If you want us to stop sending books, just say the word… it's that simple.

BOOK CERTIFICATE

Yes, Please send me FREE Zebra Contemporary romance novels. I only pay for shipping and handling. I understand I am under no obligation to purchase any books, as explained on this card.

Name _____

Address _____ Apt. _____

City _____ State _____ Zip _____

Telephone (___) _____

Signature _____
(If under 18, parent or guardian must sign)

Offer limited to one per household and not valid to current subscribers.
All orders subject to approval. Terms, offer, and price subject to change. Offer valid only in the U.S.

Thank You!

CNHL2A

lll.....l.llll....ll.l.ll.l.l.l...l.l..ll.l.l..l.ll.l..lll...l

Zebra Contemporary Romance Book Club
Zebra Home Subscription Service, Inc.
P.O. Box 5214
Clifton , NJ 07015-5214

PLACE
STAMP
HERE

"What do you want?"

Honesty forced her to admit, "Nothing, really. I was calling to see how things were going. But if what I just overhead is any indication, I already know the answer. What was that all about, anyway?"

"They want to go to Sunday school," he answered on a weary note.

"Let me guess," Maddie murmured, smothering the rise of irritation. "When they asked, you refused to take them. Naturally, you have too much work to do."

"As a matter of fact, I do," he retorted stiffly. "I have a half-dozen horses that need shoeing, and the tank out at Serrado Canyon to check on. That may not sound like a lot of work to you, but it is when I have to keep track of these monsters at the same time."

"If they want to go to Sunday school, you should take them, MacCallister. Not because it's what they want, but because it will be good for them."

"I told you, I don't have time." The words were clipped and tight.

Maddie hesitated, then plunged ahead—against her better judgment. "I have a deal for you, MacCallister," she said.

"What's that?" He sounded leery.

"You get the children ready for Sunday school and I'll take them."

Eben snapped up the offer. "Done."

"I'm talking about dressed for church," Maddie warned. "That means with their hair brushed and their good clothes on."

He didn't hesitate. "What time?"

She glanced at the clock on the nightstand. "I'll be there in forty-five minutes. But don't expect any help from me when I get there. If they aren't ready when I drive in, I'll leave and you can have the fun of explaining why they aren't going to Sunday school after all."

"They'll be ready," he stated and hung up.

Smiling to herself, Maddie placed the receiver back on its cradle, then sobered at the knowledge of what she had just done—she had found another excuse to see Eben.

"You keep this up, Madeline Marie," she told herself sternly, "and you'll get your heart broken again. This time there won't be an Allan Williams around to pick up the pieces."

With a sigh, she absently ran a hand through her hair, felt its dampness, and glanced at the clock in sudden panic. She had less than twenty minutes to dry her hair and get dressed. Hurriedly she set the cup on the nightstand and raced to the bathroom.

Exactly forty-five minutes later Maddie pulled up in front of the old adobe house and stepped out of the Jeep Cherokee. The twins ran out the front door to meet her, their black patent leather shoes clattering across the flagstone veranda. They looked like a pair of little dolls in identical, lace-edged dresses of burgundy velvet with matching velvet headbands shimmering through their blond curls.

"We been waiting—" An exuberant Joy began the sentence.

Hope finished it. "—and waiting for you, Maddie."

"We thought you were—"

"—gonna be late."

"You thought wrong. I'm here." Maddie opened the rear passenger door for them before throwing a curious glance toward the house. "Where's Dillon?"

"He's coming." Joy scrambled into the backseat.

"Uncle Eben made him—"

"—wear a tie."

"He hates it." Hope climbed in after her sister.

"Uncle Eben got mad at him," Joy confided a bit smugly.

" 'Cause he wouldn't stand still," Hope explained with a knowing nod of her head.

Joy sighed in adultlike exasperation. "Uncle Eben had a real hard time—"

"—getting it tied right."

"He finally did, though," Joy concluded, as if she had never once doubted the outcome.

"I'm glad he did," Maddie said, then instructed, "Be sure to fasten your seat belts. Do you need help with them?"

"No."

"We can do it." As Hope worked to shove the clasp in place, Dillon came out of the house, one hand tugging at the knotted tie at his throat.

Eben was right behind him, carrying the baby. "Touch that tie, kid"—Eben warned—"and you'll find yourself cleaning the barn every night for a week.''

"How come I have to wear a tie?" Dillon grumbled. "I never had to wear one to church at home."

"But you look very handsome in one," Maddie told him.

"Who cares?" He tried to sound indifferent, but she noticed the quick squaring of his shoulders and the small, proud lift of his chin.

"Why don't you ride in the front seat with me, Dillon?" she suggested.

Eben frowned. "Aren't you going to put the baby in the front seat?"

"The baby?" Maddie said, her surprise quickly giving way to amusement when she saw that Eben had Tad dressed in a spiffy little blue outfit complete with a matching billed cap. "I hate to tell you this, but Tad is a little young for Sunday school. I don't think they have classes for his age group."

"So?" Eben asked, looking uncertain.

"So—I said I would take the children to Sunday school. Tad is obviously not old enough."

"But you're going to take him anyway, aren't you? He's already all dressed up."

Maddie cocked her head to one side, her lips curving in a chiding smile. "Do I look like a babysitter to you, MacCallister?"

His gaze made a slow and thorough sweep of her, traveling from head to toe and back again, taking in the sleek hairstyle, the flattering lines of her cashmere sweater dress, and the beautiful, desirable picture she made. A car door slammed shut behind her.

"You look like you belong in my bed," Eben said at last, too low for the children to hear.

Suffused with heat, Maddie stared at him, transfixed by the sudden flare of desire in his eyes, utterly speechless.

An instant later, anger flickered in his expression, thinning the line of his lips. "Dammit, Maddie, a woman of your age shouldn't look that good."

She laughed, a little shakily. "You always were good at giving backhanded compliments, Mac-Callister. A woman of my age," she repeated in mockery, conscious of the rapid thudding of her heart. "Thank you very much." Turning, Maddie started around to the driver's side. "I'll bring the children back as soon as Sunday school is over."

"But—what about the baby?" Eben frowned in protest.

"He's all yours." Maddie opened the car door and ducked inside, calling gaily back to him, "We'll see you in a couple of hours. Have fun!"

Eben muttered a few choice expletives as she drove off. Hearing them, little Tad jabbered a reply and waved his hands in the air. Eben glanced at the happy baby and sighed.

"Looks like we're stuck with each other," he said, then lifted his glance again to the trail of alkali dust kicked up by the fast-traveling sports utility van. "I guess I should be grateful for small favors. I could have had the whole bunch of you on my hands this morning. Trouble is—you know she planned this, don't you?" he advised, arching one eyebrow.

Tad laughed and waved his hands some more.

"I suppose you think that's a good joke, too." Eben wasn't amused.

All of a sudden Tad got big-eyed and quiet. Eben smiled at his serious expression.

"I guess it is kinda funny," he admitted. "Just the same, you and me have a lot of work to do. It's time we got started." He studied the baby for a long, thoughtful second. "But if you're going to be tagging around with me for the next two hours, I'll need to figure out how to do that and still have my hands free."

He carried the baby back in the house, an idea forming.

Chapter X

"Where's Uncle Eben?" Straining against the seat belt, Joy stretched to look out the side window as Maddie drove into the ranch yard.

On the other side, Hope did the same, mirroring her sister's eager anticipation. "I can't wait to show him—"

"—what we made for him—"

"—in Sunday school."

"I bet he'll really like it," Joy declared with a pleased nod.

"They're nothing but stupid pictures," Dillon jeered.

"Don't you listen to him," Maddie countered quickly. "Your pictures are beautiful."

And if Eben didn't echo her praise, Maddie fully intended to throttle him.

Parking close to the adobe house, she scanned the area by the barn where Eben usually shod his horses. But there was no sign of him, or any of his shoeing paraphernalia. Maddie seriously doubted that he had already put shoes on all six horses, not when he had Tad to watch.

She spied his old blue pickup parked near the chicken coop. Its presence indicated that, if he had gone to check the tank at Serrado Canyon, he had already returned.

But where was he?

"Do you see him, Maddie?" Joy had her seat belt unfastened before Maddie switched off the engine.

"He's probably in the house."

Her response sent both twins scampering out of the car straight to the house. Climbing out of the Jeep Cherokee, Maddie glanced around the yard once more, then followed Dillon into the house. The twins met her at the door, wide-eyed with concern.

"He isn't here, Maddie," Joy said in a confused and worried voice.

"We called and called—" Hope began earnestly.

"—and he didn't answer." Joy shook her head, apprehension clouding her eyes.

"He didn't?" Maddie murmured, conscious of the silence that permeated the house and reluctant to admit she was at a loss for an explanation. "What about—"

"Tad isn't here either." Joy answered her question before Maddie had a chance to finish it.

"Are you sure?" Unconvinced, Maddie took a step toward the bedrooms.

"We looked in his crib," Joy told her.

Hope gave a slow shake of her head. "Tad wasn't there."

"He isn't anywhere."

"Do you think something happened to them?" Hope's eyes turned a liquid blue.

"Did they die like Momma and Daddy?" Joy's chin quivered.

"Of course not." Maddie rushed to dismiss that thought from their minds.

"Then where are they?" Hope asked, her voice wavering on a fearful note.

Before Maddie could answer, Dillon spoke up, taking a positive track for a change. "They're probably in the barn somewhere."

At this hour of the day, Maddie knew that was unlikely, but the twins didn't agree. Relief sprang instantly into their expressions.

"I'll bet that's where they are." Joy seized at the thought.

"Come on." Hope grabbed her hand, pulling her toward the door. "Let's go see."

Before the twins could launch themselves, Maddie stopped them. "Not in your good clothes you aren't going to the barn," she said, striving for a note of normalcy. "You have to change first."

Without protest, the twins switched directions

and raced for their bedroom. Dillon wasn't far behind them, tugging furiously at the hated tie.

Alone, Maddie made a quick search through the house, half-hoping that Eben had left a note somewhere. Finding none, she walked back to the front door and took another look outside.

But there was still no sign of him when Dillon and the twins rejoined her, dressed in their everyday clothes. Together the four of them started for the barn. Halfway across the ranch yard, Maddie heard the rhythmic pounding of hoofbeats.

"Look." Joy pointed excitedly to the horse and rider cantering in from the eastern desert. "Here comes Uncle Eben now."

"But where's Tad?" Hope frowned.

That was precisely what Maddie wanted to know when she saw that Eben's hands were clearly free. Furious at the thought that he had ridden off and left the baby alone somewhere, she went to meet him. As he drew closer, she noticed the large hump on his back. All of her anger dissolved in a laugh of relief.

"Where have you been, Uncle Eben?" Joy asked when he swung out of the saddle.

"We thought you were at the barn," Hope crowded close, staring at the big gray horse.

"We been looking and looking for you."

"What's that thing on your back?" Hope asked when it began moving.

"Your brother," Eben replied, then said to Maddie, "Give me a hand, will you? I rigged up this blanket sling to carry Tad in, then rode out to check the tank and see how well this sling worked."

"You've got Tad in there," Joy said in astonishment, catching a glimpse of her brother's face when Maddie helped Eben out of the makeshift baby carrier.

"You gave him a ride on your horse," Hope realized, envy coloring her words.

"Can we go for a ride?" Joy asked, all big-eyed at the prospect.

"Please, Uncle Eben. Please," Hope begged.

Maddie saw Eben's refusal forming and moved to the horse's head, rubbing a hand under its forelock. "This is Duffy, isn't it?" she asked, certain she recognized the dark gray gelding.

"I know what you're thinking, Maddie," Eben began, his voice full of warning.

"Good." She smiled in easy defiance. "Because I know Duffy won't mind if you let the girls ride in the saddle while you lead him to the barn."

The twins jumped up and down, bubbling with excitement. Eben was trapped and he knew it.

He tried to be angry about it, but it was impossible when Maddie's playful smile was so persuasive and oddly intimate. She had always been able to coax him into doing things.

Not always, he corrected himself, remembering that he had stood fast on one thing—he had refused to marry until his finances improved, convinced it wasn't fair to ask Maddie to scrimp and save and do without the way he did.

For the first time, Eben wondered whether he might have been wrong.

"Well?" she challenged lightly, forcing his thoughts back to the present.

"I'll make you a deal, Maddie," he said, using the same words she had said to him on the phone that morning.

"What's that?" Her eyes sparkled with amusement.

"I'll give them a ride as far as the barn if you'll go to the house and put on a fresh pot of coffee."

"Deal," Maddie agreed readily.

One at a time, Eben picked up the twins and set them in the saddle. After making sure Joy had a tight grip on the saddlehorn and her sister's arms were around her, he gathered up the trailing reins and headed for the barn leading the gray horse. Dillon watched them, his chin tucked low on his chest.

Maddie noticed his glum, half-resentful expression and guessed at its cause. "Would you like a ride on the horse, Dillon?"

"Getting led around is kid stuff," he said, feigning contempt.

She started to argue, then thought better of it. "In that case, why don't you help me make the coffee?"

"Naw." He kicked at a rock and wandered off, hands shoved in his pockets.

In the kitchen, Maddie sat Tad on the floor and let him crawl around while she made coffee. Just as it finished brewing, the twins charged into the house, bursting with excitement over their horse-back ride and eager to recount every single detail of it.

Joy wrapped it up with, "Duffy's really a nice horse, Maddie."

"Uncle Eben said we could ride him again, too," Hope added.

"Maybe," Eben qualified, joining all of them in the kitchen.

Joy looked at her sister, their thoughts connecting. "That means—"

"—we have to be good." Hope nodded in immediate understanding.

"That's okay, Uncle Eben." Unconcerned, Joy climbed onto a chair.

"Yeah, we got to be good anyway—" Hope announced calmly.

"—'cause Santa Claus is coming."

"Not to this house, he isn't." Eben stepped over Tad to reach the coffeepot.

"Don't be that way, Eben," Maddie murmured in quick reproach.

"Why not?" He arched a challenging eyebrow.

"Because," she said. His attitude wasn't a subject she wanted to discuss with him in front of the children.

"Now there's a good reason," he mocked.

A sudden, loud gasp came from Joy. "We almost forgot."

"We made you something, Uncle Eben—" Hope remembered as well.

"—at Sunday school."

Both girls tore out of the room, leaving Maddie and Eben alone in the kitchen with Tad. He played happily on the floor with some plastic bowls he had dragged out of a lower cupboard.

The kitchen suddenly seemed a little too quiet to Eben. Or maybe he was too conscious of Maddie, too conscious of the way her dress softly shaped itself to her body.

He took a sip of his coffee, but it was a different heat that coursed through his blood.

"Aren't you going to have some?" He noticed that she hadn't poured herself a cup.

"No." When she avoided his eyes, it made him wonder if she weren't equally aware of him. The possibility didn't make him feel any more comfortable. "Did you see Dillon outside when you came in?" Maddie asked.

Eben nodded that he had. "He was throwing rocks at a cactus."

"I think he felt left out when you gave the girls a ride on the horse, and didn't offer him one."

"I'm surprised you didn't drag him to the barn and insist that I give him one," he said dryly.

"I thought about it," Maddie admitted. "But he claimed that being led around was kid stuff."

"It is."

"It is, but that's all he can handle now," she reminded him.

"Our situation was different. We were both born on a ranch." He gestured with his cup in the direction of the absent children. "They're town kids."

"Just the same, you need to think about teaching them how to ride," Maddie said.

"I don't have time." Truthfully Eben couldn't remember being taught how to ride. It was something he had grown up knowing.

"I didn't say you had to start tomorrow." There was a telltale edge to her voice, the kind that forecast the start of an argument.

Eben was ready for one, anything to release the tension prickling through him. His mouth opened to form a sharp retort when the twins burst into the kitchen with their usual clattering clamor.

"See what I drawed for you in Sunday school, Uncle Eben." Screeching to a stop before him, Joy held up a crudely drawn picture, colored with crayons.

"I drawed you one, too." Hope waved her paper in the air.

"Hers is different than mine," Joy explained with a self-important nod.

"Show him yours first."

Needing no second urging, Joy thrust her paper forward, holding it high for Eben to see. "It's a picture of Baby Jesus in the manger." She shifted around so she could look at the drawing while she identified its defining features. "Here's Jesus, and that's Mary and Joseph. Over here's the angel and the star—I drawed it like your spurs," she said in an aside.

Hope crowded in, reminding her, "You forgot to say about the little boy and the sheep."

"I didn't forgetted," Joy declared in a huff. "I

was just showing him the other stuff first.'' Turning, she directed her attention back to the picture. ''That's the boy and the sheeps. And right there— that's Annabelle.'' With a triumphant flourish, she pointed to a tan blob with stick legs.

Eben gave the drawing a cursory glance, nodded, and concentrated on his coffee. A long, drawn-out discussion of the drawing was the last thing he wanted.

He was ready to strangle Maddie when she asked, ''Who is Annabelle?''

''Uncle Eben's cow,'' Joy replied.

''We named her that,'' Hope added, beaming with obvious pride.

''Dillon's learning how to milk her.''

''When we get bigger—''

''—Uncle Eben's gonna show us—''

''—how to do it, too.''

''I'll bet you're *all* looking forward to that.'' Maddie glanced at Eben, a teasing light dancing in her eyes.

''Uh-huh,'' Joy agreed, adding, ''Right now, we get to feed the chickens—''

''—every morning.''

''But we can't get their eggs,'' Joy declared with a definite shake of her head.

Hope sighed in regret. ''When we try—''

''—they peck us.''

''And that hurts.''

''I'm sure it does.'' Maddie nodded in sympathy while Eben fought to keep from exploding at the way she encouraged their mindless chatter.

"Okay, Hope, it's your turn to show Uncle Eben the picture you made him." Joy stepped back to give her sister center stage.

"I drawed the Wise Men," Hope told him, holding up her drawing for his review.

"I couldn't put them in mine," Joy interrupted with the quick explanation.

" 'Cause they were still traveling, following the star right there." Hope pointed to her rendition of it.

"They didn't have airplanes when Jesus was born," Joy inserted.

"So I drawed them on horses," Hope said, clearly pleased with her choice.

"Dillon says she should'a put them on camels." Joy checked to see if Eben agreed with that.

"But they could'a rode horses, couldn't they, Uncle Eben?" Hope reasoned.

"I suppose." His smile was as thin as his patience. At the same time, he found it hard to be irritated with them, not when they looked at him with such innocent, trusting eyes.

"I would'a drawed Duffy like Joy did Annabelle, but I didn't know Duffy when I made this," Hope explained, referring to the gray gelding. "He's a nice horse. I like him a lot."

"What do you think, Uncle Eben?" Joy asked to get his reaction.

"Do you like what we made you?" Hope chimed in, clarifying Joy's question.

"The girls did a beautiful job, didn't they?" Maddie prodded in a tone that warned him not to hurt their feelings.

Annoyed that she would think he could be that callous, Eben offered a somewhat gruff, "They're very nice. Both of them."

"They're yours to keep." Joy offered him the picture she had made for him.

Hope quickly followed suit. "We drawed them for you, Uncle Eben."

"Thanks." Collecting both pictures, he laid them aside.

"You can put them on the 'frigerator," Joy said helpfully.

"Want me to get some tape for you?" Hope offered.

"Not right now. Maybe later," Eben stalled. "You two run outside and play for a while."

"Okay." Joy headed toward the door.

But Hope lingered, her glance running brightly to Maddie. "Want to come play with us, Maddie?"

"Not today." She smiled to take any sting out of her refusal. "It's time I was going home."

"Not yet." Eben laid a restraining hand on her arm, checking the slight movement she made toward the door.

She halted, her startled glance flying to his face, her lips parting in surprise. He found himself staring at them, remembering too vividly the taste and texture of them.

"Why not?" Her voice had a husky and disturbed quality to it.

It pleased him, especially in view of the havoc

her nearness was causing in him. "We need to talk," he told her, then said to the twins, "Go on, outside with you."

Untouched by the undercurrents sizzling in the room, the twins bounded from the kitchen, made a detour to their bedroom to collect their doll Eloise, then slammed out the front door. Through it all, Eben kept his gaze locked on Maddie.

"What did you want to talk to me about?" The huskiness was gone from her voice, replaced by a note of bland interest. It told him her guard was up.

Angered by that, by the attraction she still held for him, his memories of the past—both the good and the bad ones—her insinuations that he was somehow to blame for her leaving, and a thousand other things, he pushed the answer through his teeth. "Us."

Abruptly he pulled her into his arms and brought his mouth down in a hard, covering kiss. She resisted him for no more than an instant, then leaned into him, accepting his roughness and echoing the fierce hunger in it.

He wanted to drive into her and take what in the past had always been his alone to claim. She longed for it as well. Her response made that clear.

But there was no satisfaction in making her want him. She had wanted him before—and left. He wanted to punish her for that, to hurt her as she had hurt him. But even as his arms tightened around her, he felt the emptiness of it.

"Why?" he muttered against her lips, anger and

pain combining to rip him apart again—anger that he could still care for her and pain that it wasn't returned. "Why did you have to come back at all?"

Dragging his mouth from hers, he fought to level out his breathing and bring the pounding of his heart under control. There she was before him, head thrown back, exposing the long curve of her throat, her lips swollen and wet from his kiss and her eyes still half-closed.

"I was doing fine—I had gotten over you. Now—" He broke off the thought that pride wouldn't allow him to complete.

But the pain was still there, the kind of pain that was both physical and emotional. One could be assuaged, the other couldn't.

"Why didn't you stay away?" he demanded harshly.

"Damn you, MacCallister," she said in a voice made husky by her own conflicting emotions. "You're always so quick to blame me. As far as you're concerned, everything is my fault."

"It is." It stunned him that she could believe otherwise. Confused and angry, he demanded again. "Why? Why did you leave me?"

With sudden strength, Maddie pushed back from him. "Why?" She stared at him, incredulous.

"Yes, why? Dammit, Maddie, I have a right to know," he snapped.

She laughed in disbelief, angering him further. "I can't believe you are even asking me that. The answer is so obvious any fool could figure it out."

"Now I'm a fool, am I?" He ground out the words.

"Obviously not if you have to ask." Behind the curve of her lips, there was a hint of pity.

"Then tell me—why did you leave? Why did you marry Williams?" he persisted. "Did you love him as much as you claimed to love me?"

"Not in the beginning, I didn't," she admitted with thoughtful candor. "I liked him, though. Allan was warm and kind—and he made me laugh." Idly she studied the grim set of Eben's mouth. "You have to remember that—at the time—I wasn't looking for love. I had already found out how much love could hurt. In a way, I guess I was running from it."

"But why?" Eben demanded again, tormented by the question she had yet to answer.

She swayed closer to him. "Can't you see that I left because I was convinced you didn't love me?"

Astounded by her answer, Eben had to repeat it. "That *I* didn't love you?! Whatever gave you a fool idea like that?"

"What else could I think?" she reasoned. "Every time I talked about getting married, you would put me off, insist that we had to wait, that maybe next year we could get married. But when next year came, it was the same answer as before. If you didn't want to marry, then it was obvious you didn't really want to share your life with me—that you were just using me to satisfy your physical needs. As far as I was concerned, it was clear you didn't want a wife; you wanted a mistress."

"That's ridiculous," he denied. "I couldn't afford a wife."

"Yes." She smiled wryly at his response. "That was always your favorite excuse."

"It wasn't an excuse; it was the truth," Eben insisted.

"Here's another truth for you, darling." Rising up on her toes, Maddie kissed him lightly on the mouth. "You were so busy chasing security that you threw away my love."

"I did no such thing," he rushed to deny that. "You walked out on me."

"It always comes back to what I did to you, doesn't it?" she countered with a touch of sadness. "You can't see at all what you did to me."

"I didn't do anything," he said quickly, forcefully.

"Be honest, Eben." Maddie chided. "Security was always more important to you than I was."

"That isn't true." He was stunned that she thought that.

"Isn't it?" Her dark and gentle eyes were full of reproach.

Her soft question shook his certainty as little fingers seized the leg of his jeans. Distracted by the tug on his pants, Eben glanced down. A gurgling Tad stared back at him, wobbling upright on unsteady legs while he held on to Eben's jeans with both hands.

"Eben, look," Maddie exclaimed. "Tad is standing! Did he just pull himself up?"

"How should I know? I wasn't paying attention."
He still wasn't.

When he glanced up again, Maddie wasn't there.
Eben located her a fraction of a second later,
crouching next to the baby, a hand cupped at Tad's
back, ready to offer support.

"Is this the first time Tad's done this?" she asked
with a touch of wonder in her voice.

"Done what?" Eben frowned.

"Pulled himself up, of course."

"At dinner the other night, he grabbed hold of
the chair and stood up. Why?"

"Why?" she mocked, then shook her head in
amazement and cooed to the baby, "You did that,
and your uncle wasn't even impressed, was he?"

Grinning, Tad let go of Eben's jeans and
stretched his arms out to Maddie. She caught him
an instant before he lost his balance.

"Look at you." Maddie held him upright while
he stomped the floor in an imitation of a war dance.
"You're growing up so fast, Tad. You haven't even
mastered the art of crawling and here you are trying
to walk already."

"How can you do that?" Eben stared at her,
dumbfounded.

"Do what?" Scooping the baby up, she straightened, buried her mouth in the baby's neck, and
blew. Tad giggled wildly.

"Make this lightning transition from arguing to
fussing over the baby." Eben was still too drugged
by the taste of her and the sensation of her body
against him to easily make the leap.

"It's simple." Maddie continued to smile and make gonna-get-cha faces at the baby. "I'm a woman. Or hadn't you noticed?"

"I noticed," he said dryly, aware that Maddie had always been too much woman for him to ignore. That had been true in the past, and it was still true now.

"Oh-oh." She blinked at the baby, then peered inside his pants. "I thought so. It's time for Uncle Eben to change your diaper." She started to pass Tad to him, then stopped and looked inside his pants again. "Wait a minute. That's a safety pin. These are real diapers."

"Of course they are."

She sighed in amusement. "Why doesn't it surprise me that you couldn't stand the thought of spending money on disposable diapers?"

"Do you have any idea how much those throwaway things cost?" Eben countered as she transferred the baby into his arms. "The way this kid goes through them, you can spend a fortune on them and all of them wind up in the trash. With cloth diapers, you wash them and use them again. And you won't find a better cleaning rag either."

A droll laugh slid from her throat. "Eben MacCallister, the master recycler."

Reacting to her jibing tone, he challenged, "What's wrong with that?"

"Nothing, I suppose," Maddie replied, studying him with thoughtful eyes. "It's just the irony of it. When it comes to *things,* you never throw them away, no matter how old or worn out they are. If they break down, you fix them, put in new parts, and get every ounce of use out of them. But when it comes to people, the first time they let you down, you're finished with them. Young, old, new, or used, you don't care. Out they go.''

"Is there supposed to be some message in that?'' he asked with an edge of sarcasm.

Maddie looked at him for a long, silent second, then smiled. "Let's just call it—food for thought.'' Her smile deepened. "See you later, MacCallister.'' She headed for the door.

"Wait a minute. We aren't through talking yet,'' he protested, although for the life of him, he didn't know what was left to say.

"I tell you what.'' Maddie paused in the doorway, one hand resting gracefully on the jamb. "If you want to talk some more, call me.'' Her warm smile turned lightly knowing and taunting. "But of course, you won't. Because that would mean you would have to make the next move, wouldn't it? And people only get one chance with you. As far as you're concerned, I already blew mine. Of course''—Maddie lifted her shoulders in an elegant shrug—"I see it the other way—you blew yours.''

"Do I detect a little pride there, Maddie?'' Eben mocked, needing to retaliate in kind. "It sounds like you want to make certain that I know you quit instead of getting fired.''

"Then let me make it a little clearer.'' Her voice turned a little cool and firm. "I didn't move back here hoping that you might give me a second chance, MacCallister. On the contrary, you will be very lucky if *I* give you one."

"Really?" Irritation graveled his voice.

"Really." Her smile became broadly saccharine. "Now, put that in your pipe and choke on it."

With a wave of her fingers, Maddie was out of the kitchen, leaving him seething.

Tad chose that moment to realize his diaper was soaking wet. His screech of protest rose loud and strong, covering the slam of the front door.

Chapter XI

The conversation with Maddie haunted Eben for days, turning him more snappish and irritable than usual.

On Wednesday morning, a moving van pulled into the ranch yard, interrupting one of Eben's training sessions with a two-year-old filly. Eben's mood went from sour to foul when the driver claimed that union rules prohibited him from unloading the shipment of the children's various belongings.

Left with no other choice, Eben had to pull Ramon and Luis from their work in order to get the truck unloaded. On top of that, the driver insisted that Eben count the number of boxes, verify it matched the figure on the bill of lading, and inspect them for damages before he could sign for them.

By the time the van left, Eben had lost a good hour's work.

But that wasn't the end of it.

The instant the twins saw the boxes, they swarmed around him, giving him no peace until he found their Barbie dolls. Naturally, the dolls were in the last box he opened. In the meantime everything had been unpacked. Which meant, it all had to be put somewhere.

Before he knew it, the morning was gone.

To make matters worse, both the house and the yard had become an obstacle course, strewn with toys, tricycles, a bike, a high chair, playpen, baby swing, walker, another crib, and more kid paraphernalia than Eben knew existed.

Twice he almost called Maddie to pick up the baby crib she had loaned them. Each time, the memory of their last conversation stopped him. There was no way he wanted Maddie to think, even for one minute, that he wanted her to give him a second chance when he was the one who had been wronged.

As a consequence, the dismantled crib from El Regalo still sat in the bedroom.

On Sunday morning, Eben took the children to Sunday school himself, came back to the ranch, rigged up a canvas shade near the corral, and drove back to church to pick up the children. That afternoon, he installed Tad and his playpen under the canvas shade, and instructed Dillon and the twins to play nearby so they could be within sight of their baby brother. Then Eben squeezed in some extra training sessions with the older colts while still keeping an eye on the children.

When Monday rolled around, Eben was feeling optimistic. The morning sessions with the remaining three-year-olds went so smoothly, he decided to turn all but two of them out to pasture until a week before the sale, at which time he would bring them in and tune them up. This left him free to concentrate his efforts on the two-year-olds.

At noontime, he gulped down the lunch Sofia brought him, and climbed aboard a skittish sorrel colt fifteen minutes later. He was on his third horse of the afternoon when Sofia ran up to the corral, all anxious and flustered, one hand cradling the protruding mound of her stomach.

"*Señor* Mac! *Señor* Mac!" She sagged against the railing, out of breath. "You must come quick!"

"What's wrong?" Catching sight of her pale, strained face, Eben instantly thought the worst and turned in the saddle, shooting a glare at Ramon, waiting at the corral gate with the next horse. "Dammit, Ramon, I told you if she has that baby—"

Sofia quickly corrected his inaccurate conclusion. "Your telephone has a message, *Señor* Mac. It is *importante.*"

"Important? How would you know?" he said with impatience.

"It is the teacher at the school. She says you must call her at once. It is *muy importante.*" Sofia waved a scrap of paper. "I write down the telephone number for you."

School. Dillon. The kid was sick. There had been an accident. He was hurt.

A dozen scenarios played through Eben's mind, each one more dire than the last, as he rushed to the house, placed the call, and waited for the teacher to come on the line.

"This is Eben MacCallister," he began, but got no further than identifying himself.

"Mr. MacCallister," the woman broke in, her voice thick with reproval. "I am pleased that you *finally* managed to find time to speak to me."

"I beg your pardon," Eben countered, stiffening at the hint of sarcasm in her voice. "I called as soon as I received your message."

"So you did—this time," she added with critical emphasis. "Unfortunately you weren't as prompt in responding to all of the notes I sent home with your nephew. He informed me that you were too busy to bother with them."

"What notes?" Eben frowned in surprise. "Dillon hasn't brought me any notes."

"I can assure you, Mr. MacCallister," she stated coolly, "notes were sent home with him—every single day for the last four school days."

"And I can assure you that they were not received by me," he repeated, the muscles in his jaw tightening. "Now, what seems to be the problem?"

By the time Eben had finished listening to the teacher's litany of complaints against Dillon, his temper was at a slow boil. The instant the conversation concluded, he slammed the receiver down and snatched his riding gloves off the kitchen counter.

"I'll throttle that kid," he muttered and took two strides across the room, then stopped as the twins came barreling into the kitchen, dragging strings of old-fashioned Christmas lights, the large kind used in outdoor displays.

He stared at the multicolored bulbs, recognizing them instantly even though it had been years since he'd seen them, years since he'd thought about the boxes of lights and Christmas decorations gathering dust upstairs.

His father used to drape the entire house with lights every Christmas, and scatter more decorations all through the inside of it until it was impossible to turn without bumping into something Christmas. Carla had loved it, and continued the tradition after their father died.

To Eben, it had been a waste of time, energy, and money, but he had never raised any objections when his sister dragged down the boxes every year. He had opposed her on only one point—that the outside lights were plugged in only on Christmas Eve.

"Uncle Eben! Uncle Eben! Look what we found!" they cried, talking on top of each other in their excitment.

"What are you doing with those lights? Where did you get them?" he irritably snapped out the questions, glowering at the pair.

"We found 'em—" Joy rushed to begin the explanation.

"—upstairs in a box," Hope finished it, positively agog with the discovery.

"Upstairs?" His frown darkened at their blithe announcement that they had been exploring the bedrooms in the converted attic. "What were you doing up there?"

Catching the disapproval in his voice, Joy shrugged and adopted an air of innocence. "Looking."

"You got lots of bedrooms up there—" Hope continued, for once not picking up on her twin sister's sudden reticence.

"—with lots of boxes in 'em," Joy added cautiously.

"I know what's upstairs, and you two don't belong up there," Eben stated in no uncertain terms. "Do you understand me?"

"Yeah." Joy nodded, then tried to divert him. "But we found these—"

"—Christmas lights up there." Hope held her tangled string.

"You got lots and lots of 'em, Uncle Eben."

"Can we hang 'em up outside tonight?" Hope asked eagerly.

"No." He walked around them and headed for the door.

After an instant of shocked silence, they ran after him, the light strings clattering across the floor behind them. "But it's almost Christmas."

Eben planted both feet and swung back on them. As one, they skidded to a halt in front of him, eyes wide with uncertainty.

"Where is Sofia?" he demanded, his glance shooting to scour the living room in search of the young Mexican woman. "She's supposed to be watching you two."

"She's with Tad," Joy explained, alert to the annoyance on his expression.

"She said we were to go play somewhere—" Hope inserted quickly.

"—and to be quiet."

"She's trying to get Tad to go to sleep."

Joy shook her head in regret. "But he doesn't want to take a nap."

"Tad's a trial." Hope sighed.

"Maybe you could hang up the lights tomorrow?" Joy suggested.

"No. Not tomorrow or the next day or the day after that," Eben stated curtly.

"But you got to," Joy insisted plaintively.

"It's Christmastime," Hope reminded him.

"At Christmas, you got to—"

"—hang up lots and lots—"

"—of lights."

"I don't *got* to do anything," he declared with force.

But Joy heard another refusal forming and leaped in, "It isn't hard, Uncle Eben."

"We'll help you," Hope volunteered.

Eben cut off their offer, his hands slicing through the air. "I don't need any help because I'm not hanging up any lights."

"But it's Jesus' birthday," Joy argued.

"And Momma said that—"

"—Jesus was the Light of the World."

"And you gotta hang lights—"

"—so people can see how—"

"—bright He's shining everywhere." Hope's arms swept in a big circle, swinging the string of multicolored lights still clutched in her hands. It barely missed her sister's head.

"I think He can shine just fine without the help of a bunch of lights," Eben snapped, already a step beyond exasperated.

"But—"

Eben exploded, "No lights!"

Both girls jumped, their eyes going saucer-round. He stopped himself, wiping a hand down his face while he struggled to temper his anger.

"Look, lights require electricity, and electricity costs money. And I haven't got the money to waste on a lot of Christmas lights."

He wanted to kick himself for talking about finances to a couple of precocious four-year-olds. But facts were facts. He didn't have the spare time to hang the lights, and he definitely didn't have extra money to pay for the additional electricity the lights would take. "Is that clear?" he finished.

The sad-eyed pair nodded. Their mouths were turned down about as far as they could go. Eben wondered if they had been taking lessons from Maddie in how to make him feel like a heel. Thinking about her made him angry all over again.

Surveying them, he took note of the limp strings of Christmas lights and gestured to them. "Take those lights and put them back where you found them. And stay out of the attic."

"Yes, sir." Joy's lower lip jutted out in a pout of abject disappointment. She turned to her sister. "Come on, Hope."

She took her hand. Side by side, the girls set off, trailing the strings of lights, the bulbs chattering across the tiled floor behind them. Eben had to harden himself against the sight of their bowed heads and slumped shoulders.

"Don't drag the lights over the floor like that, either," he ordered, feeling like some ogre in a fairy tale even as he said it. "You'll break the bulbs and there'll be glass chips everywhere. Pick them up and carry them right."

Eben watched, half-irritated by their slowness, while they reeled in the strands and grappled to get their small hands around the bunched cord. One look told Eben they would never succeed. He walked away so he wouldn't have to witness their failure.

Annoyed with himself, irked by the twins, and furious with Dillon, he returned to the corral. In such a mood, he knew better than to climb on a young horse. But he did it anyway.

The horse sensed his repressed anger, and things went from bad to worse. Within minutes, the usually calm and responsive two-year-old was in a sweat, fretting and fighting Eben at every turn. Before he undid weeks of training, Eben stepped out of the saddle and shoved the reins into Ramon's hands.

Ramon laid a calming hand on the jumpy colt

and eyed Eben with wise caution. "You want I should bring you the next one, *Señor* Mac?"

"No." He shot a look at the winter sun, gauging the time by its position in the sky. Noting the afternoon was nearly gone, Eben jerked off his gloves. "Turn them all out. That's it for today. You and Luis get an early start on the evening chores."

Leaving the corral, Eben struck out for the house, slapping the gloves against his leg with each angry stride. With nerves stretched as taut as an electrified wire and muscles tensed with the urge to hit something, each *chink* of his spurs acted as a goad to his temper.

Halfway to the house, he stopped, recognizing that he had no more business being around Tad and the twins in this mood than he had handling the horses. He swung away, changing directions, and spotted a boil of dust far down the ranch lane. His gaze zeroed in on it, his eyes narrowing and his mouth thinning when he recognized the telltale yellow of the school bus bringing Dillon home.

Deciding that if anyone deserved to feel the rough edge of his tongue, it was Dillon, Eben stopped to wait for the bus. It swung into the yard and made a circle before it rolled to a halt amid a grinding of brakes and swirling alkali dust.

When the doors swished open, Eben had a glimpse of a harried woman driver; then his eye was caught by the boy coming from the rear of the bus, a backpack slung over one shoulder. Along the way, Dillon took a punch at another boy, then knocked the books out of the arms of a girl sitting near the front.

Eben stepped onto the bus. "Pick up those books."

Surprise wiped the smirk from Dillon's face. "Wha—?"

"You heard me." Eben spun him around and pointed him toward the jumble of books, conscious of the bus driver's grateful look. "Pick them up."

"But I didn't—"

"I saw you do it," Eben warned, cutting off Dillon's attempt to deny responsibility. "Now pick them up."

The harshness of his voice had the dark-haired girl backing away to resume her seat and Dillon crouching down to gather up the scattered books and papers.

No one in the bus said a word. The only sounds came from the idling engine, rustling paper, and thudding books.

When Dillon went to give the girl her books, Eben said, "Apologize to her, too."

"Sorry," Dillon mumbled and started to turn away.

Eben turned him back. "You're sorry for what?" he said, insisting on a more specific apology.

"I'm sorry your books fell," Dillon said in a faintly defiant jeer.

Eben tightened his grip on Dillon's shoulder, his fingers digging a little. "Wrong. Try again," he ordered.

Grudgingly, Dillon muttered, "I'm sorry I knocked your books to the floor."

"It's okay," the girl murmured, embarrassed for him.

Head down, Dillon ducked away from Eben and clumped down the steps out of the bus. Eben followed, nodding to the driver. "Sorry for the delay."

"I'm not," she told him, a weary smile lifting her lip corners. "This is the quietest the bus has been since I loaded up."

The doors whooshed shut behind him. As soon as Eben was well clear of the vehicle, there was a shifting of gears and the bus rumbled out of the yard. Dillon had taken off for the house at a jogging run.

Eben yelled over the diesel's drone, "You come back here, kid."

Dillon ran another couple steps, then appeared to have second thoughts about the wisdom of that and turned back around.

"What do you want now?" Dillon frowned in veiled belligerence.

"What do you think I want?" Eben countered in cool disapproval.

"How should I know?" Dillon replied with a shrugging lift of his shoulders that reeked of insolence.

For now, Eben let that pass. "Do you have any homework to do tonight?"

Dillon looked him in the eye and lied, "Nope."

"That isn't what your teacher told me."

Guiltily dropping his gaze, Dillon shifted uneasily. "Yeah, well, I already got it done."

"Where is it?" Eben challenged smoothly. "I'd like to see it."

Dillon's head came up, some of the cockiness returning. "I left it at school."

Eben took a step toward his truck, motioning for Dillon to follow. "Come on. We'll go get it."

"All right, so I don't have it done," Dillon admitted with a flash of resentment. "It's no big deal anyway."

Facing him again, Eben stood with his hands on his hips, one leg bent. "Your teacher tells me you haven't turned in one single homework assignment."

"So? What do you care?" Dillon jeered in open rebellion.

"Your teacher also told me you have been disruptive in class," Eben stated.

Dillon feigned an uncaring shrug. "She's a pain."

"She said you've been talking in class, fighting with other students, throwing papers and spit balls—" Before he could finish the list of offenses, he was interrupted.

"I never started that stuff. She's always picking on me. She hates me."

"Do you deny that you marked up your desk, glued the pages of one of your textbooks together—"

"It was an accident," Dillon insisted. The bottle tipped over—"

"—and somehow managed to spill glue over every single page in the book, I suppose," Eben said in dry disbelief.

Dillon was smart enough not to attempt a defense of that. "Other kids do the same thing, but they never get in trouble. Only me."

"What happened to all the notes your teacher sent home with you?" Eben demanded.

"I threw 'em away," Dillon declared in another show of defiance. "You would'a been too busy to read them anyway, so what difference does it make?"

"You're going to find what difference it makes," Eben fired back, his temper boiling over. "You are going straight into that house and you aren't going to budge from it until you get every bit of your homework done tonight. And I'm going to look at it and make certain it's done right. Tomorrow morning, you and I are going into school and get every single assignment that you failed to turn in. This weekend you will make up every one of them. There will be no playing, no bike riding, no nothing until it's done. Is that clear?"

"I won't do it!" Dillon yelled, his eyes filling with hot, angry tears.

"You'll do it, or I'll tan your hide blue," Eben warned.

"I hate you! Do you hear? I hate you!" Dillon stormed. "I wish we'd never, ever come here. I hate it and I hate you!"

"Hate me all you want," Eben told him, "but you're still going to do that homework."

Without another word, Eben took Dillon by the arm and marched him to the house. In the kitchen, he pulled out a chair and sat Dillon on it, then opened the backpack and spread out his papers and pencils on the table.

"Get busy," he ordered.

"I won't," Dillon said, blubbering softly, his elbows on the table and his head in his hands, hiding tears and a quivering lip.

"You'll sit there until you do." Too angry to trust himself further, Eben walked out of the kitchen, straight to the door.

"Uncle Eben!"

"Uncle Eben!"

The twins raced outside after him.

"What?" Turning, he glared at the pair, in no humor for more of their nonsense.

"When are we gonna get our Christmas tree?" Joy asked brightly.

"We found lots of stuff to hang on it." A bright red ornament dangled from a metal hook hanging off one of Hope's fingers.

Eben's gaze fastened on it. "Where did you get that? I thought I told you to stay out of the attic."

Joy blinked once in surprise. "But you said we had to put the lights away."

"And when we did—"

"—this other box just fell open," Joy explained with a palms-up gesture of absolute innocence.

"I'll bet it fell open." With the help of four little hands, Eben thought in irritation and swung away from the pair.

"How soon are we gonna get our tree?" Joy scampered after him, coming up on his right.

"We aren't getting a tree." He kept walking, determined to escape their incessant chatter.

"But we gotta have a tree for Christmas," Hope said from his left, the pair flanking him like a set of stereo speakers.

"We aren't hanging up any lights, and we aren't having any tree." His voice was sharp with impatience.

"But we've got to," Joy declared in alarm.

"If we don't—"

"—where's Santa gonna leave our presents?"

Eben stopped, challenging, "Look around you. This is the desert. We don't have trees and snow and all that other Christmas stuff here."

"But—" Joy began worriedly.

"No more buts," he cut in before Hope could add her voice to the protest. "I'm not throwing money away on a dead tree and that's final. Keep it up and there won't be any Christmas either."

He walked off. This time, the twins didn't follow. Behind him, Eben heard the first sniffling sob and shut his ears to it.

Trouble. He'd had nothing but trouble since those four kids arrived.

Dressed in boots, sharply creased blue jeans, and a short calvary-style jacket with leather fringe on the shoulders, Maddie entered El Regalo's large commercial kitchen through its side door.

Here, there were no vega-studded ceilings, no valuable Navajo blankets on the walls, no potted cactus towering in the corners, no trace at all of the rich Southwest atmosphere that was the hallmark of El Regalo Guest Ranch. The kitchen's acres of stainless steel, chrome, and snow-white tile gleamed and flashed under bright fluorescent lighting.

At this hour of the afternoon, there was the usual bustle of predinner activity in the kitchen, complete with the clatter of pans and the spicy scents of cayenne, cilantro, and a tinge of onion. Maddie paused next to a long table where the pastry chef added the last decorative flourishes to a cheesecake.

Her glance skipped over him to seek out Guy Bonnelle, El Regalo's tall and skinny master chef. She heard the boom of his laughter an instant before he emerged from the large pantry.

"Hey, Maddie." In one glance, he took in her outfit and teased, with typical good humor, "How's the Indian scout today?"

"Her sharp eyes spotted the first group of riders coming in," she responded with an answering smile.

He checked the watch on his wrist. "Your news is about five minutes late. Fran already alerted us."

Fran Sawyer was El Regalo's general manager— and had been for the last seventeen years. There was little that went on at the guest ranch that ever escaped her notice, as Maddie had quickly learned.

Beyond going over the monthly balance sheets,

approving a new advertising campaign or a major purchase, Maddie had few other duties as owner. If anything, she served as extra window dressing, mixing and mingling with the high-paying guests, adding to the atmosphere.

But her presence certainly wasn't required.

"I should have guessed Fran had already notified you," Maddie admitted, then started to mention that ice was needed in the small cantina bar, a favorite gathering place for the guests coming off a trail ride. Fortunately she noticed the busboy at the ice machine, scooping cubes into a steel bucket, before she said anything.

Fighting that familiar useless feeling, she walked over to inspect the hors d'oeuvres a sous-chef was arranging on a silver serving tray. She scanned the assortment of canapés, identifying the usual choices of ham pinwheels on pumpernickel rounds, Sevruga caviar on blinis, cheese with port wine on toast points, and profiteroles with tuna mousse.

A second tray, already prepared, offered a more traditionally Southwestern assortment. As Maddie started to glance at it, her eye was caught by the bay scallops with basil cream cheese on the first tray.

"Didn't I see a notice that one of our guests is allergic to shellfish?" she asked.

Guy Bonnelle directed a hawklike look at the sous-chef. "I told you to label the scallops *before* you put them on the tray."

The man reddened. "I forgot," he said and hastily removed the scallops from the tray, then rushed to find the proper labels.

"Thanks," Guy said to Maddie.

She shook her head, dismissing his thanks. "You would have noticed it when you inspected the tray."

On that point, Maddie was certain. Highly allergic to strawberries himself, Guy Bonnelle was meticulous when it came to food allergies of their guests.

"Probably," he agreed. "But it's better that the mistake was caught now rather than later."

"Mrs. Williams, you have a phone call." One of the kitchen assistants held out the receiver to her.

Surprised and curious, Maddie walked over to the kitchen extension, paused long enough to unclip an earring, then took the receiver and carried it to her ear.

"This is Maddie Williams. How can I help you?"

A sobbing voice wailed, "I want my mommy!"

There was more bawling in the background, punctuated by a baby's angry screams.

"Joy? Is that you?" Maddie guessed instantly and frowned in concern. "Honey, what's wrong?"

The child babbled an answer, but she was crying too hard. Maddie couldn't understand a single word she said.

"Sssh, now. Everything's going to be okay. Just stop crying a minute and tell me what happened," she urged, but the girl's second attempt was no more intelligible than the first. Maddie tried a different tactic. "Where's your uncle?"

The question brought a fresh burst of wailing.

"Where's Sofia?" she tried again.

In between sobs came, "I—don—knooooow."

Had Eben gone off and left the children in the house alone? She was going to kill him with her own bare hands if he had. Fury pushed Maddie's jaw forward.

"Joy, listen to me," Maddie insisted, clutching the phone a little tighter. "I'm coming right over. Do you hear—I'll be there just as soon as I can."

She slammed the phone down and flew out of the kitchen.

Chapter XII

Maddie broke every speed limit between El Regalo and Star Ranch, pulling into the yard in record time. Immediately, she spied Eben at the paddocks throwing hay to the penned horses.

The sight of him fueled her sense of outrage that he had left the children in the house unattended. What if one of them had gotten hurt or become deathly ill?

Before the churned-up dust began to settle, Maddie piled out of the Jeep Cherokee, dodged a tricycle in her path, nearly tripped over a large toy dump truck, and pushed a soccer ball away from the screen door so she could open it. Following the sound of sniffling sobs, she headed for the kitchen, stepping over a stuffed tiger and skirting a toy baby carriage, loaded with children's books.

"Hope? Joy? It's Maddie," she called anxiously.

Instantly Tad let loose with an angry howl as chair legs scraped the floor and feet clattered to meet her. The weeping twins launched themselves at her legs before Maddie could reach the kitchen doorway.

Crouching down, she hugged them to her and glanced up when Sofia appeared in the doorway. The woman looked frazzled and at her wit's end as she rocked a tired and bawling, red-cheeked Tad from side to side in her arms.

Maddie had a moment's relief that the children hadn't been left alone. But something was clearly wrong.

"What's going on here, Sofia? What happened?"

The young Mexican girl looked on the verge of tears herself as she lapsed into her native tongue, then caught herself and started over again.

"Los niños, they will not stop crying. I ask, but they do not tell me why. The little one, it is his teeth, I think, but—" She looked at the twins and lifted her shoulders in a shrug of absolute bewilderment.

"Where is Dillon?" Maddie asked Sofia, and continued to try to comfort the weeping twins.

"La cocina." Sofia nodded in the direction of the kitchen.

"Come." Taking the clinging girls by the hand, Maddie led them into the kitchen.

Dillon sat slumped in a chair, his schoolbooks

and papers scattered across the table in front of him. None of them looked as if they'd been touched.

"What happened, Dillon?" Maddie asked. "Do you know why the girls are crying?"

He shook his head, the corners of his mouth going down another notch. "They came in here bawling their heads off," he said, then added acidly, "*He* did it, though."

The spite in his voice left Maddie in little doubt that he meant Eben. Still, she insisted on clarifying it. "Who did it? Your uncle?"

Nodding, Dillon looked pleased at the sudden grimness in her expression. "He yelled at them about something."

Swallowing her annoyance with Eben, Maddie led the twins over to a chair, sat down, and gathered them onto her lap. Both girls were a sight, their faces pale and drawn, their cheeks drenched with tears, and their noses running.

A Kleenex box sat on the table amid a pile of wadded-up tissues, evidence of previous attempts to dry their eyes and noses. Maddie made her own attempt, pulling two tissues from the box and wiping first Hope's nose, then Joy's freckled one.

"What did your uncle say to you?" Maddie asked gently while Sofia walked the floor behind her, trying to quiet the cranky baby. "Maybe I can do something to help."

Hope screwed up her face and started to cry all over again while Joy gave her a sad and doubtful look.

"He . . . said," she began, hitching in a sobbing breath between almost every word, ". . . we can't . . . have . . . Christmas."

"We don't . . . got snow or . . . trees," Hope inserted in an echo of her sister's pattern.

"This is . . . a desert, he said," Joy added as a tear slipped off spiked lashes and dribbled down her cheek.

"And you don't have . . . Christmas—"

"—in a . . . desert."

"Your uncle told you that, did he?" Maddie murmured tightly.

Simply killing the man was too good for him, she decided. A long, slow torture would be much more appropriate.

"Uh-huh." Both girls nodded.

"Well, I'll tell you something—your uncle is absolutely wrong," Maddie informed them, stroking a hand over Joy's blond curls. "I know that for a fact."

"You do?" Hope gave her a wistful, yet skeptical look.

"I do." She nodded decisively.

"How?" Joy questioned, willing to be convinced.

"Because Christmas started in a country that looks very similar to the land you see right outside the kitchen window," Maddie replied.

"It did?" Hope brightened a little.

"Yes."

"How do you know?" Joy cocked her head to one side, a curious frown pleating her brow.

"I know because Christmas began with the birth of Jesus, and he was born in—"

"—Befflehem," the girls chorused.

"And Bethlehem is a town in the Judaean Hills where it's rocky and dry just like it is here." Maddie smiled at their rapt faces, pleased to notice their rapidly drying tears. "Do you remember what Mary rode when Joseph took her to Bethlehem?"

"A donkey," Joy answered quickly.

"I was going to say that," Hope pouted.

"Hope, do you remember when you drew your picture of the Three Wise Men on horses, what did Dillon tell you that you should have drawn instead?" Maddie asked.

She had to think a minute. "He said the Wise Men rode camels."

"And where do camels live?" Maddie prompted.

Instantly all smiles, they both answered, "In the desert!"

"So we can still have Christmas—" Joy pressed her hands together in rapturous excitement.

"—even if we don't got snow and trees," Hope finished in delight.

"That's right. And I will make certain your uncle knows it." That was more than a promise; it was a solemn oath, despite the benign smile Maddie wore.

"Christmas!" Joy cheered jubilantly

"We're gonna have—" Hope took up the cry.

"—Christmas!"

The twins tumbled off her lap. Giddy with happiness, they jumped up and down, clapping their hands. An exhausted Tad stirred briefly in Sofia's arms, then went right back to sleep as the girls rushed out of the room.

With that settled, Maddie had one final mystery yet to solve. "Sofia, did the twins ask you to call me?" she asked.

"They called you?" Her head came up in a gesture of surprise. "I did not know this, *señora.*"

Dillon sank a little lower in his chair, burying his chin against his chest and avoiding Maddie's eyes when she glanced his way. But she observed the guilty movement.

"Do you know anything about this, Dillon?" she asked in quick suspicion.

"Why should I?" he replied, turning cagey.

"Because, as bright as your sisters are, they couldn't have made that phone call all by themselves," she replied. "Someone had to help them. Since Sofia didn't do it, I have a feeling that someone was you. Was it?"

He wiggled uncomfortably in the seat and stared at his hands. "I couldn't get them to stop crying. They wanted Mom and—" He broke off that sentence, hesitated, then said diffidently, "Finally I asked if they would like to talk to you."

Which raised another question in Maddie's mind. "How did you find my number?"

"It's on a paper next to the phone. Your name's right beside it, so I knew it had to be yours." He darted her a worried look. "You won't tell, will you? He said he'd beat me if I got off this chair."

"I won't tell." An iron calm settled over Maddie—the same kind of burning calm that precedes a battle.

Dillon studied her, his eyes suddenly blue and wicked. "You're gonna give him a piece of your mind, aren't you?" Satisfaction gleamed in his smile.

Charmed by his impish look, Maddie smiled back. "I have a feeling it may be a whole chunk, not just a piece." Grinning conspiratorially, Dillon started to scoot off his chair. "Whoa there." Maddie stopped him. "Where do you think you're going?"

Still grinning, Dillon replied, "I thought it'd be kind'a fun to watch you do it."

"Well, you thought wrong," she told him, standing up. "If your uncle told you to stay in that chair, then that's where you sit until he tells you otherwise."

"Aaw, man," he moaned in protest, the scowl returning, but he pushed back onto the chair seat.

The ancient tractor sputtered and coughed to a halt, positioning the flat rack level with the last horse pen. Keeping one hand on the scarred steering wheel and a leg rigidly extended to hold down the brake pedal, Ramon turned sideways in the tractor seat and watched as Eben snapped the twine around a bale and tossed a quarter of its hay into the pen. It landed with a rustling *plop*, raising small snake-heads of dust.

Straightening, Eben lifted his hat and swiped his

mouth across the sleeve of his shirt, then settled the hat back on his head, conscious of the gritty hay chaff that clung to his clothes and skin.

But he was more strongly aware of the stretch and pull of tired muscles. Next to chopping wood, manhandling sixty- and seventy-pound bales was the best way he knew to get rid of a lot of pent-up anger. And it was definitely working this time.

"Ready, *señor?*" Ramon called, his voice vibrating as the rough-running engine shook the tractor seat.

Before Eben could reply in the affirmative, there was a movement in his side vision, something that reminded him strongly of the flipping swing of buckskin fringe. He swung around to identify it and saw Maddie dressed like an Indian scout in a navy wool jacket trimmed with fringe.

A sharp kick of pleasure rocketed through him. It was purely an involuntary reaction.

His first impulse was to jump off the rack and go meet her. Then she shouted, "MacCallister, get off that hayrack! I want a word with you."

Her heated words were like the rasp of a matchhead across coarse sandpaper. They produced an instant fire that pushed him off the rack.

He hit the ground and waved for Ramon to go on, then strode to the fence where Maddie waited for him.

"What are you doing here?" The low thunder of his voice startled a roadrunner and sent it streaking in the opposite direction.

Maddie ignored it completely and launched

right into her tirade. "How dare you tell those girls that people don't celebrate Christmas in the desert? That is the cruelest thing I have ever heard!" she declared. "It was bad enough when you tried to convince them there was no Santa Claus. But to take away Christmas—"

"What are you talking about?" Anger and confusion chased across his face.

"As if you didn't know," she scoffed in temper. "Those poor girls were practically in hysterics by the time I got here. You should have seen them bawling their eyes out, their hearts broken because you told them they wouldn't have a Christmas."

"I never said any such thing," Eben indignantly denied the accusation.

"Next, you'll try to convince me it was all their imagination, I suppose. Let me tell you something, MacCallister." Maddie jabbed his chest with her finger. "Little girls don't make up something as horrible as that. No Christmas!" she repeated in outrage. "You ought to be staked over an ant hill or—"

"Dammit, Maddie, I never said that," he protested again. "They were harping at me to buy a Christmas tree and I told them we weren't going to have any tree. But that's all I said."

Maddie paused, studying him with suspicion. "I don't buy that," she said at last. "Two little girls wouldn't take a simple statement like that and turn it into no Christmas," she declared, then attacked his second statement. "And what's wrong with buying a tree?"

"What's wrong?" Eben lifted both hands in disbelief. "Do you know how much the stores want for a Christmas tree now? I am not going to spend that kind of money for a dead tree."

"Then buy a live one and plant it after Christmas," Maddie argued.

"And watch it die for lack of water?" he scoffed at the suggestion, regarding it as ludicrous. "This is the desert, Maddie. Use some common sense. It would be a waste of money."

"Money, money, money—that's all you can talk about," she said in disgust, her eyes flashing with temper. "You and your precious money. You just can't stand the thought of spending it on something as foolish as a tree or Christmas, can you, MacCallister?"

"Will you stop painting me to be like some damn Scrooge," he exploded. "I plan on seeing that those kids have gifts on Christmas."

"Good." Maddie snapped a satisfied nod. "I'm glad I shamed you into that, at least."

His mouth dropped open. Before he could react, she pivoted on her heel, the fringe at her shoulders flaring out, then settling in a fluid sway of motion when she walked off.

Recovering, Eben ducked between the fence rails and went after her. He caught her by the elbow and spun her back to face him.

"For your information, Miss High-and-Mighty Know-It-All, you didn't shame me into anything," he hurled in anger.

"Didn't I?" She arched an eyebrow in cool, taunting skepticism.

Furious, Eben fired back, "No, you didn't."

"No?" Maddie folded her arms tightly in front of her, fingers tapping in temper. "Then, where did they get the impression they wouldn't have any Christmas at all?"

"How should I know how their little minds work?" Eben countered in exasperation. "Sure, I told them this was the desert, that we don't have snow and trees like they're used to. I was probably short with them. They've been driving me crazy with all this nonsense about lights and trees."

"They are children, MacCallister. You need to make allowances."

"That's easy for you to say," he retorted. "Try living with them."

"If you're looking for sympathy, MacCallister, you're out of luck. If I pity anyone, it's those children living with you." Her dark eyes glittered with reproach. "Threatening Dillon that you would beat him if he got off that chair, what kind of a monster are you?"

"That kid deserves a beating." On this subject, Eben was confident of his grounds. "I got a phone call from his teacher today. He's on the verge of becoming a juvenile delinquent."

"Don't exaggerate."

"Who's exaggerating?" he retorted. "He hasn't turned in any homework at all; he's been picking fights in class, smarting off to the teacher, and destroying school property. And in case you haven't figured it out yet, he's only been in school a week!''

"He's only doing it to get attention," Maddie reasoned, inwardly concerned by the list of offenses.

"Well, he has my attention now," Eben promised, an old anger ridging his jawline.

"If you had shown him some before, this probably wouldn't have happened," she argued in Dillon's defense. "He's only seven years old. It isn't enough to give him a warm bed, food, and clothes. He needs you to spend time with him, show him some affection, Eben. If you continue to ignore Dillon, he'll rebel all the more just to make you notice him."

"I don't have time—"

"At this rate, you'll never have time," she cut in impatiently, irritated by that old, overused excuse he kept trotting out.

He paused a beat, his mouth tightening in sudden grimness. "I don't know why I'm talking to you at all. None of this is your business." He stalked off, heading to the barn.

But Maddie wasn't finished, not by a long shot. "That's your answer to everything isn't it? You just walk off."

"I'm tired of arguing," he fired back. "No matter what I say or do, you manage to find fault with it. You never used to be this way, Maddie."

"You're absolutely right. I wasn't. That was my mistake." A half-step behind him, Maddie crossed the barn's threshold and breathed in the dry, musty redolence of hay, grain, and penned animals, but she was too upset with him to notice it. "I should have confronted you a long time ago instead of keeping it all inside."

Eben swung back, fastening his hot, blue eyes on her. "So, why didn't you?"

"Why?" she repeated in a strangled outrage.

Inches separated them and the barn's thickening shadows surrounded them, as if shutting out the world. Her glance ran over the man before her. Every magnificent inch of him radiated challenge.

But it was more than his craggy good looks that tugged and twisted at her. Just as in the past, it was her own physical and emotional response to him.

"Because I was so besotted with you, so anxious to please you, that I couldn't bring myself to say or do anything that might upset you," she admitted with a trace of self-disgust, determined now to clear the air between them. "I thought I had to be that way for you to love me. But that didn't work either, because you still didn't love me enough to marry me."

"We're back to that idiocy, are we?" Eben stated, quick and harsh. "You know damned well I loved you. How many times does a woman have to be told something before she believes it?"

"Words mean nothing when they aren't backed up with action," she came back just as quickly.

The sharpness of her answer touched off the sparks that had been flying between them for the last five minutes. Burned by them, Eben hauled her against him.

"So, I didn't back them up with action—not even when I held you I suppose?" he mocked when Maddie bowed away from him. With an arm banding her waist, he caught her chin and jaw in his large hand and held it, the glint of more than just anger in his eyes. "Or when I kissed you?"

His mouth slanted onto hers with a raw urgency to its possession. But in that initial instant of contact, Maddie heard that half-smothered groan of longing he tried to swallow. For the first time, she sensed the depth of his pain.

Eben lifted his head, his ragged breath moist and heavy against her skin. "Didn't I back it up with action when I lay with you, Maddie?"

With her fingertips, she traced the slashing groove near the corner of his mouth and whispered in gentle reproach, "Sex is not proof of love, Eben."

His gaze bored into her, steel-hard and glittering. "Only marriage is, right?"

Angered, he pushed her away from him and half-turned, fighting to bring himself under control.

Afraid that he would walk off again, Maddie laid a hand on his arm. There were too many unanswered questions between them. In the past, she had lacked the courage to ask them. Because of that, she had the uneasy feeling she had caused as much hurt as he had.

"Marriage is one way, Eben," she said, then paused, searching for the right combination of words. "There's something that I never understood—if you truly loved me, why didn't you come after me, Eben? Why did you let me go?"

"What other choice did I have?" he countered with rancor, all stiff and tall, still resisting any suggestion he was to blame. "You made it clear, it was marriage or nothing. I couldn't marry you, not back then."

A sigh, riddled with some of the old bitterness, escaped from her lips.

"Yes, you couldn't afford a wife." That had always been his stock answer. Maddie had hoped for something more.

"No, dammit, I could not afford a wife," he insisted with force. "You don't know how bad it was back then—and I didn't want you to know." Some of that old rigid pride resurfaced to harden his expression. "There were weeks on end that eggs, beans, and milk gravy were all that Carla and I had to eat. I couldn't afford to butcher a steer so we could have meat on the table unless one broke a leg. I loved you, Maddie. I couldn't ask you to live like that. It would have been wrong."

"But I could have helped," she protested. "I could have worked, brought in extra money—"

"We've been through all this before, Maddie." His voice was clipped and tight, rejecting any further discussion on that point. "It wouldn't have worked. Not for long. If I had any doubts about that, Carla settled them for good. This was her home, but she couldn't take living like that," he reminded Maddie. "She ran off the first chance she had. Eventually you would have come to hate living like that, too. In time, you would have hated me." Pain was back in his eyes. "I couldn't risk that. It would have hurt more than losing you did."

He believed that. Maddie could see it in his eyes, hear it in his voice. Suddenly, everything else began to make sense for the first time.

"That's why you didn't try to win me back when you found out I was engaged to Allan, isn't it?" she said, seeing it all so clearly now.

His expression darkened with some of the old remembered bitterness and anger. "How could I compete with Williams?" He looked away, pride not letting him meet her eyes. "With all his money, he could give you more than I could ever dream of doing."

"But don't you see, Eben?" Maddie murmured, her heart twisting at the foolishness of his pride— and her own. "I didn't marry Allan because he was rich. His money simply proved that he loved me even though I had nothing to give him in return but myself. Right from the start Allan knew I didn't love him. How could I when I was still in love with you? But he loved me anyway." She smiled at that memory. "Unconditionally. Just as I was. And he was willing to take the chance that I would come to care for him. He trusted me, Eben, when you didn't."

"His money made it easy for him." The lingering resentment in his voice was at odds with the regret that now glittered in his eyes.

Her mouth curved in a gently chiding smile. "Now, you insult me, Eben." She cupped a hand to his cheek in a loving caress. "I am not a woman to be bought."

"I know that." He ground out the words, irritated that he had put his foot in his mouth again. It turned him half-humble.

Before he could apologize, Maddie eliminated the need. "We were both guilty of doubting each other. I guess it comes from being young and foolish."

"Maddie." The simple utterance of her name contained a wealth of things Eben wanted to say, but didn't know how to verbalize.

She solved the problem by kissing him. At the touch of her lips, his hands slid around her with an adoring gentleness she had almost forgotten. This was the other side of Eden, the man who stroked and kindled, who wanted to give pleasure as well as receive it.

Glorying in the searing tenderness of his kiss, she molded herself to him. This was the man she loved, every sweaty, dusty, virile inch of him. He was the man she had never stopped loving. She had giver her heart to him a long time ago—and somehow forgotten to take it with her when she left.

He wasn't an easy man to love sometimes. He could be proud and hardheaded, even downright rude on occasions. But the intervening years had taught Maddie that no one was perfect; certainly she wasn't. Better than anyone, she knew the mistakes she had made.

Love allowed her to look beyond Eben's faults

and see that his heart was good. More than just good, it was strong and vulnerable, too.

"I'm not letting you go a second time, Maddie," he told her, emotion thickening his voice.

Even as she thrilled to his declaration, honesty prompted her to warn him, "I've changed, Eben. I'm not that meek, young girl you once loved. I talk back now. I'll argue with you, give you my opinion whether you ask for it or not."

"That's been very clear." His mouth crooked ruefully. "Lately there hasn't been much you have agreed with me about."

"Do you mind?" she asked, her breath catching high in her throat.

"Oh, I mind, all right." He nodded, his eyes darkening with a possessive light. "But I can learn to live with it. It'll be a lot easier than living without you."

His mouth claimed hers in another long and deep kiss as renewed desire flowed freely between them. Maddie wrapped her arms tightly around his neck, holding on to this feeling they had almost lost.

Even after their lips parted, they stayed in the embrace, each breathing hard and smiling a little at this giddy rush of young love reborn.

"Stay here tonight." His hands moved over her back, vaguely irritated by the barrier of her wool jacket and blouse when he wanted nothing between them to interfere with this new closeness.

Regret was in her smile. "I can't. The staff is putting on an amateur show for our guests tonight.

I'm the emcee. And no," Maddie inserted before he could ask, "I can't get out of it."

"Tomorrow night, then," Eben said, smothering his annoyance.

She heard herself saying, "Sorry, that's the big dinner and dance before Saturday's gymkhana and barbeque."

A stiff impatience swept through his expression. "With all the help you have at that dude ranch, there has to be someone who can stand in for you."

He was absolutely right; her presence wasn't mandatory; there were others who could assume her duties. Maybe it was pride, a misplaced sense of caution, or simply a need to assert her independence that refused to let her do that and give him the impression that she was once again at his beck and call.

"Are you saying—work shouldn't come first?" Maddie teased lightly.

He saw the trap instantly and backpedaled. "I'm not saying that at all. I was just hoping—"

"Then you'll be glad to know there is a very good chance I can sneak away on Saturday after the barbeque." She smoothed the collar on his shirt, adjusting it to lie perfectly. "I could come over then, and you could throw a couple logs in the fireplace, get a good blaze going. We could pop some popcorn, keep the kids occupied stringing it for garland until their bedtime rolls around and—"

"String popcorn for what?" Eben frowned in

sudden suspicion. "I told you I'm not buying a tree."

"Not even a little bitty tree?" she coaxed. "After all, it is Christmas."

"We're not having a tree, and that's final." But he knew he hadn't heard the end of this. "Don't you dare go behind my back and get those kids a tree, Maddie. Because if you do—"

"You'll what?" She slid her hands inside his shirt and pressed closer, snuggling against him, making him aware of the way their bodies fit together.

"I'll throw it out." Aroused and fighting it, Eben wasn't sure how to deal with this new, aggressive Maddie, especially when it was clear she knew exactly what she was doing to him. "I swear I will."

"You wouldn't be that cruel." She nearly purred the words.

"Maddie." He had intended to say her name in warning; instead it spoke of his need.

A husky, faintly triumphant laugh came from low in her throat.

Eben swallowed it, his arms circling her in a crushing grip that tried to absorb her into him. The roaring in his ears masked the crunching scuffle of leather soles on the desert's sandy soil and muted the seeking cries of young voices.

The barn door's rusty hinges squealed a warning an instant before sunlight glared against his eyelids and a little girl called, "Uncle Eben?"

They sprang guiltily apart to the sound of twin gasps. Joy and Hope stood just inside the barn, their mouths agape with surprise. Joy recovered first.

"You were kissing each other—"

"—just like Mommy and Daddy," Hope finished, clearly intrigued by the discovery.

"Momma said she kissed him—"

"—'cause she loved him."

"Do you love Maddie, Uncle Eben?" Joy cocked her head at a wondering angle.

Conscious of the redness creeping up his neck, Eben dodged the question. "What are you two doing here? You're supposed to stay close to the house."

"Sofia said we could come." Joy continued to watch him with bright, speculative eyes, a pleased smile curving her lips.

"Yeah, Dillon wants to know—" Hope began, recalling their original purpose.

"—if he's gotta milk Annabelle tonight—"

"—or if he's gotta stay at the table."

"He's been there a long time, Uncle Eben," Joy reminded him, taking her brother's side.

"I'll milk the cow tonight," Eben replied. "You tell Dillon that I expect his homework to be done by the time I'm through with the chores."

With a sigh of regret, Joy promised, "We'll tell him."

"Did Maddie 'splain that we get to have Christmas?" Hope bubbled with a kind of shy excitement, not altogether sure he wouldn't still veto it.

"I never said you couldn't have Christmas," Eben asserted, defensive again.

Joy opened her mouth to argue, but Maddie stepped in. "It was all a misunderstanding, girls."

"Are we gonna get a tree then, too?" Bright-eyed at the possibility, Joy clamped both hands together in a prayerfully expectant pose.

"No tree." Half-expecting Maddie to take up the cry, Eben fired a quick glance at her. "I told you that, and I mean it."

"But we got to have a tree—"

"—to put our presents under," the twins reasoned.

Joy didn't give him a chance to speak. Recognizing that he was deaf to her pleas, she turned to different ears. "Maddie, can't you talk to Uncle Eben—"

"—and 'splain that we need a tree?"

Amusement danced in Maddie's sidelong look, accurately gauging his level of irritation. "This isn't a good time to talk to your uncle about getting a tree," she told them. "He can get very stubborn when you push him too hard."

Frowning, Joy mulled that over. "But we aren't pushing, Maddie."

"We're just asking," Hope declared, all big-eyed with innocence.

"And the answer is still 'no,' " Eben inserted, a little testily.

"But, Uncle Eben," Joy began in her best wheedling tone.

"I said—"

Maddie smoothly broke in, her hand sliding into his palm. "We know what you said, Eben—and we aren't going to argue about it anymore today, are we, girls?''

With heavy sighs, Joy and Hope grudgingly agreed. Turning, Maddie gave his hand a small squeeze.

"I'll see you on Saturday," she whispered.

Dragging her glance from him, she moved away and herded the girls out of the barn.

He forgot all about the tree the twins wanted. His thoughts centered solely on the promise that had been in Maddie's eyes. It had been years since he had looked forward to the weekend coming. Now, Saturday couldn't get here soon enough.

But it seemed a long way off when he reached the house, milk pail in hand, and discovered that Dillon had yet to start his homework. In this battle of wills, Eben was determined that he wasn't going to be bested by a mere seven-year-old.

Chapter XIII

Blond hair, the pale gold of cornsilk, glistened in the room's lamplight. Perched a bit precariously on the vanity's dainty stool, Eben pulled the softly bristled brush through Joy's silken curls. She sat on his knee, dressed in a lavender and pink nightgown, her head bowed against the drag of the brush.

Hope was on the floor near his feet, instructing Tad in the game of "pattycake." Tad waved his hands in an uncoordinated attempt to copy her clapping action. Occasionally his fingers touched each other, but his little palms never quite connected. Undeterred by his failure, Tad laughed with glee, showing off his newest tooth.

Pausing, Eben shifted Joy, turning her on his

knee to get at the last section of hair. With the first stroke of the brush, the bristles caught in a snarl. Unable to stop the downward impetus in time, he pulled her hair.

Joy sucked in a quick breath, her hand flying protectively to her hair. "Ouch! That hurts, Uncle Eben."

"I know. Just hold still a minute," he told her. "We're almost through."

Starting at the ends, the way he would with a matting snarl in a horse's mane, he worked loose the knotting tangle in her hair and brushed the freed strands smooth.

Inevitably during this nightly ritual Eben thought back to all the times he had fixed their mother's hair when Carla was their age. Barrettes, braids, ponytails, hairbands—at one time, he had mastered them all. And here he was learning to do it all over again. Oddly enough, he didn't mind anymore.

He was careful not to delve too deeply into the possible reasons behind it—or acknowledge the vaguely warm and fuzzy feeling that drifted through him while he brushed the twins' hair.

But inwardly he knew it was all tied up with his memories of Carla—memories of the old days when they had been close, as close as a brother and sister could be. Whether he wanted to admit it or not, he sometimes saw flashes of Carla in her daughters.

Except for the powder blue of their eyes, the twins didn't bear that much physical resemblance to her. There was a roundness to the shape of their faces while hers had been more angular, like his. Their hair was blond and curly; Carla's had been light brown and straight.

But Joy had her mother's positive outlook, her confidence, enthusiasm, and resilience. As corny as it sounded, considering the joy she found in life and living, she couldn't have been more aptly named.

As for Hope—there had been another side to Carla as well. A sensitivity, a slight reserve, an idle dreamer living in quiet anticipation with thoughts going around in her head that she didn't always share with him.

Thoughts that Eben wondered about now.

Try as he might, he found it harder and harder to summon up the old anger, the old sense of betrayal when he thought about Carla now. All because of the twins.

The discovery turned him slightly brusque when he lifted Joy off his knee and set her down.

"We're all done," he announced. "Time for bed."

"Not yet." As expected, the protesting wail came from Joy.

"Please, Uncle Eben," Hope immediately added.

"No. It's bed for both of you," Reaching down, he scooped Tad into his arms, drawing a surprised squeal from him.

Joy sighed in disgust. "How come Dillon gets to stay up?"

"Because he has homework to finish," Eben replied, shifting Tad to ride high on his ribs.

"But he's got school tomorrow," Hope reminded him with a touch of sternness.

"That's why he has to get his homework done." Little fingers grabbed at his lower lip, the ragged edge of a nail scraping it. Eben pushed the baby's hand down and made a mental note to clip Tad's fingernails. "You two, get your doll and hop into bed."

Shaking her head in adultlike exasperation, Joy declared, "First, we got to say our prayers, Uncle Eben. Remember?"

"Then you'd better get at it," he told her. "You're running out of time."

Without any show of haste, the twins knelt beside the canopied bed, clasped their hands together in prayer, and closed their eyes before offering up their bedtime prayer that somehow managed to get longer every night.

Tonight, God was asked to bless not only their own family members, but He was also expected to include Sofia, Ramon, Luis, Annabelle the cow, and Duffy the horse as well. Before they finished, the twins added Dillon's teacher, which Eben thought was appropriate.

Anticipating the concluding "Amen," he started forward to hustle the girls into bed. But it didn't come.

Instead Joy peeked out of the corner of her eye and added to their already lengthy prayer, "And

God, will you please work on Uncle Eben about getting us a Christmas tree?"

"We really need one," Hope declared fervently, keeping both eyes tightly closed.

"Amen," they chorused and hurriedly scrambled into bed, diving under the covers while Eben fought off a couple of guilty twinges.

Neither girl so much as glanced in his direction until Eloise the doll was nestled securely between them. Then each regarded him with a look of beguiling innocence.

"Nice try." More amused than irritated by their ploy, Eben sat on the edge of the bed. Keeping one arm hooked around the baby, he adjusted the covers around each twin with his free hand. "But you're still not getting a tree," he stated as much for his own benefit as theirs.

"It isn't Christmas yet," Joy informed him, supremely confident.

"There's still time for God to work on you," Hope added with a faint smile.

It was blackmail, the emotional kind. And he wasn't about to surrender to it.

"Don't get your hopes up," Eben warned them.

"But that's what Christmas is all about," Joy reminded him.

"Hope and Joy," her sister added with a satisfied nod.

"That's us," Joy inserted proudly, then impulsively sat up and planted a dry kiss on his cheek. "Good night, Uncle Eben."

Hope instantly followed suit with a kiss of her own. "Good night, Uncle Eben."

"Good night." He stood up, the sensation of their soft lips lingering on his cheek, awakening a tenderness he refused to recognize.

Halfway to the door, Eben heard the scuttle of movement in the hall. But there was no one in sight when he came out of the bedroom. He listened for a moment, catching a betraying rustle of sound coming from the kitchen.

"What do you think your big brother's up to?" Eben glanced at the heavy-eyed baby in his arms. Tad looked at him and yawned, then went back to gnawing hungrily on his fist. "Let's go get your bottle and find out, shall we?"

In the kitchen, he found Dillon slumped in the same chair, still sulking and giving every appearance that he had been there the whole time.

"I got my homework done. Are you satisfied now?" he grumbled in sarcasm and avoided Eben's eyes.

"Where is it?" Eben glanced briefly at the papers on the table as he crossed to the refrigerator.

"Right there." Dillon flipped a hand in the direction of the papers. "Can I leave now?"

"Not until I look it over," Eben replied.

First, Eben retrieved the baby's bottle from the refrigerator, set it in a pan of water on the stove, turned on the burner under it, then went to check Dillon's assignment, half-expecting to find it haphazardly done. After perusing it carefully, he saw that all but two of the answers appeared to be correct.

"It looks fine." He nodded in satisfaction. "You can put your stuff away and get ready for bed."

"Now that I got this done," Dillon eyed him uncertainly, "you aren't going to take me to school in the morning, are you?"

"Of course." Water bubbled in the pan, rattling the baby bottle it surrounded.

"But I can ride the bus," Dillon declared when Eben walked over to turn the burner down and test the milk.

"Not tomorrow, you aren't."

"But I don't want you to take me," Dillon protested, anxiety showing in his expression.

"That's too bad," Eben told him. "You have a lot of homework to make up, and I intend to get every single assignment from your teacher."

"But she never said I had to make them up," Dillon argued.

"That's right, she didn't. I'm the one who said you were going to do it." Eben shook a couple drops of milk on his wrist. It felt warm, but not hot.

"But that's not fair!"

"Fair or not, you're going to do it." Eben slipped the nipple into Tad's mouth. He sucked on it greedily, his eyes quickly closing in tiredness and contentment.

It was a feeling Dillon didn't share. "I am not doing that homework!" He grabbed his papers and pencils off the table, jammed them in his book bag, and ran out of the kitchen.

Seconds later, a bedroom door slammed shut.

The battle over the missed homework resumed the following day.

On Friday, Dillon spent the entire evening at the kitchen table, staring at the stack of missed assignments without touching a single one.

Judging by the mutinous set of Dillon's chin, Saturday gave every indication of being a repeat of the previous evening.

"I said to bring your schoolwork in here and get busy." Eben tried to stare the boy down.

"I'm not doing it." Dillon glared in defiance while an uneasy Sofia cleared the last of the breakfast dishes from the table.

"That's your choice, kid—"

"My name's not 'kid,' " Dillon protested vigorously. "I hate it when you call me that!"

Eben paid no attention to the outburst and picked up where he left off. "As long as you understand, you will sit at that table until it's done."

"I will not." Dillon belligerently folded his arms and planted both feet solidly on the floor.

"I can help you, Dillon," Sofia offered quickly, clearly sympathizing with him. "Together, we can do it very fast, no?"

"No." He turned on her, hot tears glittering in his eyes. "It's Christmas vacation. I don't have to go back to school for two weeks. And I'm not going to do any stupid homework!''

''If you had done it when you were supposed to, you wouldn't have to be doing it now,'' Eben reminded. ''Now get your things and get started.''

''I won't!'' Dillon shouted in full rebellion. ''I'm never going to do it. Not ever!''

He bolted from the kitchen. Eben took two angry strides after him, yelling, ''Come back here—'' then broke off when the screen door banged shut behind the boy.

He had a brief glimpse of Dillon's tearstreaked face as he ran stumbling and crying toward the rear of the house. Sighing, Eben turned back and instantly encountered the twins' reproachful looks.

''What's wrong with Dillon?'' Joy's expression put the blame squarely at his feet.

''Nothing. He's just mad.'' Eben was more than a little angry himself.

This was Saturday; Maddie was coming over tonight. He could just imagine how she would react when she walked in and saw Dillon still sitting at the table.

''Do you wish that I should go after him, *Señor* Mac?'' Sofia inquired hesitantly.

He thought about that, then sighed again and shook his head. ''No. Let him cry it out by himself. He'll be fine.''

''But he is a little boy,'' she protested, her words an echo of the phrase Maddie had used. ''He could get lost. He does not know the desert.''

"He won't go far," Eben stated with more confidence than he felt.

Outside, he surreptitiously scanned the rock-pillared slope behind the house, searching for some sign of the boy. He detected a patch of blue near a jumble of tall, wind-scoured boulders. It was the same shade of blue as the shirt Dillon had been wearing.

Eben marked the spot in his mind as he made his way to the corral to begin the morning training session. When he climbed aboard the second horse, the scrap of blue was no longer visible.

Somewhere around midmorning, Sofia ventured a few yards behind the house, shadowed closely by the twins. The sound of her voice calling for Dillon rang across the clear desert air.

But Eben heard no answering shout.

The stubborn little fool, he thought. Didn't he realize people were worrying about him? Or was that part of Dillon's plan? To scare them a little, get some attention and sympathy.

If the kid didn't show up soon, Eben promised himself that the kid would get plenty of attention. And he intended to apply it to the backside of his pants—assuming the kid was all right, of course.

Lunchtime came with still no sign of Dillon.

An anxious Sofia hovered beside Eben's chair, clutching the coffeepot in both hands, his cup already filled to the brim.

"The little one, do you think maybe he is lost?" The concern in her voice was palpable.

"Maybe." Eben dipped his spoon into the bowl

of soup, conscious of the twins watching him, their eyes big and round and silently accusing, their food before them untouched.

Over in the corner, Tad gripped the webbed side of his playpen and pulled himself up, then squealed to attract their attention.

But no one glanced his way.

He tried one more shriek, then plopped back down on the playpen's padded floor and grabbed the tail of a stuffed lion, giving it a good shake before drawing it to his mouth.

Sofia returned the coffeepot to its burner and peered out the window. "Dillon did not eat all of his pancake this morning. He must be very hungry by now," she said worriedly.

"Probably." Eben avoided the twins' staring eyes.

He told himself it was a relief to finally eat a meal without listening to their constant chatter. But their continued silence worked on his nerves.

"Maybe he falls, *Señor* Mac," Sofia said, her eyes dark with a new dread. "Maybe he lays somewhere hurt. Or maybe a snake bites him."

Eben had already gone through the whole dire list of possibilities. "At this time of year, the rattlesnakes would be denned up."

But he also knew there was always the outside chance Dillon might have stumbled on one sunning itself on a rock.

"Uncle Eben?" Joy's voice was small and hesitant.

"What?" His glance bounced off her fearful face.

"Did Dillon go to heaven—"

"—like Mommy and Daddy?" Hope's voice wavered with the hint of a sob.

"Of course not," Eben replied, deliberately gruff, then tried to sidetrack them with more mundane matters. "You two get busy and eat your lunch."

Joy glumly pushed her soup bowl away. "I'm not hungry, Uncle Eben."

"Me neither," Hope mumbled and scooted back in her chair, tucking her chin low.

Truthfully Eben didn't have much of an appetite either. But he had the uneasy feeling he would need the energy this food could give him.

Chin quivering, Joy turned soulful eyes on Eben. "I want my brother."

"He'll be back soon." If Eben had to drag the kid by his hair.

"Maybe you should go look for him, *Señor* Mac," Sofia suggested tentatively.

"I plan on doing that very thing just as soon as I'm done eating." He dipped his spoon into the suddenly tasteless soup again, wondering if he'd be able to force another drop down.

"You are?!" Surprise and delight mixed with the relieved breath that rushed from Sofia.

"Of course." It irritated him that she had thought he wouldn't. "Luis and Ramon will be bringing the horses up here to the house any time now. I left orders to saddle them up as soon as they finished their lunch."

"I am so glad you do this, *Señor* Mac," Sofia

declared. "I have been very worried that something has happened to Dillon."

"More than likely he's up there getting a good laugh out of the trouble he's causing," Eben muttered.

The last couple bites of soup sat like lumps in his throat. Eben knew he couldn't get another swallow down, and pushed back from the table.

Ten minutes later, Ramon and Luis rode up to the house leading Duffy, the big steel-gray gelding. Eben handed a rifle to each of them with instructions to use a three-shot signal if either located Dillon, then gave the extra pair of binoculars to Ramon and wrapped the strap to his pair around the saddle horn.

After making sure they all carried plenty of water, he tightened the cinch and swung aboard the gray. He gathered up the reins and lifted his gaze to the slope where he had last spotted that patch of blue.

"Where do you wish us to look first, *Señor* Mac?" Ramon inquired, his face an expressionless mask. Like Eben, only his eyes showed the concern they were all feeling.

Eben didn't have to waste time about his answer to that. He had already figured out the initial areas to be searched.

Working on the assumption that Dillon wouldn't have circled back around the house to the barn and pasture areas, he concentrated their efforts on the rough country behind the adobe house. He directed Luis to scour the scrub desert on their left with its maze of arroyos. Ramon, he sent to the broken country on their right, studded with catclaw, cactus, and thinly scattered clumps of grass.

For himself, Eben chose the slope of rock towers behind the house, the same area where he had first seen that patch of blue. It was a decision based on more than the sighting of what might have been Dillon's shirt, but also the memory of all the times as a boy when he had gotten mad at his father and run off.

Only once had he struck out for town. All the other times, he had climbed among the wind-eroded rocks, seeking a high place as if to get above his troubles. It had seemed an instinctive thing.

Eben could only hope that Dillon was led by the same instincts.

He touched a spur to the surefooted gray horse. It set off at a quick walk, automatically skirting the large clump of thorny prickly pear a few yards beyond the house. Stones rolled and clattered, dislodged by the gelding's iron-shod hooves.

Busy scanning the tangle of boulders rising before him, Eben never glanced back to see the twins standing beside Sofia, watching the three searchers ride away.

Within minutes Eben was too far away to hear the strident ring of the telephone inside the house.

Joy heard it and instantly brightened. "Maybe that's Dillon."

She tore back into the kitchen, with Hope right at her heels. Together the two of them pushed a chair over to the counter. Joy scrambled onto its seat, snatched the receiver off the hook, and pressed it tightly to her ear.

"Hello? Is that you, Dillon?" she said excitedly.

"No, dear, it's Maddie."

Crestfallen, Joy relayed the bad news to her sister. "It's only Maddie," she told her, then said into the phone, "Me and Hope thought you might be Dillon."

"Why would you think that?" Maddie wondered with a confused laugh.

" 'Cause he's gone." Joy caught hold of the phone cord and twisted her fingers into its spiraling coil.

"Gone. Gone where?"

"We don't know." Joy's chin began to quiver.

"You don't—" Maddie broke off that sentence to demand, "Is your uncle there?"

"No, he went to look for Dillon. Ramon and Luis went, too."

"How long has Dillon been gone?" Maddie asked. "Do you know?"

"All morning," Joy admitted as tears formed in her eyes. "He got mad at Uncle Eben and ran out of the house. He didn't even eat all his pancakes. You haven't seen him, have you, Maddie?"

"No. I'm sorry—"

"You don't think he went to heaven to see Mommy and Daddy, do you?" The tears rolled off her lashes and trickled down her cheeks.

"I'm sure he hasn't—"

"That's what Uncle Eben said, too, but I know

Dillon misses them," Joy declared with a definite whimper in her voice.

"Of course, he does, but—"

When Hope started to cry, Joy stopped trying to hold back the tears and wailed into the telephone, "I want my brother!"

"Sssh, don't cry, honey. Your uncle will find him. Honest, he will," Maddie rushed to assure her. "Now, you and your sister need to go find Sofia, and tell her I'll be right over. Okay?"

A garbled " 'Kay" was Joy's response before she hung up.

After three hours of riding, Eben hadn't found a trace of the boy. He let the gelding pick its own way among the forest of rocks.

Overhead, a hawk wheeled in the sky. But Eben took no notice of it, his gaze constantly moving and shifting, scanning the area immediately ahead and to either side of him, alert for any hint of movement.

He cupped a hand to his mouth and shouted Dillon's name, just as he had done a dozen times before. Reining in the gelding, he listened for a reply with no expectation of hearing one.

If the kid wanted to be found, he would have answered before now. And if he didn't—that was another problem entirely.

There were too many hiding places. The kid could play cat-and-mouse with him forever, slipping behind a rock while Eben rode around the front of it.

But there was always the possibility that Dillon was lying somewhere, injured and unconscious. That was what kept Eben looking.

Again, he dragged the binoculars from their leather case and glassed the craggy land ahead of him. Lowering them, Eben checked the sun's angle and gave himself one more hour to find the kid. If he hadn't located him by then, he would have to call the authorities, get a chopper in here, and see if they couldn't spot the kid from the air— while there was still some daylight left.

Eben didn't want to think about the kid spending the night out in the desert without a coat, not at this time of the year. Or any other time, for that matter.

A stone rattled somewhere behind him. Swiveling in the saddle, Eben glanced back in time to see a flash of blue and a mop of pale brown hair before the boy disappeared behind a jagged pillar.

Dillon was alive. Unharmed.

Relief washed through him, followed by a swamping wave of anger for all the needless worry the kid had caused everyone.

"Dillon!" Eben roared and sank the spurs into the gray, setting the horse on its haunches and spinning it around, then sending it back over the trail.

As the gelding came around the stone tower, Dillon jumped to a smooth rock below it, slid down its canted side to the base, then hugged its face while he began inching around it. On the other side of that rock, there was a good twenty-five-foot drop to a talus slope.

"Dillon, you get back here right now!" Eben shouted and reined the gelding in, unable to pursue the boy any farther on horseback.

Dillon threw him a half-frightened look and disappeared behind the rock face. Peeling out of the saddle, Eben went after him on foot, jumping from rock to rock as Dillon had done.

Suddenly there was a sharp, startled yelp, broken off in midcry. Eben's blood ran cold when he heard the telltale rattling of falling rock.

"Dillon? Dillon!" He looked, but saw only a fast-sliding avalanche of stones clattering down to the slope—and not a young boy's body. "Dillon, are you all right?" he shouted. "What happened?"

But all he heard in reply was a series of short, panting grunts, tinged with panic.

Exercising caution, Eben worked his way down the rock to its base and found the problem. The narrow ledge that Dillon had inched along had caved in, leaving him with only one small toehold.

Dillon was literally holding on by his fingertips. Eben could see him—the whiteness of his face and the terror in his eyes—but he couldn't reach him.

"Hang on, kid," he instructed grimly. "I'm getting a rope. I'll be right back."

Dillon was too terrified to answer.

Eben scrambled up the rocks to the big gray horse, removed the coiled rope and tied one end of it to the saddle horn, then went back down, playing out the length of rope as he went.

Rigging up a crude rappel, Eben took up the slack in one hand and pulled on the other, signaling the gelding to keep the rope taut. He walked over the edge of the rock well clear of Dillon and lowered himself down.

As soon as he was level with the boy, Eben moved sideways to reach him. He ran out of rope short of the kid. By stretching, Eben could just reach Dillon's right wrist.

"Dillon, listen to me," Eben ordered with forced calm. "I'm going to grab your right hand. When I do, I want you to try to inch a little closer to me."

"No." It was a sob, spoken with eyes scrunched tightly shut.

"I can't get any closer," Eben stated with barely contained impatience. His own thoughts were full of worry about how much longer Dillon could hold on. "You'll have to trust me."

"You'll let go and I'll fall," Dillon whimpered.

"I won't let go," Eben promised. "I swear to God, I won't, kid."

Dillon's eyes snapped open, a fear-born anger blazing from them. "You don't believe in God. You don't believe in nothing!"

There were a lot of things Eben could have said, but he knew Dillon wouldn't listen to any of them. Probably with cause.

Searching strictly by feel, Eben found a solid bit of footing, tested it, then let out the last bit of rope and wrapped a couple turns of it around his arm, feeling the stress it put on his shoulder joint.

He wasn't normally the praying kind, but he said a quick one right before he made the swing toward the boy. A split second later he hooked an arm around Dillon and jerked him off the rock.

A strangled outcry came from the boy. Pain, like a hot fire, stabbed Eben's arm and shoulder from the strain of their combined weights. Using his toes and knees, he fought to ease some of it.

"Wrap your arms around my neck," he told Dillon, jaws clenched, pushing out the words. "And hang on."

He felt the boy's frightened trembles as Dillon wrapped arms and legs around him. With his second hand free at last, Eben grabbed on to the rope, gathered his strength, and started up, pushing with his feet and hauling on the rope with his arms.

Long seconds later, they reached safety.

Eben sagged against the canted rock, muscles quivering from the effort, the knot of fear in his stomach finally loosening. He let go of the rope, then pried Dillon's arms from around his neck.

"We made it, kid." His voice had a husky emotional rasp to it. "You're okay now."

But there was no response from Dillon as he buried his chin a little lower and refused to even look at Eben.

Concerned, Eben peered at the boy's white and tearstained cheeks, smudged with dirt.

"What's wrong? Are you hurt?" he asked, unable to find any obvious sign of injury.

"No," Dillon replied, in a small, unusually subdued voice.

"All right, then." Satisfied that the kid was suffering from nothing more than a good scare, Eben pushed to his feet and started gathering up the loose rope, discreetly giving Dillon a chance to pull himself together.

Dillon sat without moving. "I guess you're gonna beat me now for running off instead of doing my homework," he mumbled.

Stunned, Eben exploded, "What?!"

"I said—" Dillon began, twice as hesitant.

"I know what you said," Eben snapped the answer. "What I don't know is how you could think—" He bit off the rest of it, too furious to trust either his control or his temper.

With quick, angry jerks, he took up the last of the slack in the rope, then crossed the rocks to the waiting horse. He looped the coiled rope over the saddle horn and glanced back at Dillon.

"I'm going back to the ranch," he stated curtly. "Are you coming with me or not?"

After a long run of seconds, Dillon nodded, none too happily. "I'm coming."

Still angry and frustrated, Eben deliberately turned away and concentrated his attention on the dark gray gelding, but he was conscious of the scrape of shoe leather behind him. When Dillon joined him on the trail, Eben tossed him the canteen. Startled, Dillon recoiled from it, but it hit him in the hands. Recognizing it, he caught the canteen by its strap.

"There's some water in there if you're thirsty," Eben stated, then pulled the rifle from its boot.

Dillon's eyes got big when he saw the blue gleam of the barrel. "What are you doing with that?"

"I have to signal Ramon and Luis. They're both out looking for you," Eben replied, each word sharply clipped.

Pointing the rifle into the air, Eben fired three shots, waiting a full count between each one. The air rang with their traveling echoes.

Chapter XIV

Despite the signaling gunshots, Maddie didn't draw an easy breath until she saw with her own eyes that Dillon was safe and unharmed. Then it slipped from her, in a wavering sigh.

Dillon sat in front of Eben in the saddle, his expression somewhat tense and resentful, a guilty drop to his chin. But her searching glance found no hint of injury.

Relieved, Maddie hugged Tad a little closer, a small smile curving her lips as Joy patted at her leg.

"Maddie, look," she pointed to the big gray horse carrying a double burden.

"There's Dillon," Hope cried while Sofia murmured a quick prayer of gratitude and crossed herself.

"I see him," Maddie said but her attention had already shifted to Eben.

Some of her uneasiness returned when she saw his stone-hard face, all tight-lipped and grim. Maddie knew without asking that Eben and Dillon had resolved none of their differences. If anything, the gulf between them appeared wider.

She had hoped—Maddie sighed, not entirely sure what she had hoped.

Deep in her heart, Maddie was convinced that Dillon was trying to force Eben to show that he cared about him—much as she had done all those years ago when she had left Eben. Judging from Dillon's downcast expression, he hadn't been any more successful at it than she had.

When Eben rode up to the house with Dillon, the twins ran to welcome them, all puffy-eyed from the tears they had cried over their runaway brother. Maddie drifted closer, watching as Eben swung out of the saddle, then lifted Dillon and set him on the ground.

The twins were on him in an instant. But Dillon pulled free of their clutching hands and headed straight for the kitchen door, ignoring their clamoring voices.

Equally silent, Eben caught up the gray's reins and turned, his eyes softening a little when their glance fell on Maddie. "I didn't expect to see you here," he said, then shot a knowing look toward the house, surmising, "I guess the twins called you again."

"I'm the one who called this time." The reason she had phoned no longer seemed to matter. "Where did you find Dillon?"

At the mention of Dillon's name, an anger tightened his expression again. "Playing hide-and-seek up in the rocks. The fool kid was so busy trying to dodge me, he nearly broke his neck," he muttered. "If I hadn't spotted him, he'd be at the bottom of a twenty-five-foot drop. Luckily I managed to get to him before he fell."

"Thank God." A breath feathered from her lips, her eyes widening at the picture Eben had painted even as Maddie tightened her hold on Tad. "Poor Dillon," she murmured in empathy. "He must have been scared to death."

"If he wasn't, he should have been," Eben declared, a hardness banding the muscles along his jaw.

Maddie sensed at once that there was more to this story than he had told her. "What happened, Eben?" she asked, instantly suspecting the worst. "Don't tell me you bawled him out for running away?"

"You're as bad as he is." He treated her to an icy glare.

"What do you mean?" she asked, suddenly questioning her own conclusion.

"I mean—that after I plucked that kid off the face of a rock, he thought I was going to beat him!" There was righteous indignation in his voice and expression. "Good grief, I have never once raised my hand to that kid."

"Maybe not, but you've raised your voice enough times," Maddie reminded him, looking at the situation from Dillon's side.

"But I have never hit him," he repeated insistently.

"And I'd be willing to bet you never have said a kind word to him either," she accused, angry now on Dillon's behalf.

"What has that got to do with anything?"

She stared at him, utterly amazed that he could ask such a question. "How can you be so dense, MacCallister?" she declared. "If you constantly yelled at a young horse, that animal would be afraid of you whether you had ever struck it or not. What makes you think a young boy would react any differently?"

Eben stiffened, resisting any suggestion that he was, in some way, at fault. "If you think I'm going to praise that kid after all the trouble he's caused, you can think again, Maddie."

"I never said you should," she countered, annoyed that he had taken her comment to the extreme, "but you can praise him for the things he's done right."

"Maddie," he began, half in anger, then paused and looked away, drawing in a deep and weary breath. "Look, I just spent the last four hours combing those rocks for him. Then I had to risk my own neck rescuing him. If you want to know the absolute truth, I was more scared than he was.

So, right now the last thing I want to do is argue with you, Maddie. If you want to read me the riot act, save it for later, okay?"

For the first time, Maddie looked beyond the anger that hardened his features, and saw the emotional pain it skillfully masked.

Eben MacCallister was not the kind of man who could come right out and say he'd been hurt by Dillon's reaction—and he would certainly never admit that he had been worried about Dillon. But it was clear he had been, even if he hadn't shown it.

She was briefly irritated with the way he kept his feelings locked inside, seldom expressing them. And on those rare occasions when he did, he invariably disguised them in anger.

It was a form of self-protection, she supposed. A sadly misguided one.

"Sorry," Maddie said, finding it easy to be generous. "I guess I was so upset and worried about Dillon, I took it out on you."

He studied her for a long second, a gentle warmth slowly stealing into the desert blue of his eyes. "I'm glad you're here, Maddie." The husky sincerity of his voice flowed over her like a caress.

A little thrill traveled through her. Sparkling with it, Maddie smiled. Unlike Eben, she had never been skilled at hiding her feelings. But experience had taught her not to be a pushover.

"I'm glad I'm here, too," she said, then added with a truthful, yet teasing lightness, "However, that doesn't mean I don't think you were partially to blame for Dillon running off." Her smile widened at the snap of temper in his eyes. "But that's something we can battle about later. Right now it's enough that you are both safe and unharmed."

Looking at her, Eben shook his head, a dry amusement showing. "I should have known the new Maddie wouldn't back down."

"No, she wouldn't," Maddie confirmed softly. "I hope you don't have a problem with that."

"I thought I would, but—I don't," he replied with unusual candor, then turned self-conscious and concealed it with a masking gruffness. "That doesn't mean I agree with you."

"Heaven forbid," she laughed and the sound drew a gurgling coo of agreement from Tad.

Eben glanced at the baby in her arms, then swung his gaze back to Maddie. Something nameless and intimate passed between them. Moved by it, Maddie could only look at him.

In the end, Eben was the one to break the contact, turning to the patient gray horse.

"I'd better be seeing to Duffy. He needs a good rubdown after that ride," he said and moved away, leading the gelding.

As she watched him, a small hand patted lightly at her chin. Smiling, she caught hold of the little fingers seeking to explore her mouth and smiled at the bright-eyed baby.

"What's the matter? Do you think I haven't been paying enough attention to you?" she asked Tad in a voice warmed by the heady glow she felt.

His smile, the twinkle in his eyes, their expectant

look, all said playtime. Laughing, Maddie obliged him, burying her face below his ear and blowing on his neck. Tad giggled wildly and wanted more.

But Maddie shook her head. "I think we should go see how your brother is." After a last glance at Eben's retreating figure, she made her way to the side door leading into the house.

Seated on a kitchen chair, Dillon twisted and squirmed. trying to avoid the washcloth in Sofia's hand while a sister hovered anxiously on either side of him.

"It's nothing but a little dirt," he grumbled in protest, embarrassed by the attention. "I can wash myself."

Sofia paid no attention to him, murmuring a concerned, "Your cheek," when a wipe of the wash-cloth revealed the redness of scraped skin. "I will get something to put on this."

The instant she laid the washcloth aside and started from the room, Joy grabbed it up to finish the job.

"Oh, no, you don't." Dillon snatched the cloth out of her hands in a flash and scrambled off the chair.

"But I just want to help," she wailed.

"I don't want your help." Dodging her reaching hands, Dillon scrubbed his face with the washcloth. "Just go away," he declared with force, then saw Maddie and ducked his head with a shame-faced look. "Why can't everybody just leave me alone?"

"We were worried about you, Dillon." Maddie lowered Tad to the floor. Immediately he went down on all fours and crawled over to his brother, jabbering all the way.

"You didn't need to worry. I was okay." The scowl was back, this time tinged with a lurking sadness and lingering hurt.

"But we didn't know that," Maddie gently reminded him.

Joy quickly took up the argument, her tears still close to the surface. "We thought you—"

"—got lost." Hope clutched at his arm.

He jerked it away from her, snapping an impatient, "I wasn't lost, okay?"

But his answer only added to his sisters' confusion.

"If you weren't lost—" Joy said.

"—how come you didn't come back?"

"Because I didn't want to, that's why." Troubled and confused himself, Dillon lashed out at them.

Joy's lower lip trembled. "Why not?"

"Yeah. How come you ran away and left us?" Hope stood back, suddenly uncertain and afraid to trust him.

"Because you two are a pain. You're always hanging on me and bugging me about stuff." Despite the anger in his voice, his chin quivered with the nearness of his own tears.

Before their crushed feelings could turn into full-blown wails, Maddie stepped in. "Don't you pay any attention to him, girls. He didn't mean that. Did you, Dillon?" she said, giving him a pointed look.

"I did so!" he insisted and sniffled back more threatening tears.

"No, you didn't," Maddie stated, then explained to the twins, "He's only trying to sound tough so you won't notice that he's a little scared and confused just like you are."

"I'm not scared," Dillon denied as the tears filled his eyes despite all his attempts to hold them back. "I'm not scared of nothing."

Reluctant to challenge his claim, Maddie was relieved to see Sofia when she returned to the kitchen, a tube of antiseptic ointment in her hand. Maddie took advantage of the distraction to redirect the conversation.

"I'm sure Dillon is hungry after missing lunch. Why don't you fix him a sandwich, Sofia, while I put that on his cheek?" she suggested, then added, "Girls, you can help her." Turning to Dillon, Maddie waved him back to the kitchen chair. "Hop up there."

"I don't need that." He glared at the tube of ointment she took from Sofia.

"Probably not. But we're going to put it on just the same." With a hand on his shoulder, Maddie guided him to the chair.

Grudgingly he climbed onto it while she pulled a second one close to his and sat down. She took her time unscrewing the cap, squeezing some ointment on her finger, then set the tube aside and tilted his chin to examine the abrasion on his cheek.

"I'm glad you weren't hurt any worse than this," she told him.

"Yeah," Dillon mumbled in answer, steadfastly avoiding her gaze.

"You were lucky that you didn't fall and wind up with a bunch of broken bones," she said.

He flashed her a guilty look, then winced when she smoothed the antiseptic cream onto the section of scraped flesh.

"He told you, didn't he?" Dillon accused, not bothering to mention Eben by name.

"Yes." With slow, gentle strokes, Maddie spread the ointment over the entire area, discreetly watching Dillon's expression. "That must have been very frightening, clinging to the rock like that."

He nodded, shutting his eyes at the memory. "I was scared," he admitted, the words barely above a whisper as an involuntary tremor shook him.

"I know." But instinct told Maddie that he needed the comfort of more than just words.

Obeying it, she lifted his nearly fifty-pound frame and pulled Dillon onto her lap. After a token resistance, he submitted almost gratefully to the embrace of her arms.

She simply held him for a moment, resting her cheek against his head. "When you ran off and didn't come back, we were all just about as scared as you were—not knowing where you were or if you were lost or hurt," she murmured.

"*He* wasn't." The mumbled words were riddled with accusation and resentment, but underneath it all, there was an ache.

"I think you're wrong, Dillon." Lifting her head, Maddie combed aside a lock of his hair, smoothing it into place. "Your uncle Eben was as worried about you as the rest of us were."

Not believing that, Dillon shook his head. "He hates me."

"Sweetheart, that's not true," she insisted softly, hurting for him.

"Yes, it is." He stared at the floor, the corners of his mouth pulled all the way down in a look of abject misery.

"If your uncle hated you as much as you think he does, he would have been glad that you had run away," she reasoned. "But instead he went out to look for you. Why do you suppose he did that?"

Dillon had an answer. "He probably wanted to make sure I was gone."

"All right." Maddie paused, realizing that Dillon was going to take some tall persuasion. "What about when he rescued you off that rock? That was a dangerous thing to do, wasn't it?"

"I guess." His shoulders lifted, trying to shrug that off, but Maddie could see he was mulling that one over in his mind.

"If he really hated you, why didn't he just let you fall?"

Dillon frowned in thoughtful concentration, then finally admitted, "I don't know."

"I think that your uncle didn't let you fall because he didn't want you to get hurt." She wrapped her arms a little more closely around him.

"And the reason he didn't want you to get hurt is because he really cares about you."

Dillon had to think about that long and hard before acknowledging a hesitant, "Maybe. But he's still mad at me, though."

"Dillon, he's not mad at you," she corrected. "He's mad about some of the things you've done."

"You mean, like not doing my homework," Dillon guessed, hanging his head a little lower.

"That, and misbehaving in school and running away, making everyone worry about you," she listed the rest. "None of that was right, was it?"

"No." He sighed heavily in admission.

"Everyone makes mistakes, Dillon," Maddie told him. "When you do, then you have to try extra hard not to make them again."

Joy walked up to the table, proudly carrying a plate with a sandwich on it. "We fixed you a peanut butter sandwich, Dillon—"

"—with pickles." Hope followed with a tall glass of milk.

"It's just like the ones—"

"Momma used to make." Hope pushed the glass onto the table next to the sandwich plate.

"Sofia's cooking—"

"—some soup for you, too."

Frowning, Joy cocked her head to stare at him. "How come you're on Maddie's lap?"

Hope peered at his face, then drew in a surprised breath of discovery. "Have you been crying?" she asked in astonishment.

When Dillon hurriedly swiped at the tear marks

on his face, Maddie covered for him. "The medicine stung a little when I put it on his cheek."

"Did you blow on it?" Joy wondered, confident of the solution.

"That's what Momma always did." Hope nodded with an air of great wisdom.

"I sure did. That's why I had Dillon on my lap," Maddie fibbed, keeping a steadying hand on him when he scooted off it to the floor.

When he slid back onto his own chair, both girls crowded in beside him, plying him with questions, wanting to know where he had gone, whether he had seen any snakes, and always coming back to their sense of abandonment with variations on why had he left them.

A subdued Dillon responded with more shrugs than specific answers, taking full advantage of the sandwich in his hand and the bowl of homemade beef noodle soup Sofia set before him, to keep his mouth full so he wouldn't have to reply.

His sandwich was half-finished when Eben came in the side door, all three rifles cradled in the crook of his arm. Dillon froze for an instant, his glance rushing to Eben then, just as quickly, sliding away as he hurriedly picked up his spoon and concentrated on his soup.

Eben's glance at Dillon was equally brief before he swung it to the coffeemaker on the kitchen counter. But Maddie noticed that the fiery glitter of irritation was gone from his eyes. Only a hint of sternness remained in his expression, an expression that was otherwise calm and composed.

"Would you mind putting on some coffee?" he asked. "I could use a cup."

"I will do it." Sofia moved quickly to comply with his request.

Eben nodded his thanks and continued through the kitchen, heading for the master bedroom to return the rifles to the locked gun cabinet.

Moments later he was back. The almost musical *chink* of his spurs marked each stride as he crossed to the coffeepot and poured himself a cup.

To Dillon's chagrin, Eben carried it to the table and sat down directly across from him. Taking off his hat, he hooked it on the back of an adjacent chair and combed the flatness from his hair with his fingers. An unruly lock fell across his forehead. Maddie smiled when she saw it, aware that Dillon's hair exhibited the same tendency to stray.

"Uncle Eben," Joy began. Unlike her brother, she suffered no uneasiness in his presence. "We keep asking Dillon where he went—"

"—and how come he didn't come back," Hope added.

"But he won't tell us," Joy declared, a frown of frustration creasing her forehead.

"Yeah, make him say," her sister urged.

Eben took a sip of his coffee, eyeing Dillon over the cup's rim. "Answer your sisters."

"I was eating, and you're not supposed to talk with your mouth full," Dillon asserted, taking refuge in good manners. Immediately he picked up his sandwich and took a big bite.

"You picked a convenient time to remember

your table manners," Eben observed dryly as Tad crawled over to his chair and pulled himself up.

Automatically Eben reached down and lifted the toddler onto his lap, then pushed his coffee cup back before Tad could make a grab for it.

"After you get that bite down," he told Dillon, "you can stop eating long enough to tell them what they want to know."

Stalling for time, Dillon chewed and chewed, half-hoping that if he delayed long enough, everyone might forget he was supposed to answer.

The tactic might have worked on the twins, who immediately switched their attention to Eben, bombarding him with questions, wanting to know everything from why it had taken him so long to find Dillon, to whether he'd seen any snakes. But Eben wasn't so easily sidetracked.

Yet, watching the interplay between Eben and the children, Maddie saw what would have been obvious to anyone looking on—this was a family.

Tad and the girls knew it. Only Dillon and Eben were unconvinced of it, both for the same reason—they were afraid.

In Dillon's case, he secretly craved the security that had been ripped from him when his parents died; Eben, on the other hand, was determined to maintain his independence and limit the degree of attachment he felt to anyone. His impatience and flashes of irritation were his armor to keep the children from getting too close; they worked on Dillon.

Dillon opened his mouth to take another bite

of sandwich before anyone noticed he had swallowed the last one. But Eben's quick eyes caught him in the act.

"Hold it right there," he warned. "You've got some answering to do."

"I forgot." Dillon lowered the sandwich, staring at it the whole time. "I hid up in those tall rocks," he told the girls, keeping his responses deliberately brief. "And I didn't come back because I didn't want to."

"Why didn't you want to come back?" Joy studied him with puzzlement.

"Because I wanted to be by myself, that's why," he retorted.

"How come you didn't answer when Sofia called?" Hope frowned.

"Because I didn't want her to know where I was. I was hiding, I told you," Dillon reminded her, exasperation creeping into his voice.

"Weren't you scared of being all alone?" Joy was wide-eyed at the prospect.

"Do you see what happens?" Dillon looked at Eben in a show of despair. "You answer one question, and they ask another. How am I supposed to eat?"

"You should have thought of that before you ran off," Eben replied without any hint of sympathy, but he took pity on Dillon just the same and asked the twins, "Do either of you know where Tad's drink cup is? I think he wants some milk."

Distracted from her interrogation of Dillon, Joy said, "It's by the sink."

"Sofia washed it," Hope explained.

"I'll get it." Joy jumped off her chair.

"No, I will," Hope protested and scrambled to beat her to the sink and Tad's drink cup.

While the twins fought over possession of the cup, Sofia retrieved the milk pitcher from the refrigerator, and Eben installed Tad in his high chair. Dillon was careful not to draw any further attention to himself and gave the whole of his own to eating the rest of his meal.

He did his best to drag out the task, but all too soon, as far as he was concerned, he had finished both his sandwich and the soup.

"You are full, yes?" Sofia gathered up the empty soup bowl and sandwich plate.

"Yes." Dillon nodded, then hesitated and stole a glance at Eben, encountering his watchful eyes. He had trouble meeting it squarely, but he tried. "Do I still have to do my homework?"

An eyebrow went up. "First you caused trouble at school," Eben began in a reasonable tone. "Then you rebelled here at home and ran away, worrying everybody when you didn't come back. Ramon, Luis, and I spent the better part of the day looking for you. And now you're asking whether you still have to make up your homework? Do you really think that's the kind of behavior that deserves to be rewarded?"

Dillon hung his head. "No."

"I'm glad to hear that." Eben studied him for a long second while Maddie tensed, ready to intervene if he came down on Dillon too hard.

Dillon had been through a lot today. Perhaps he didn't deserve to be rewarded, but he didn't need any further punishment.

"Since tonight is a special night," Eben stated, "you only have to finish one day's assignment."

Joy's ears perked up at his choice of words. "How come tonight's special?"

"Because"—Eben's glance sought Maddie, his eyes smiling—"Maddie is going to stay and have dinner with us."

Both twins rushed to her, cheering in approval. But Dillon didn't share their excitement over the news. Gloomy-eyed, he stared at his schoolbooks, then released a heavy sigh of resignation and reached for them.

"Not now." Eben stopped him, surprising both Dillon and Maddie. "We'll need to set the table for dinner in a little while. Since this is a special occasion, we want the table to look extra nice. You can do your homework after we eat," he told the boy. "In the meantime, put your school things on the counter."

For a moment Dillon could hardly believe his luck, then rushed to clear away his papers and books as if afraid Eben might change his mind. But the twins were captivated by something else Eben had said.

"Are you going to put flowers and candles on the table—" Joy began eagerly.

"—like Momma and Daddy used to do—"

"—when she fixed him a 'mantic dinner?"

Eben glanced at Maddie, his eyes darkening with

a look that was intimate, possessive, and oddly tender. Little ripples of response skidded up her spine.

"I can rustle up some candles, but I don't know about the flowers. I'm afraid it's the wrong time of year."

She felt that quick, familiar tug of desire snd smiled with it. "We can skip the flowers tonight."

Joy sucked in a breath, her expression exploding with the light of a sudden idea. She grabbed her sister and whispered something in her ear. Hope's face lit up, too.

As one, they raced from the kitchen.

"Where are they going?" Eben asked as Tad banged his empty drink cup on the high chair's tray and squealed long and loud.

"I don't know." Maddie went to lift Tad out of his high chair.

Eben gestured to Dillon. "Go see what your sisters are up to."

"How come I always got to do stuff?" Dillon complained, then winced in anticipation of Eben's censure.

Eben obliged him, eyes narrowed. "That's your job."

"I'll check on the girls," Maddie volunteered, explaining, "I have to go that way anyway. Tad's diaper needs changing."

"All right," Eben conceded after a slight hesitation. "Dillon can give me a hand with the chores instead."

Wisely Dillon didn't protest, but Maddie noticed he didn't show any enthusiasm either.

"Go easy on him," she murmured to Eben as she moved by him, fully aware he wouldn't welcome the advice. She saw his flicker of annoyance and added a soft, "Please."

As far as Eben was concerned, he had already been easy on the kid, but he held his silence until they were outside. With Maddie's gentle admonition still ringing in his ears, he unconsciously tempered his words.

"It's time you understood, Dillon, that there's a lot of responsibility that comes with being the oldest," he lectured. "That means you need to watch out for your sisters and baby brother—always set a good example for them."

"I know. But it isn't fair, though." Dillon grumbled, kicking at a rock.

"No, it isn't, but that's the way it is." Eben gave him a stern look. "Tad and your sisters look up to you because you are the oldest. They depend on you to be there for them—especially with your mom and dad gone now. You know as well as I do that your parents are counting on you to look after your brother and sisters."

Those words sounded all too familiar. Eben tried to think where he had heard them, then remembered his father had told him much the same thing—years ago.

Looking at Dillon, Eben recalled the awful heaviness he had felt back then—a heaviness all mixed up with an achy kind of loneliness and despair.

"You can do it," he said, but his father had told him that, too.

Eben remembered that he had desperately wanted to believe he could. But he had known it was too much—known he was too young. Worse than that, his father had never said three very important words. Words that might have made all the difference.

Eben said them now to Dillon. "I'll help you."

Dillon looked up, studying him with a mixture of skepticism and hope. "You will?"

"As much as I can," Eben promised. "But you have to do your share of looking out for them, too."

"I guess it won't be too bad," Dillon decided, and attempted a maturelike shrug. "I'm kinda used to it anyway."

"I've noticed," Eben replied, a dozen different scenes flashing through his mind—like the night he had found Dillon already on hand to comfort his sister after a bad dream had awakened her, or the time Dillon had sprung to his sisters' defense, ordering Eben not to shout at the twins.

Dillon glanced at him in surprise, then just as quickly looked away. He didn't say a word, but he walked a little straighter, a definite glow of pride in his eyes.

Chapter XV

Flames leaped and crackled over the stack of split logs in the fireplace. Their flickering light cast a warm glow over the living room. Eben settled back against the worn leather sofa and idly watched the fire's changing patterns, his long legs stretched in front of him.

From the hallway came the sound of footsteps. His head turned toward it, his glance seeking and finding Maddie's emerging figure. The firelight reached out to fall softly on the varied hues of gold in her sweater.

He liked the way the material clung, enhancing her straight posture and slender shape. Most of all, he liked the quickening of her expression when she saw him ensconced on the sofa.

"Are the twins finally asleep?" he asked, drawing his legs up to create a path for her between the coffee table and the sofa.

"They're in bed, but I'm afraid it's asking too much to think they are actually asleep." Her smile was wry with shared humor. "How about Tad?"

"Once I got the bottle in his mouth"—Eben snapped his fingers—"he was out like a light."

"Lucky you," she murmured in idle envy, and glanced at the light that spilled into the living room from the kitchen doorway. "Dillon is still hard at work, I see."

"He's almost done, I think," Eben said as Maddie sank gracefully onto the seat cushion beside him. Leaning forward, Eben picked up the two glasses on the end table and handed one to her. "I fixed us a drink."

"Wonderful." She took a sip of the watered scotch and made an approving sound in her throat. Her glance made a slow encompassing scan of the subtle intimacy of the darkened living room and the fire's yellow blaze. "This is nice. The perfect end to a perfect evening."

Eben smiled crookedly, automatically curving his arm around her shoulders, drawing her more snugly against his side. "Dinner was about as far from perfect as you can get."

"Not to me," Maddie declared, smiling at the memory of it. "It may not have been a quiet dinner—"

"Not with four yammering kids sitting in," he inserted dryly.

"—but we did have the requisite candlelight, flowers, and a white tablecloth," she reminded him.

"It wasn't white for long," Eben recalled, then arched a quizzical brow. "Where did the twins come up with those spindly stalks of fake roses?"

Maddie pressed a silencing finger to her lips and whispered, sharing the information in strictest confidence. "I'm not supposed to tell you. The roses are from their matching cloche hats. By the time I discovered what they were up to, they already had one of the roses off. I tried to convince them that we didn't need flowers, but they insisted that it wouldn't be a *'mantic* dinner without them," she said, copying their pronunciation of romantic.

"I don't know how *'mantic* it was, but it was definitely memorable," Eben declared on an amused sigh.

"Personally, I loved it. It beats the other kind, hands down." Maddie spoke from experience. Lately she'd had too many of the quiet, uneventful kind.

His sideways glance skimmed her face. "I guess you've known both kinds—the fancy and the absurd," he murmured, well aware it had been her late husband who had shown her the elegant dinners with an intimate table for two, sparkling crystal, and gleaming white linen.

"Yes." She met his gaze, aware that her late husband hadn't crossed her mind. She felt a fleeting rush of guilt, and refused to hang on to it. "Maybe I shouldn't say it, but this one is my favorite."

"You're crazy," he said, amazed and pleased.

Her eyes danced. "Probably."

But it was nonetheless true. Dinner that night had been silly and special—one to remember—and cherish. It had been years since she had felt needed and useful—but most of all, wanted and loved, especially by the man beside her.

Gazing into his eyes, she saw the warm glint of desire that had been in them from the moment she arrived. When he dipped his head toward hers, she moved to meet it. As their lips brushed, there was the stuttering bounce of a chair being pushed across the kitchen's tiled floor, followed by the slap of paper and books coming together.

With a small, wry grimace, Eben pulled back, murmuring, "Something tells me Dillon is about to walk in on us." Maddie laughed, soft and low in her throat. Eben studied her, an eyebrow arching. "What's so funny?"

"Us. Me," she said, then explained, "I feel like a schoolgirl, caught necking on the couch."

An answering smile deepened the corners of his mouth as Dillon sauntered into the living room, exhibiting a touch of his old cockiness while feigning nonchalance. Eben transferred his attention to him.

"Did you finish your homework?" he asked, already guessing the answer.

"All done. See?" Dillon pushed the papers toward him, then watched when Eben glanced through them, all the while struggling to appear unconcerned and indifferent.

"Good job, Dillon." Eben smiled in approval and handed them back.

Dillon ducked his head, hiding the sudden beam of pride, then tried to dismiss the importance of the compliment with an idle shrug. "It was easy. I'd already done most of this stuff at my other school."

"Then it shouldn't take you long to finish the rest of your homework tomorrow."

"I guess not." His shoulders moved again, filling the moment of hesitation. "Do I have to go to bed now?"

Eben nodded. "It's late."

"Yeah." Dillon nodded and sighed in resignation, then glanced at Eben and almost smiled. "Good night."

"Good night."

An on-looking Maddie heard the note of warmth in Eben's voice and observed the softening of his eyes, though the rest of his expression never altered.

"That was a rather startling transformation," she murmured once Dillon was out of earshot.

Eben gave her a slightly puzzled look; then the line between his brows cleared. "You mean, Dillon. I guess it is, in a way."

Actually she had been referring to both of them, but Maddie didn't bother to clarify that.

"You must have said something to him," she guessed. "The girls and I barely had the dinner table cleared off when he dragged out his schoolwork."

"We had a little man-to-man talk when we went to do chores." Even as he said it, Eben knew that wasn't an accurate description. It had been more like a boy-to-boy talk.

He pushed the memory aside, preferring not to think about it now, telling himself it was because Maddie was beside him—where he had always wanted her to be—and the children were in their rooms.

Setting his drink aside, he glanced sideways at her, his eyes full of amusement, challenge, and a building desire.

"What was that you were saying a minute ago about necking on the couch?" he murmured.

With a low, throaty laugh, she reached across him to place her glass on the end table beside his. He took advantage of the change in her position to draw her across his lap.

The laughter died on her lips as he bent to tactilely reexplore their softness. There was nothing furtive in the kiss, nothing desperate. It was the kind that said they had all the time in the world, that nothing had to be hurried or rushed.

She slid her fingers into his hair, reveling in the clean slickness of it. This was no dusty, sweaty cowboy with a half-day's growth of beard scratching her skin that now held her in this arms. He had showered and dressed for this date. A small thing, perhaps, but it was proof that he wanted tonight to mean something.

To Maddie, it meant everything.

Inside she felt as fluttery and excited as she had

when she was young and all these sensation were new. But added to it this time was a soaring lift of her heart that wasn't generated by the roaming caress of his hands or even his sensual nibbling of her neck.

Nothing mattered now, certainly not the mistakes of the past regardless of whether they had been hers or his. Here and now was all that counted, cradled in his strong arms and devoured by the amorous heat of his mouth.

She felt so gloriously happy she wanted to shout it to the world. And all because of him, and the second chance they had been given. Which was something she had never dared to hope would happen. Not after all this time, after all this heartache.

Emotion shivered through her like a living thing, all warm and glowing. With each breath she drew it strengthened.

"I love you, Eben," she murmured against his lips, unable to contain it any longer.

The minute she said it, Maddie realized that she loved him even more than before. Back then, she had been blinded by the emotion itself, convinced it automatically meant the "happily ever after" part of it would follow. Life had taught her better.

"You'd better love me." Eben lifted his head fractionally to gaze at her, his voice as thick and husky as her own. "Because I love you too much to let you go a second time."

"I'm glad, because I don't want to go." Her

fervent declaration brought his mouth down in a hard, driving kiss that sought to claim.

"We're getting married," he said, breathing heavily, and her heart soared, her lips parting on the quick words of agreement. But it all died when he added, "Just as soon as I get the ranch paid off."

"No," she said without emotion, hiding the leap of fury and deep hurt.

"What?" Surprise and disbelief momentarily froze him.

Taking advantage of it, Maddie twisted out of his arms and sat up.

"You heard me," she told him. "We either get married immediately or we don't get married at all."

"Wait a minute—"

"No, I won't wait." She stood up, needing to put distance between them before she was tempted by his nearness.

"All we're talking about here is a month!" Eben came to his feet as well, eyes blazing.

"I wouldn't care if it were only a week! I'm not waiting."

"What kind of a fool attitude is that?"

"It's my fool attitude." Maddie turned on him, lashing out in a mix of outrage and pain. "Why did I ever think you had changed even a little, MacCallister? You never listened to one thing I said to you, did you?"

"Of course, I listened," he said. "Before, you

thought I didn't love you when I asked you to wait. Now you know better.''

"Tell me something—what happens if you can't come up with the money?" she challenged. "What happens if you lose the ranch?"

"I'll come up with it," he declared. "Have some faith in me."

"Why should I?" she fired back. "You don't have any faith in me!"

"That isn't true—"

"Isn't it?" she challenged. "How many times do I have to tell you that it's you I want to marry? I don't care about this ranch."

"I do! It's a part of me—a part of who and what I am. I have spent my whole life scratching and clawing, going without and saving every dime I could to keep this place—and now I'm supposed to give it up because *you* don't care about it?!"

"I never said that," she protested angrily, then paused, sensing the futility of further argument.

She had the funds to write a check that very moment to pay off the ranch, but Eben would never accept the money from her—just as he would never marry her if he lost the ranch. She was sure of that.

Part of it was due to his stubborn male pride, but the majority of it came from the fact that his sense of self-worth was tied up in the ranch. Looking at him, Maddie experienced a host of conflicting emotions—pity, anger, sorrow, bitterness—and a love that wouldn't die, even now.

"I never realized until this moment how very much like your father you are," she said sadly.

"That is a lie," he denied with vehemence.

"I wish it were." Sorrow crept into her voice, the sorrow of regret. "But it isn't. Just like him, you believe that no one could care about you unless you have things. In your father's case, he spent money he didn't have, buying presents and picking up someone else's tab, while you scrimp and save, trying to hold on to it and amass enough money to own this ranch outright. Not because you want to be out of debt, but because you want people to look at you with respect and admiration—something you're convinced they will never do unless the ranch is yours. Things aren't important, Eben. People are."

His face was hard stone and his eyes were cold as ice chips. "Are you finished?"

She looked at him for a long second. "No, Eben. We are."

Fighting tears, Maddie turned and walked out of the house.

Eben made no move to follow her. When the door clicked shut behind her, he swung about and faced the fire, all icy rage. From the hallway came the whisper of bare feet on the floor. His gaze cut to the source of it, locking on a pajama-clad Dillon, poised in the opening.

"You're supposed to be in bed," Eben snapped.

Dillon ducked his head in guilty acknowledgment. "I know, but—are you gonna lose the ranch?"

"No." The answer came back hard and fast.

Then, for no reason that Eben could explain, he added, "Not if I can help it."

"We'd have to move, wouldn't we?" Dillon surmised. "That's why you've been so worried about money."

"We aren't moving, and we aren't losing this ranch. Maddie doesn't know what she was talking about. Just forget about it and go back to bed," he ordered, unable to temper the sharpness in his voice.

After a second's hesitation, Dillon dropped his gaze and made the slow walk back to his room. Alone again, Eben grabbed the poker and stabbed at the blazing logs, scattering them to let the fire die.

But the fire Maddie had started wouldn't be so easily extinguished. He felt the pain of it slashing through him like a thousand razor cuts.

She was wrong. Dead wrong.

He had been a fool to let her back into his life and open himself up to being hurt again. He had proposed and received a lecture for an answer when all he had wanted was her understanding and support.

With the snap and pop of a dying fire behind him, Eben snatched up his drink glass and downed a swallow of scotch. But its fiery burn did little to ease the tearing pain inside.

His fingers tightened on the glass, whitening with the pressure he put on them. As he started to hurl his drink at the fire's glowing embers, he saw Dillon coming out of his room, carrying a small tin box.

"I thought I told you to go to bed," he growled, needing privacy to nurse his deep wounds.

Avoiding his eyes, Dillon walked straight to the coffee table and placed the tin box on top of it.

"You can have this," he said and pried off the box's snug-fitting lid, revealing a bunch of coins and crumpled bills. "There's twenty-one dollars and forty-four cents here. I was gonna use it to buy a present for my sisters, but . . . they like it here. They wouldn't want to move."

Thunderstruck, Eben stared at the contents of the tin box, frozen by the memory of all the times he had handed his precious savings over to his father to pay some bill that was owed.

"I don't want your money," he declared half-angrily.

Dillon looked up, his eyes gentle with understanding. "It's okay. You can pay it back, Uncle Eben. That's what Mom and Dad did sometimes when they couldn't come up with all the rent money." He smiled, looking quite proud of himself. "Good night."

It was that proud and pleased look on Dillon's face that stopped Eben from shoving the tin money box back into his hands. Once he had given just as selflessly, warmed by the feeling his contribution was important. That was long before he realized that his father would more than likely squander it on something else.

He didn't want the money. He didn't need it. But he didn't know how to give it back without hurting the boy's feelings.

There had to be a way. But he couldn't think. That was Maddie's fault.

The kid believed in him. Trusted him. Why couldn't she?

Angry, frustrated, and hurting, Eben drank down the last of the scotch, then stared into his empty glass. He felt the urge to get falling-down drunk. Before it could become more than an urge, his glance fell once again on Dillon's tin money box.

After a second's hesitation, he set the glass down long enough to put the lid back on the metal box, then carried it and the empty glass into the kitchen. The glass he put in the sink, and the box he set on the countertop, pried off its lid, and dumped out the money.

Under no circumstances was he going to use a dime of it. At some point, later on, he'd give it back to Dillon. Until then he would stick it in an envelope and put it away for safekeeping.

Eben pulled open the catch-all drawer near the telephone and rummaged through its assortment of receipt books, bill of sale forms, blank stationery, postage stamps, pens, and pads in search of an empty envelope. But the first one he uncovered was the envelope addressed to him, the one with the letter inside that Carla had written to him.

Recognizing it, he started to impatiently shove it aside, but something stopped him. Maybe it was Maddie's accusation that he was like his father. Maybe it was his inability to summon the old resentment toward his sister that he had once felt so strongly. Or maybe it was Dillon giving him this money, taking him back to his own childhood.

Eben couldn't explain his reason for taking the envelope out of the drawer and removing the handwritten letter from it. He wasn't even sure it was a conscious decision.

But it was there, unfolded in his hands, and he read again that same opening line:

Dear Eben,

I hope you never have to read this letter, but if you do, then you know why I have written it.

You see, I know our children couldn't be in better hands than yours, Eben. You were the best big brother a girl could have. And you didn't do too bad being a mother and father to me, either.

I wish I was saying this to you face to face. I've called a dozen times and hung up before you could answer. I've written even more letters and tore them all up.

I had such big dreams when I left the ranch, Eben. When I took the money, I was certain it would be only a matter of months before I'd be able to pay you back with interest—

That remembered anger curled through him at the mention of the money. His fingers dug into the paper as he came close to wadding the letter up, shoving it back in its envelope, and throwing both in the trash. With an effort, Eben forced himself to read on.

—but it turned out that I wasn't the next Patsy Cline or Reba McEntire. I wasn't going to show up one day in a shiny new Cadillac and present you with enough money to pay the ranch off.

To be honest, I think I knew it wasn't going to happen a couple months after I got to Nashville. But I refused to give up. I kept knocking on doors and singing every chance I had.

I got that from you, Eben—the courage to chase my dream and the determination to stick with it even when things were going bad, even when everyone else was telling me to give it up. But I kept remembering how you fought to keep the ranch, how hard you worked and how much you sacrificed. Every time I wanted to curl up in a corner and feel sorry for myself, I thought about you and tried again—

You crazy little fool, Eben thought.

Yet, for the first time he understood some of the things that had driven her. And for the first time, he felt a kind of reluctant admiration for his sister.

I didn't succeed, but I guess you've figured that out by now. I'm sorry I took the money, Eben, but I'm not sorry I went to Nashville, because that was where I met Nolan Rogers, my husband. You would like him, Eben. He's a wonderful man and a fabulous musician—and a terrific father to the kids. He's as bad as I am—he can't stand being apart from them for more than a day. In fact, two days after we brought Dillon home from the hospital, Nolan took a job in Branson so he could be home every night instead of somewhere on the road, doing a bunch of one-night stands.

By now, I guess, you've already met the children. I wish I could be there. I'm not worried about the twins. Hope and Joy love everything and everyone. Ever since I told them I grew up on a ranch, they have been after us to come visit. Be warned, Eben, they'll probably turn out to be as horse-crazy as I was. I know the girls can be a handful, but they are such a wonderful handful. And I know that no matter what happens, they'll bounce back from it quickly. That's the blessing of being a twin, I suppose—they always have each other.

As for Dillon—oh, Eben, he reminds me so much of you. He's such a little man for his age, so quick to assume responsibility. You should see the way he looks after the girls, just as you did for me. It worries me sometimes that he is too serious, more interested in solving someone else's problems than playing with other kids his age.

I can't tell you much about the new baby, except that the doctor told us we're going to have another boy. A happy, healthy one, I hope.

Something happens when you have children, Eben. Maybe you've already found that out. I hope so. Because you'll know what I'm talking about when I say that having children changes you. You don't spend nearly as much time thinking about yourself and what you want. Suddenly you're responsible for another human being. In this case, four of them.

You start thinking about what will happen to

*them if something happens to you. Or worse yet, if
something happens to both you and your spouse—*

The handwriting changed subtly. The pen
strokes appeared firmer, tighter, as if the words
were more carefully thought out before they were
transferred to paper.

*—Maybe this isn't fair of me, Eben, when I owe
you so much already. And I don't mean just the
money. Nolan and I have talked about naming one
of our friends as the children's guardian if anything
should happen to us. They are good people, but—
I know the kind of home they would have with you.
It's the kind I would want for them.*

*I hope by the time you read this that we have been
able to save enough money to pay back what I took.
But, if we haven't, I hope you understand that I'm
giving you something much more precious to me—
my children.*

Love them, Eben, as you loved me.

                              Your loving sister,
                              Carla

He started at her signature a long, long time,
fighting a tightness in his throat. Slowly and carefully, he folded the letter and slid it back in its
envelope. But he didn't put it away. Instead he
held it, his eyes watering.

Pride—they'd both had too much of it.

That was something Maddie still didn't understand.

Chapter XVI

The two-year-old chestnut gelding pricked its ears at the solitary cow in the corral. Eben walked the young horse to it. With a snort and a dip of the head, the cow swung away and trotted off, staying close to the fence. Eben let the horse stop and turn with the cow, staying parallel with it.

To the horse, this was a game. To Eben, it was a training session, with the cow doing most of the instructing, teaching the horse the necessities of running stops and rollbacks.

Eben sat back, letting instinct and reflex take over. Thought wasn't required, which was just as well. He hadn't been able to get Maddie off his mind for the last three days.

There was a feeling of emptiness inside he couldn't

seem to shake no matter how much he tried to tell himself he didn't need her, that he could get along just fine without her. He'd done it before and he could do it again. Then he would think about Carla's letter and the ache would start all over again.

Braking to a stop, the cow squared around to face the horse and rider. For a moment, the horse and cow were eye to eye, locked in a staring contest, mucles bunched, ready for the next move. The chestnut gelding swiveled an ear, catching the squeak and clatter of the little red wagon Dillon pulled behind him.

Eben shot an identifying glance at the boy and the small caravan that followed him. The twins skipped alongside the wagon, chattering away to Sofia. Tad was tucked in the crook of her arm.

A bucket bounced and rattled inside the bed of the toy wagon. Dillon dragged something in his other hand, but at this distance, Eben couldn't make out what it was as the unusual cavalcade trooped out of sight.

Briefly he puzzled over the scene, then dismissed it as the cow jumped to the right and the chestnut leaped after it. Whatever those kids were up to, Sofia was with them. There wasn't much chance they would come to any harm.

Unbidden came the thought that Maddie would have gone after them, found out where they were going and why.

Eben clamped his jaws together, angered that she had crossed his mind again. She had all kinds of leisure time to do such things. He had work to do, and he'd already lost enough time at it.

Work. It's always work with you, isn't it? came the echo of her taunting words.

The memory of them was like a spur, goading him into action just to prove she was wrong about him. At the same time, Eben was furious with himself for thinking he needed to prove anything to anyone. Carla had trusted him; that was enough.

Yet he kept an eye out, watching for Sofia and the children to return. But there was no sign of them when he finished the chestnut's training session.

Nagged by their absence, Eben took a break against his better judgment. As he moved away from the corral, one of the twins ran into view and raced straight to the house. The back door slammed shut behind her. He lengthened his stride, determined to find out what was going on.

Before he reached the house, the girl ran out of it, clutching a bulky jacket tightly to her. Eben frowned, conscious of the noonday sun shining high and hot.

"What are you doing with that coat?" he called.

A freckle-nosed Joy slowed her steps long enough to explain, "Dillon needs it to keep from getting poked."

The puzzled furrow between his brows deepened. "Poked with what?"

"The cactus," she replied, as if the answer was obvious, then took off.

Thoroughly confused, Eben went after her,

rounding the tall clump of palo verde only a few steps behind her. He stopped short, his glance quickening over the scene.

In the palo verde's scant shade, Sofia shifted uneasily, one hand automatically patting Tad's back. Hope crouched beside the red wagon, her attention centered on a sweaty and dust-streaked Dillon.

He had on an old pair of Eben's work gloves that came halfway up his forearms. A shovel lay near his feet, not far from the shallow hole that had been dug in the desert's sandy soil.

But it was the low-growing, treelike cactus, commonly called a teddy bear cholla, lying on the ground that claimed Eben's attention. Its roots were half dug out and half chopped.

"What's going on here?" he asked in confusion.

Dillon spared him a glance as he took off the gloves in order to put on the jacket. "I'm having trouble getting this cactus in the bucket. I keep getting poked."

"What do you want with the cactus in the first place?" Eben frowned.

"It's our birthday present," Joy replied, aglow with pleasure.

"Your birthday present?" Eben struggled to make sense of this.

"Yeah," Dillon confirmed, proud and a little self-conscious. "You see, I knew what they wanted more than anything was a Christmas tree. And I knew you didn't have the money to get one. So, I figured I could get 'em a cactus for a Christmas tree. After all, we're living in the desert," he concluded, convinced it made perfect sense.

"That's got awful sharp spines on it for a Christmas tree," Eben pointed out.

"That's okay," Joy assured him.

"Jesus wore a crown of thorns," Hope reminded him.

"Not when He was a baby, though," Eben countered while he privately marveled at her reasoning.

"I figured I could get some scissors and cut 'em off." Dillon shrugged into his jacket and reached for the gloves. "First, though, I got to get it to the house."

Eben's first impulse was to tell Dillon to forget it, that there was no way he was going to allow him to bring that cactus into the house.

Before he could give voice to it, Joy spoke up, all starry-eyed, "Isn't it beautiful, Uncle Eben?"

Hope nodded in quick affirmation. "It's the bestest Christmas tree—"

"—in the whole world."

Their fervency stopped him. There were a dozen good, solid reasons why a cactus was a bad idea. But he couldn't get a single one of them out of his mouth. In his mind, he could see Carla laughing and applauding their choice. It was just the kind of thing she would have done.

"The way you're going at that, you'll never get that cactus in the bucket," he informed Dillon, stepping in. "Go get Ramon. Tell him to get that heavy tarp from the barn and bring it here."

A little more than an hour later, the many-branched cactus stood in the living room, the worst of its barbed spines singed off with an old butane torch Eben had.

It should have looked strange and out of place with its blackened stalk and charred edges. But to Eben's eye, it seemed to fit with the room's white-plastered walls, hand-hewn vegas, and Indian rugs. It secretly pleased him.

The twins were overjoyed with their *tree* as they crowded around Dillon, bubbling with thanks. A little embarrassed, he pushed them away.

"Uncle Eben and Ramon helped, too," he reminded them.

Eben barely had time to brace himself before the girls launched themselves at him, hugging his legs and gushing their thanks while a grinning Ramon looked on. Like Dillon, Eben felt awkward and a little uncomfortable.

"You're welcome, but let's not get carried away with this," he said with an emotional gruffness that deterred neither twin.

Joy tilted her head all the way back to look up at him, both arms still wrapped around his leg. "I'll bet nobody else—"

"—in the whole world—" Hope continued, her earnest voice stressing the phrase.

"—has got a tree—"

"—like ours."

Eben thought that was a safe bet. "It's one of a kind, all right."

"We knew you'd get us a Christmas tree," Joy told him, at last letting go of his leg.

" 'Cause we asked God to talk to you about it."

"And He did," they said in unison.

As one, both girls turned to admire their tree, but it was Joy who declared, "Now we got a place to put our presents."

Presents. With a kick of shock, Eben realized this was Christmas Eve. It put an edge on his nerves, gripped them with a compelling sense of urgency.

"Come on, Hope." Joy grabbed her sister's hand and pulled her toward the hallway. "Let's go get the decorations."

"No!" Eben called them back in a voice that was sharp and quick. Startled, they swung back to face him. "I have to go into town for a little bit," he continued in a more reasonable tone. "While I'm gone, I don't want any of you going near that cactus. It still has some spines on it, and I don't want you getting hurt. We'll decorate it tonight."

"All of us?" Joy asked.

"Yes, all of us," he confirmed.

Her smile grew wide. "Just like a real family, huh?"

"Yeah," Eben replied, much more softly.

With the excitement of decorating the cactus-tree and the anticipation of Christmas morning and a birthday celebration, it took a while for the twins to wind down enough to willingly crawl into bed. Eben heard them whispering to each other as he left the room, pulling the door partway shut behind him.

Moving quietly, he went down the hall and looked in on Dillon. He was already in bed, the blankets pulled high around him. When the light spilled through the open doorway, Dillon rolled over, sober-faced and subdued.

"Are you going to bed now?" Dillon asked.

Eben shook his head. "I'm going to clean up the mess in the living room first."

"Do you want me to help?"

"No, I want you to go to sleep."

Dillon stared at the covers for a moment, then lifted his gaze to Eben again. "They think there's gonna be presents under the tree in the morning. They're too young to understand about not having money."

His words had the ring of an adult, but his eyes belonged to a boy.

"There'll be some presents," Eben told him, catching that flicker of uncertainty that doubted Christmas morning would hold any wonder for him. "Good night, Dillon."

Haunted by the look in Dillon's eyes, Eben went back to the living room and made his way through the opened boxes of Christmas decorations, few of them used, scattered around the floor. He stopped when he reached the cactus-turned-Christmas tree.

Chains of crudely cut paper rings looped its branches, sharing the space with a double strand of twinkling lights. Here and there, an ornament hung off it, almost lost in the waterfall of silver tinsel that draped it. Balanced precariously atop its uppermost branch was a cardboard star covered with aluminum foil. At its base, a striped serape covered the bucket of desert sand that it held it erect.

It had been years since there had been a Christmas tree in this house. The longer Eben looked at this odd one, the more beautiful it seemed.

Which was crazy. The thing bordered on ridiculous.

Not to the twins, though, he thought, remembering the joy that had been on their faces while it was being decorated. And not to Carla—she would have wholeheartedly approved of it.

In that moment, he knew Maddie was definitely wrong; things were important.

Galvanized by that realization, Eben picked up the box at his feet and went to work.

The harsh, persistent jangle of the telephone finally penetrated through the layers of deep sleep, rousing Maddie. She rolled over with a groan and peered at the digital clock on her nightstand.

Four in the morning.

She nearly buried her head under the pillow, convinced it was a wrong number. But it was the thought of the phone continuing to ring that had her groping for the receiver.

"H'lo," she mumbled in a voice foggy with sleep.

"Maddie, it's Eben." The familiar sound of his voice snapped her awake, her heart lifting, then just as quickly sinking to the depths.

"Do you know what time it is?" she said sharply.

"Yes. I'm sorry about that, but—it's the kids."
Somewhere in the background, Tad was screaming
his head off. "Something's happened. Can you
come over right away?"

She hardened herself against the tug of his voice,
and the background cries. "No."

"Maddie, please. I need you—the kids need
you," he hastily corrected himself. "Hurry."

A fresh scream of pain was cut off in midcry by
the disconnecting click of the telephone. Maddie
stared at the receiver in her hand, a sick, scared
feeling rising from the pit of her stomach. She
knew Eben MacCallister. After their last argument,
he would have turned to her for help only if she
was the last possible resort.

Something had to be terribly wrong.

She flew out of bed and raced to the closet,
grabbing a pair of jeans off their hanger and a
sweater off the shelf. Barely five minutes after the
phone call, Maddie slid behind the wheel of the
Jeep Cherokee.

At that hour of the morning, the roads were
virtually empty. She scanned them constantly, half-
expecting to meet an ambulance along the way.

When she finally made the turn onto the ranch
lane, she noticed the unusual glow in the distance.
Her first thought was a fire, but the light stayed
steady, without that wavering leap of flames.

The closer Maddie got to the ranch house, the
stronger and more distinctive the light became,
until she saw it didn't come from a single light,
but hundreds of lights strung all over the house,

outlining the eaves and the ramada's roof, twisting around the supporting posts. Reds, yellows, greens, blues—every color of Christmas.

Dazed and confused, she stared at the dazzling display, automatically braking the car to a stop. As she stepped out of the Cherokee, the twins burst from the house, pulling on coats over their pajamas as they raced to greet her.

"You came! You came," they chorused, jumping up and down around her. "He said you would."

Maddie grabbed the shoulders of the closest one. "Are you all right? What happened?"

Off to the side, Joy giggled. "We tricked you."

"And Tad got real mad, too," Hope told her, regret glimmering in her eyes.

"—'Cause we had to pinch him hard—"

"—to make him scream."

After the first wave of relief came anger. "This was all a trick?!"

Joy nodded in affirmation, unconcerned by the sudden, dark blaze in Maddie's eyes. "We wanted you to come see all the lights."

"Santa did it," Hope explained, waving a hand at the brightly lit house as Eben stepped out of it. Tad was bundled in his arms, sucking contentedly on a bottle.

"He did, did he?" Maddie turned, fixing a glaring look on Eben.

"Merry Christmas, Maddie." The husky caress of his voice momentarily rattled her, especially when it was accompanied by a slow, warm smile designed to melt any resistance.

Fortunately Joy distracted her before she actually succumbed to the charm of it. "We heard the reindeer on the roof, Maddie."

"They were prancing and pawing just like in the story," Hope added excitedly.

"When Uncle Eben went outside to look—"

"—he saw 'em fly away."

"Did he tell you that?" Maddie asked in disbelief, shooting another dubious glance at Eben.

"Uh-huh." Joy nodded vigorously. "And Santa left us presents, too."

"We got cowboy boots."

"See." Joy pulled up a pajama leg to show her.

"And Dillon got a cowboy hat." Hope pointed to her brother, who had come outside to stand next to Eben, a straw Stetson pushed to the back of his tousled hair.

"There's a present inside for you, Maddie," Dillon told her.

"Yeah." Joy caught her hand and pulled her toward the door. "You gotta come open it."

"Yeah, Maddie," Eben echoed her words, his smile deepening. "You gotta come open it."

She could hardly refuse, not without hurting the children's feelings. Eben had not only guessed that, but she suspected he had also counted on it.

Fuming inwardly, Maddie allowed herself to be drawn into the house. She stopped two feet inside the living room, too angry to notice the unusual Christmas tree by the fireplace. Eben paused beside her, looking much too complacent as the twins raced to fetch her present.

"It isn't right to use the children like this, Eben," Maddie declared in a voice pitched for his ears alone.

"You wouldn't have come otherwise," he replied in the same low undertone. "And heaven knows, I've done worse things."

"I'm glad you realize that," she murmured stiffly.

"I realized a good many things lately. For instance—" He leveled his gaze at her, the smoldering intensity of it tripping her pulse. "I realized earlier tonight that you were wrong. At least, you were partly wrong. Things are important—because people are important."

"I don't agree." She worked to hold on to her coolness.

"Look at those kids, their faces, and tell me the tree and all the lights and presents weren't important."

"They are only children," Maddie protested. "What do you expect, MacCallister?"

"You aren't giving them enough credit, Maddie. Children always know when things come from the heart—like that cactus tree Dillon dug up for the girls because he knew how desperately they wanted a Christmas tree this year."

Startled, she took a second look at the unusually shaped tree, its true identity half-hidden by draping tinsel and fat paper chains. Then Dillon ran up to her.

"Here's your present, Maddie." He held out a

white envelope with her name written in red pencil on the front of it.

"Thank you." Taking it, she fingered it briefly, then paused as the twins reclaimed her attention, clumping across the floor in their new boots.

"See what else Santa left us, Maddie."

Hope waved a cereal box. "We each got some Fwuit Loops—"

"—and a bag of Oreos—"

"—and a frozen pizza—"

"—but the pizzas are in the 'frigerator already—"

"—else they'll melt."

Dillon broke in impatiently. "Aren't you going to open your present, Maddie?"

"Yeah, I want to—"

"—see what it is," Hope urged.

"Me, too." Eben grinned.

Unaccountably nervous, Maddie ripped open the envelope, expecting to find a handmade card or bookmark inside it. Her mouth opened in a small *o* of surprise when she saw a gold ring crowned with a single diamond, gleaming from one corner inside the envelope.

"What is it, Maddie?" Joy teetered on her toes, straining to see.

"Can we see?" Hope crowded closer.

"Yes, can we see?" Eben took the envelope from her suddenly numb fingers, then turned sideways and practically dumped the baby in her arms. "You hold Tad for a minute," he said and reached into the envelope. ''Well, well, well, it's a ring. I wonder if it fits.''

When he caught hold of her left hand, Maddie tried to pull it away. ''If this is some new trick of yours, MacCallister,'' she began, then stopped when she heard the betraying waver in her voice. She tried again. ''I meant what I said the other night. Just because you give me a ring this time, that doesn't change anything. I still won't wait.''

''I know.'' He slipped it onto her ring finger. ''This was my mother's ring. I always planned to give it to you on our wedding day.''

Joy gasped, her eyes rounding. ''Are you going to marry Maddie, Uncle Eben?''

''Right after breakfast,'' he told them, his eyes on Maddie the whole time. ''I thought we could all pile into Maddie's car and drive down to Mexico. We'll probably have to do some searching to find somebody to marry us, but I like the idea of a Christmas wedding. How does that sound to you, Maddie?'' he asked, the timbre of his voice changing to something tender and intimate.

''What about the ranch?'' she countered, still half-afraid to believe this.

''Things are important, Maddie,'' he repeated. ''Things like a ring and a marriage license.''

''No, seriously, Eben. What are you going to do?''

There was a slight lift to his shoulders. ''If I can't come up with all the money, then I'll borrow some from you. But,'' he stressed, ''it will be a loan. I'll pay it back, every dime of it.''

"Yes," she murmured, her breath catching somewhere between a laugh and a sob.

More words weren't necessary as Eben gathered both Maddie and Tad into his arms. But it was only Maddie he kissed while the twins danced around them, and succeeded in drawing Dillon into their circle.

None of them said it, but all of them knew that while Christmas was about hope and joy, most of all it was about love.

Please turn the page for a preview of

GREEN CALDER GRASS by Janet Dailey.

A June 2003 paperback release
from Zebra Books.

Chapter One

The grass ocean rippled gold under a strong summer sun. The dirt track that cut a straight line through the heart of it was a small portion of the mile upon mile of private roads that crisscrossed the ranching empire of the Calder Cattle Company, better known in Montana as the Triple C.

It was a land that could be bountiful or brutal, a land that bent to no man's will, a land that weeded out the weak and faint of heart, tolerating only the strong.

No one knew that better than Chase Benteen Calder, the current patriarch of the Triple C and a direct descendant of the first Calder, his namesake, who had laid claim to nearly six hundred square miles of this grassland. Its size was never something

Chase Calder bragged about; the way he looked at it, when you were the biggest, everybody already knew it, and if they didn't, they would soon be told. And the knowledge would carry more weight if he wasn't the one doing the telling.

To a few, the enormity of the Triple C was a thing of rancor. The events of recent weeks were proof of that. The freshness of that memory accounted for the hint of grimness in his expression as Chase drove the ranch pickup along the hard-packed road, a rooster tail of dust pluming behind it. But the past wasn't something Chase allowed his mind to dwell on. Running an operation this size required a man's full attention. Even the smallest detail had a way of getting big if ignored. This land and a long life had taught him that if nothing else.

Which was likely why his sharp eyes spotted the sagging wire caused by a tilting fence post. Chase braked the truck to a stop, but not before the pickup clattered over a metal cattle guard. He shifted into reverse, backed up to the cattle guard, stopped, and switched off the engine.

The full force of the sun's rays beat down on him as Chase stepped out of the truck, older and heavier but still a rugged and powerfully built man.

The sixty-plus years he carried had taken some of the spring from his step, added a heavy dose of gray to his hair, and grooved deeper creases into the sun-leathered skin around his eyes and mouth, giving a crustiness to his face, but it hadn't diminished the mark of authority stamped on his raw-boned features.

Reaching back inside the truck, Chase grabbed a pair of tough leather work gloves off the seat and headed toward the section of the sagging fence six posts from the road. Never once did it occur to Chase to send one of the ranch hands back to fix the problem. With distances being what they were on the Triple C, that was the quickest way of turning a fifteen-minute job into a two-hour one.

With each stride he took, the brittle, sun-cured grass crackled under foot. Its stalks were short and curly, matting close to the ground—native buffalo grass, drought-tolerant and highly nutritious, the kind of feed that put weight on cattle and was a mainstay of the Triple C's century of success.

The minute his gloved hands closed around the post in question, it dipped drunkenly under the pressure. The three spaced strands of tightly strung barbed wire were clearly the only thing keeping it upright at all. Chase kicked away the matted grass at the base and saw that the wood had rotted at ground level.

This was one fence repair that wouldn't be a fifteen-minute fix. Chase glanced toward the pickup parked on the road. There was a time when he would have carried steel fence posts and a roll of wire along with other sundry items piled in the truck bed. But on this occasion, there was only a toolbox.

Chase didn't waste time with regret for the lack of a spare post. Instead he ran an inspecting glance along the rest of the fence, following its steady march over the rolling grassland until it thinned into a single line. In that one, cursory observation, he noticed three more places where the fence curved out of its straight line. If three could be spotted with the naked eye, there were undoubtedly more. It didn't surprise him. Fence mending was one of those never-ending jobs every rancher faced.

When he turned to retrace his steps to the pickup, he caught the distant drone of another vehicle. Automatically Chase scanned the narrow road in both directions without finding a vehicle in sight. But one was approaching, of that he had no doubt.

It was the huge sweep of sky that gave the illusion of flatness to the land beneath it. In reality the terrain was riven with coulees and shallow hollows, all of them hidden from view with the same ease that an ocean conceals its swales and troughs.

By the time Chase reached his truck, another ranch pickup had roared into view, coming from the west. Chase waited by the cab door, watching as the other vehicle slowed perceptibly then rolled to a stop behind Chase's pickup. The trailing dust cloud swept forward, briefly enveloping both vehicles before settling to a low fog.

Squinting against the sting of dust particles, Chase recognized the short, squatly built man behind the wheel as Stumpy Niles, a contemporary of his and the father of Chase's daughter-in-law.

Chase lifted a hand in greeting and headed toward the truck.

Stumpy promptly rolled down the driver's side window and stuck his head out. "What's the problem, Chase?"

"Have you got a spare fence post in your truck? We have a wooden one that's rotted through."

"Got it handled." Stumpy scrambled out of the truck and moved toward the tailgate with short, choppy strides. "Can't say I'm surprised. Just about all them old wood posts have started rottin'. It's gonna be one long, endless job replacin' 'em."

And expensive, too, Chase thought to himself, and pitched in to help the shorter man haul the steel post as well as a posthole jobber out of the truck's rear bed. "I don't see where we have much choice. It's got to be done."

"I know." Already sweating profusely in the hot summer sun, Stumpy paused to drag a handkerchief from his pocket and mop the perspiration from his round, red face. "It ain't gonna be an easy job. The ground's as hard as granite. It's been nearly forty years since we've had such a dry spring. I'll bet we didn't get much more than an inch of moisture in all the South Branch section."

"It wasn't much better anywhere else on the ranch." Like Stumpy, Chase was remembering the last prolonged dry spell the ranch had endured.

Stumpy was one of the cadre of ranch hands who, like Chase, had been born on the Triple C. All were descended from cowhands who had trailed that original herd of longhorn cattle north, then stayed on to work for the first Calder. That kind of deep-seated loyalty was a throwback to the old days when a cowboy rode for the brand, right or wrong, through times of plenty and time of lean. To an outsider, this born-and-bred core of riders gave an almost feudal quality to the Triple C.

Chase shortened his stride to walk alongside Stumpy as the pair tracked through the grass to the sagging post. "Headed for The Homestead, were you?" Stumpy guessed, referring to the towering, two-story structure that was the Calder family home, erected on the site of the ranch's original homestead.

Chase nodded. "But only long enough to clean up before I head into Blue Moon. I'm supposed to meet Ty and Jessy for supper as soon as they're through at the clinic."

"The clinic." Stumpy stopped short. "Jessy's all right, isn't she?"

"She's fine." Smiling, Chase understood Stumpy's fatherly concern. "Ty was the one in for a checkup."

Stumpy shook his head at himself and continued toward the rotted post. "It's them twins she's fixin' to have. It's got me as nervous as a long-tailed cat in a roomful of rockin' chairs. There's no history of twins bein' born in either side of our family. Or at least none that Judy and me know about," he said, referring to his wife.

"It's a first for the Calder side, too." Chase looked on while Stumpy set about digging a hole with the jobber. "Although I can't speak for the O'Rourke half."

The comment was an oblique reference to his late wife Maggie O'Rourke. Even now, so many years after her death, he rarely mentioned her by name and only among the family. This belief that grief was a private thing was one of many codes of the Old West that continued to hold sway in the modern West, especially in Triple C country.

"Twins," Stumpy murmured to himself, then grunted from the impact of the twin blades stabbing into the hard dry ground. He scissored the handles together to pick up the first scoop of soil, then reversed the procedure to dump it to one side. "Look at that," he complained. "The top two inches is nothin' but powder. It's dry, I tell you. Dry." It was a simple observation that was quickly forgotten as he reverted to his original topic. "According to that ultrasound thing the doctor did, it's gonna be boys."

That was news to Chase. "I understood the doctor was only positive about one."

"Mark my words, they'll be boys," Stumpy declared with certainty, then chuckled. "If they take after their mother, she's gonna have her hands full. They'll be a pair of hell-raisers, I'll wager— into everything the minute you turn your back. Why, from the first minute Jessy started crawlin', she was out the door and into the horse pens. She dealt her mama fits. If you ask me, it's only right that she gets back some of her own." He glanced at Chase and winked. "It's for sure you won't be

complaining anymore about The Homestead bein'
too quiet since Cat got married and moved out.
By the way, how's the little man doin' since . . .
things quieted down?''

The thwarted kidnapping of his five-year-old
grandson Quint was another topic to be avoided
from now on. But Chase knew it had left him three
times as wary of those outside the Calder circle.
After all, not only had the security of his home
been breached, but Calder blood had been spilled
as well.

"Kids are pretty resilient. Quint is doing fine."

"Glad to hear it."

"With any luck, Ty will finally be able to throw
away that sling today and start using his arm again."

The twin spades of the jobber *whacked* into the
hole. Stumpy rotated the handles back and forth
to carve out another chunk of hard soil. After it
was removed, Stumpy took a look and decreed,
"That should be deep enough." He laid the jobber
aside and took the steel fence post from Chase. "I
thought the doctors originally told Ty he'd have
to have that arm in a sling for six weeks. That
bullet he took totally shattered his shoulder. Them
surgeons had to rebuild the joint from scratch."

"True, but Ty figures four weeks is long enough.
We'll see if he manages to convince the doctor of
that."

Stumpy grinned. "He's probably *hopin'* he'll persuade Doc to split the difference and let him take
it off in another week."

"Probably."

"That reminds me." Stumpy paused in his securing of the post. "I ran into Amy Trumbo at noon. She tells me that O'Rourke's bein' released from the hospital today. Is that true?"

"Yeah, Cat went to get him. She should have him home before dark."

Chase remembered much too vividly that moment when he realized one of the kidnappers had shot his son. He saw again, in his mind, the brilliant red of all that blood, the desperate struggle to stop the bleeding and the gut-tearing mixture of rage and fear he'd felt.

But his son Ty hadn't been the only one to suffer at the hands of the kidnapping duo; Culley O'Rourke, his late wife's brother, had also been shot—in his case, multiple times.

Stumpy wagged his head in amazement. "I still don't know how in hell O'Rourke survived."

"He's got more lives than a barn cat." Chase couldn't honestly say whether he was happy about it or not. There had never been any love lost between the two men. At the same time, he knew that O'Rourke lived only for Cat, Chase's daughter and O'Rourke's niece. Maybe it was Cat's uncanny resemblance to Maggie. And maybe it was just plain love. Whatever the case, O'Rourke was devoted to her. And like it or not, Chase had O'Rourke to thank for his part in getting young Quint back, unharmed.

"I guess O'Rourke will be stayin' at the Circle Six with Cat and Logan." Stumpy scooped dirt around the post with his boot and tamped it down.

"That's Cat's plan anyway. But you know what a lone wolf O'Rourke is," Chase said. "My guess is that it'll only be a matter of days before he's back on the Shamrock."

"Is he strong enough to look after himself?"

"Probably not, but that means Cat will burn up the road, running between Circle Six and Shamrock, making sure he's all right and has plenty of food on hand." Noting that Stumpy had the job well in hand, Chase took his leave. "I'd better get moving before Ty and Jessy wonder what happened to me."

As he took a step away, Stumpy called him back, "Say, I've been meanin' to tell you, Chase—do you remember that young bull Ty sold to Parker from Wyoming last year? The one he wanted for his kid's 4-H project."

"What about it?"

"He walked away with the grand championship at the Denver stock show."

"Where'd you hear that?" Chase frowned.

"From Ballard. He hit the southern show circuit this past winter, hirin' out to ride in cuttin' horse competitions and doin' some jackpot ropin' on the side. That's how he happened to be in Denver. He saw a good-lookin' bull with the Triple C tag and started askin' questions." Stumpy's grin widened. "It was grand champion, imagine that. And that bull was one of our culls—a good'n, but not the quality of the ones we kept." With a wave of his hand, he added, "You need to tell Ty about it. As proud as he is of the herd of registered stock we've put together, he'll get a kick out of it."

"I'll tell him," Chase promised.

The high drone of a jet engine whined through the air, invading the stillness of wind and grass. Automatically Chase lifted his head and scanned the tall sky. Stumpy did the same as Chase and caught the metallic flash of sunlight on a wing.

"Looks like Dyson's private jet." Stumpy almost spat the name. "Coal tonnage must be down, and he's comin' to crack some whips. You notice he's makin' his approach over pristine range and not the carnage of his strip mines."

"I noticed." But Chase carefully didn't comment further.

"That's one family I'm glad we've seen the back of."

Chase couldn't have agreed more, but he didn't say so. Ty's marriage to Dyson's daughter Tara had been relatively brief. Looking back, Chase knew he had never truly approved of that spoiled beauty becoming Ty's wife, although Maggie had. To him, there had always been a cunning quality to Tara's intelligence, a quickness to manipulate and scheme to get what she wanted. Thankfully Tara was part of the past, another subject to be put aside, but not forgotten.

Yet any thought of Tara and that troubled time always aroused a sore point. Chase had yet to obtain title to those ten thousand acres of government land within the Triple C boundaries. The memory of that hardened the set of his jaw, a visible expression of his deepening resolve.

Without another word to Stumpy, Chase walked back to the ranch pickup, climbed in, and took off in the direction of The Homestead.

A cluster of old buildings crowded close to the shoulder of the two-lane highway that raced past them. A roadside sign to the south of them, its face pockmarked with bullet holes, identified the unincorporated town of Blue Moon. Long gone was the grain elevator that had once punctuated the horizon. It had been bulldozed to the ground years ago—as had the dilapidated structures that once occupied the back streets. In their place were a few modern brick buildings, a scattering of new houses, and a trailer court to house the employees of Dy-Corp's nearby strip-mining operation.

These were the changes Chase always noticed when he drove into Blue Moon, like the fresh coat of paint on the exterior of Sally's place. The combination restaurant and bar had long been the sole watering hole for the surrounding area. In his youth, the site had been the home of a roadhouse complete with whiskey, women, and gambling. Prior to that, it had been a general store and saloon, established by the town's first settler, Fat Frank Fitzsimmons.

Fat Frank was also the man who nailed up the first sign, dubbing the location Blue Moon. Local legend had it that the name was a gift from a passing cowboy who predicted failure for Fat

Frank's fledgling establishment, declaring that people came this way only once in a Blue Moon.

Blue Moon was still a place rarely visited by strangers, as evidenced by all the local license plates on the vehicles parked in front of Sally's. Chase found an empty space and pulled his truck into it.

Sally Brogan, the restaurant's proprietress, was at the cash register when he walked in. Her face lit up with pleasure the instant she saw him, a special light shining in her blue eyes, one that was reserved especially for Chase Calder. A widow of a Triple C ranch hand, Sally had fallen in love with Chase years ago and didn't bother to hide it anymore, even though she knew friendship was all he offered in return.

"You're late." Self-consciously she smoothed a hand over the front of her apron, as if the years hadn't added a few pounds to thicken her waist and turned her copper-red hair to a striking snow-white. "Ty and Jessy were just about to give up on you and order."

"I got on the phone and the call took longer than I expected."

Over the years, Sally had come to know Chase in all his moods. That hard, preoccupied look to his eyes was one she instantly recognized.

"Trouble?" she guessed instantly.

As if catching himself showing his feelings a little too plainly, he threw her a quick smile, his dark eyes lighting up for the first time. "Nothing that I haven't been dealing with for years."

"Old troubles are always with us." Sally came

out from behind the cash register. "It's when new ones come along that I worry."

"You're probably right." Chase waited to let her walk him to the table where Ty and Jessy waited.

Out of habit, Chase ran an inspecting glance over his tall, broad-shouldered son, seated next to Jessy. The unmistakable stamp of a Calder was there in his dark hair and eyes, and in the hard, angular cut of his features. On the green side of forty, Ty was a man in his prime. Best of all, except for the sling holding his left arm, Ty was the image of robust vigor. Chase could no longer detect any trace of the sickly pallor that had lurked below the deep tan of his son's face. There was a sense of genuine relief in that.

Beside Ty sat Jessy. As always, when Chase's glance fell on this slender woman with honeyed-gold hair, he experienced a mixture of satisfaction and approval. As slim and long-legged as a boy, she possessed a subtle beauty that went beyond simple good looks. There was a strength and a steadiness about her that radiated an aura of calm. Jessy wasn't the kind of woman to lead a man— or be led by him. But she would stand tall at his side. More than that, Jessy had been born and raised on the ranch. Like the rich tough grass that was the Triple C's wealth, her roots were sunk deep in Calder soil.

A better mate Chase couldn't have picked for his son. Or a better mother to his grandchildren, Chase thought as he took note of the protruding

roundness of her stomach, made all the more obvious by her boy-slim figure.

"It's about time you got here," Ty declared as
he slid a possessive hand across the back of Jessy's
shoulders. "Jessy was ready to faint with hunger."

"That'll be the day." Skepticism riddled his
response. With a nod to Jessy, Chase pulled out a
chair on the other side of his son and sat down.

"I'll get you some coffee." Sally started to move
away from the table.

"Better take our order first. I wouldn't want Jessy
keeling over for want of food."

A small, answering smile curved Jessy's mouth at
the twinkling glance Chase sent her direction. But
some shading in her father-in-law's expression told
her that he had more serious matters on his mind.
She doubted that a direct question would elicit a
direct answer. In that she knew her father-in-law
well. Whatever was on his mind, he would get
around to telling them about it in his own good
time.

Instead, she waited until Sally had taken their
food orders, then asked, "What kept you?"

"I got tied up on the phone," Chase replied, a
telltale grimness coloring his words. He leaned
back in his chair and began pushing around the
silverware in front of him.

"With who?" Ty asked curiously.

Chase grunted at the question, his mouth twisting in a smile that was without humor. "Which
time?" He correctly interpreted the question in
Ty's raised eyebrow. "I called to find out what

progress had been made in getting title to that land—and ended up getting the runaround.''

"They're no closer, then," Ty concluded.

"Nope." With that said, Chase made an effort to throw off the dark mood and flicked a finger in the direction of Ty's sling. "I see you still have that contraption around your arm."

"It'll come off next week."

"Actually," Jessy inserted, "Ty informed the doctor that if it didn't, he was taking it off."

"And I meant it," Ty stated, on the irritable side. "Four weeks of going around with a wing instead of an arm is long enough. It's time I started using it again."

"The doctor said he'll need at least two months of physical therapy," Jessy told Chase.

"Getting back to work is the only therapy I'll need," Ty replied.

"We'll see." Wisely Jessy didn't argue the point.

Ty flashed her a look of annoyance. Then his eye was caught by the serene calm of her expression. Just the sight of her seemed to be enough to smooth everything inside of him. Almost against his will, a smile twitched at the corners of his mouth.

"Okay. I admit I'll need some therapy," Ty conceded, "but not two months' worth."

Most times it was hard to tell what Jessy was thinking. She had always had a man's way of hiding her feelings. But not this time. The glance she slid him was alive with a mischievous sparkle.

"You're just cranky because you hate not being able to cut your own meat at the table."

The teasing jibe was all too accurate, and brought a fresh surge of irritation. "It makes me feel like a damned child," Ty grumbled.

Jessy couldn't resist another little playful dig. "That's why he ordered Sally's meatloaf instead of his usual steak," she told Chase.

"What about my meatloaf?" Sally returned to the table with their dinner salads and coffee for Chase.

Ty shot a warning look at his wife and replied, "Jessy was just telling Dad that's what I ordered."

Taking the cue, Jessy changed the subject. "Have you told Chase your news, Sally?"

"What news is that?" Chase glanced from Jessy to Sally, a mild curiosity showing.

Sally hesitated, then proceeded to refill Ty's coffee cup. "I wouldn't exactly call it news." But she was careful not to look Chase's way. "It's just that I've put the place up for sale."

"For sale." A stunned stillness gripped Chase.

"It should hardly come as a surprise." Secretly Sally was a little pleased by his reaction. "I've been talking about selling out for a couple years."

"Talking about it is one thing." Chase declared with a frown. "Actually doing it is something else again. What in heaven's name will you do? You're too young to retire." Then another thought hit him. "Where will you live? That apartment upstairs has been your only home for years."

"More like decades." Sally finished the thought with a sigh. "To be honest, I haven't decided where I'll go or what I'll do. And I probably won't until

I actually receive an offer. Finding a buyer for a place like this out in the middle of nowhere won't be easy, you know.''

"I know, but—why list it for sale now?'' Chase argued, struggling with a sense of loss he couldn't name.

"Because I'm tired,'' she replied. "Tired of working fifteen, sixteen hours a day, sometimes more. I'm tired of never having a vacation. And the clientele—it isn't the way it used to be, Chase. Most of the people who come in now are rougher, coarser.''

His expression darkened. "Has somebody stepped out of line?''

"With *me?*'' A laugh bubbled toward the surface even as she glowed at the implied compliment. "Chase, I'm not a young redhead anymore.''

"Just the same, if someone isn't showing you the proper respect, I want to know about it.''

"Of course.'' Suddenly this entire discussion was becoming painful and Sally couldn't explain why. "Would you like more water, Jessy?''

"Please.''

But Chase wasn't about to let her slip away so easily. "Are you sure this is what you want to do, Sally?''

She paused. "Chase, when you don't like your work anymore, it's time to quit. With any luck, one of the guys working for Dy-Corp has a secret dream about owning a bar and will take this place off my hands. Lord knows they get paid high wages out there.''

"If this is what you want, Sally,'' Chase began,

clearly unhappy with her decision, "I'll spread the word around that you're looking for a buyer. But—it won't be the same here without you."

She could have told him she wasn't necessarily leaving the area. She could have told him a hundred different things, but the words wouldn't come. Something in his remark had a ring of finality, and it knifed through her. At that instant, Sally knew that she had always secretly feared that if she ever sold the restaurant, she would never see Chase again, that he wouldn't come see her elsewhere because that would start talk. His comment had all but confirmed it.

"I appreciate your help, Chase."

When Sally moved away from their table, Jessy wondered if she was the only one who noticed the sudden welling of tears. Every time Jessy observed Sally and Chase together—and the love for the man that shone in Sally's eyes—it tugged at her heart. She had loved Ty from afar for too many years not to understand and empathize with the ache of that.

The memory of those times prompted Jessy to reach up and caress the strong hand resting on her shoulder, simply because she was his wife and she could. Tara was gone now; no longer did she have Ty caught under her spell.

The front door to the restaurant burst open, followed immediately by the *bang* of the screen door slamming shut, as loud as the crack of a rifle. Jessy jumped in her chair and half turned in her seat, her glance racing to the entrance.

Something inside her froze at the sight of a slender woman with sable-dark hair. It was Tara, chicly dressed in some blue concoction that looked straight off the pages of a high-fashion magazine.

Maybe it was the old fear that made Jessy dart a look at Ty. She observed the flash of surprise on his face—and something more, something like the pull of attraction. The anger of old resentment and dislike knotted Jessy's stomach.

Please look for

SHIFTING CALDER WIND

by Janet Dailey.

A July 2003 hardcover release
from Kensington Publishing.

From Best-selling Author
Fern Michaels

__Wish List	0-8217-7363-1	$7.50US/$9.50CAN
__Yesterday	0-8217-6785-2	$7.50US/$9.50CAN
__The Guest List	0-8217-6657-0	$7.50US/$9.50CAN
__Finders Keepers	0-8217-7364-X	$7.50US/$9.50CAN
__Annie's Rainbow	0-8217-7366-6	$7.50US/$9.50CAN
__Dear Emily	0-8217-7365-8	$7.50US/$9.50CAN
__Sara's Song	0-8217-5856-X	$6.99US/$8.50CAN
__Celebration	0-8217-6452-7	$6.99US/$8.99CAN
__Vegas Heat	0-8217-7207-4	$7.50US/$9.50CAN
__Vegas Rich	0-8217-7206-6	$7.50US/$9.50CAN
__Vegas Sunrise	0-8217-7208-2	$7.50US/$9.50CAN
__What You Wish For	0-8217-6828-X	$7.99US/$9.99CAN
__Charming Lily	0-8217-7019-5	$7.99US/$9.99CAN

Thrilling Romance from
Lisa Jackson

DO YOU HAVE THE
HOHL COLLECTION?

__Another Spring 0-8217-7155-8	$6.99US/$8.99CAN
__Compromises 0-8217-7154-X	$6.99US/$8.99CAN
__Ever After 0-8217-5660-5	$5.99US/$7.50CAN
__Something Special 0-8217-6725-9	$5.99US/$7.50CAN
__Maybe Tomorrow 0-8217-6054-8	$5.99US/$7.50CAN
__Never Say Never 0-8217-6379-2	$5.99US/$7.50CAN
__Silver Thunder 0-8217-6200-1	$5.99US/$7.50CAN

Call toll free **1-888-345-BOOK** to order by phone or use this coupon to order by mail. ALL BOOKS AVAILABLE DECEMBER 1, 2000.

Name_____

Address _____

City _____ State _____ Zip _____

Please send me the books I have checked above.

I am enclosing $_____

Plus postage and handling* $_____

Sales tax (in NY and TN) $_____

Total amount enclosed $_____

*Add $2.50 for the first book and $.50 for each additional book.

Send check or money order (no cash or CODs) to:

Kensington Publishing Corp., Dept. C.O., 850 Third Avenue, New York, NY 10022

Prices and numbers subject to change without notice. Valid only in the U.S.

All orders subject to availability. **NO ADVANCE ORDERS.**

Visit our web site at **www.kensingtonbooks.com**